"Isn't this exciting, Robbie? We're making history!" Anna Cross shouted in my ear as I walked near the front of a massive march of protestors. It was probably rude to use an infolink earpiece in the middle of a protest march, but Anna wanted to share every bit of the excitement she was feeling from her own part in the march.

My old N7 infolink projected an image of Anna's face directly into my eye while I could hear her perfectly in one ear but not the other thanks to noise cancellation software. She was a beautiful African American girl about my age—eighteen—with long, curly hair that had a purple stripe in it. Anna was dressed in a punkish style with a leather jacket, ripped jeans, and a t-shirt that had a vulgar message on it that wasn't my style. Anna was in New Detroit surrounded by our friends while I was in the main march in Chicago with strangers.

"We haven't accomplished anything yet," I said, with my hand cupped around my mouth to block out the noise from the crowd marching alongside me. "This is just one step of many."

"Literally!" Anna joked, pointing out the fact both marches were across the whole of their respective cities.

"I really wish you'd been able to come," I muttered, not wanting to get in argument but already a bit overwhelmed by the strangers around me.

DESTINY'S PARADOX

Book Two of the Dark Destiny Series

by C. T. Phipps and Frank Martin

CHAPTER ONE

D estiny.

It was something few of us ever contemplated. The idea that everything in the universe was predetermined and free will was an illusion. Einstein believed in block time or eternalism, which was that space and time were like a big wooden block that we were just worming our way through like a termite. Everything was happening all at once and it only seemed like we were experiencing time because our minds were tricked into thinking about it.

For me, Rob Stone, I was aware this was horseshit. I was destined to be the Scorpion, the worst tyrant in history, and a girl from the future prevented that from happening. It had taken a lot out of us, and horrible sacrifices had been made but the dark future she'd come from had been averted. Which left me to think about these sorts of weighty philosophical issues in the abstract and arguably even more important subjects.

"Did you finish Mr. Leroy's paper?" I asked Trevor as we left the dorm.

Like my grades.

Trevor looked both ways down the street in front of the university's main building and, after seeing it was free from traffic, jogged to the other side of the road.

"Finish? I haven't even started yet," Trevor said, continuing a conversation I was barely paying attention to.

Trevor Monroe was a tall, athletic, blond man wearing a jacket in the school colors—orange and black—with a button-down shirt and blue jeans. I'd never mention it to him but he kind of reminded me of Fred from *Scooby Doo*. It was amazing that show was still on the air a century after it was created. You'd think they'd have run out of guys pretending to be ghosts or real estate scams by 2070.

"It's due tomorrow," chuckled Georgia as she and I trailed behind him. "Might want to get a start on that."

Georgia Walters was waiting for us down at the crosswalk. She was a lovely African American woman wearing a conservative blue skirt and white blouse that looked a couple of decades out of date but matched the kind of retro-preppy look so many Connor University students went for.

Trevor and Georgia were the closest friends I had made during my almost four years here. They were perfect for me as they had no real interest in where I came from and were willing to let my past lie. I didn't ever want to think about who I was again, any more than I wanted to think about who I was supposed to be.

The Scorpion was never going to threaten anyone ever again. I had left behind the activist I'd been when I was Robbie, not Rob, and devoted myself to studying economics nearly twenty-four/seven since I'd been "given" a full ride here. It had been more like a bribe since I'd tried to break into the Butterfly Corporation in order to expose all their secrets. Due to complicated circumstances, I had ended up saving the company instead.

Yay me.

Now I was going to try to reform it from the inside. It was a lot better solution than trying to fix things via terrorism. That way led to my becoming history's greatest monster, the end of the world, and time travel. I hated time travel. I couldn't even watch movies or play holo vids that involved the topic anymore. All it did was bring up memories of my father dying and the nightmares that had accompanied it. Yeah, I was not about to think about that anymore. Butterfly paid for a twice weekly therapist, but it wasn't like I could share he'd been killed by an assassin from the future. Instead, I willed it away, even if it meant not thinking about Jane or the other people I'd left behind.

Trevor waited for us on the opposite sidewalk and flashed that confident smirk that drove the freshman girls crazy.

"I know, but I do my best work under pressure. Isn't that right, Rob?"

I didn't respond, thinking of Jane. We'd barely spoken after the revelation she was my daughter from the future. I missed her despite the fact she'd been so intimately tied to so many horrible events. She was my only family left.

"Rob?" Trevor waved his hand in front of my head. "Earth to Rob."

"I want to sleep with you," Georgia said.

"Wait, what?" I asked, doing a double take.

"Told you," Georgia said, smirking.

"Dammit," Trevor said, pulling out his credit card and scanning it over Georgia's infopad. "There's your twenty bucks."

"Huh?" I asked, confused.

"We had a bet over which of our methods would get you out of your zoning out faster," Georgia said. "It was a sucker's bet for Trevor."

"I'm honestly surprised," Trevor said, shaking his head. "I've never seen Rob show any interest in the opposite sex, or same sex for that matter. Not that there's—"

"I'm straight," I said, frowning. "I just don't have time for dating."

That was both true and misleading. The Butterfly FutureExec Program was a punishing program I could barely keep up with, but even if it wasn't, romance was just not in the cards for me anymore. My last girlfriend, Anna, had dumped me for accepting Butterfly's scholarship and it wasn't like I could tell her the truth of why I was committed to nonviolent reform now. Gee, Anna, it's because of time travel and my becoming the next Hitler. Is the world becoming a cyberpunk dystopia ruled by megacorporations that bad by comparison?

Except, yeah, it was.

3

"Who said anything about dating?" Trevor said, wiggling his eyebrows suggestively. It was the weirdest damned thing and I had to wonder where he learned it. "Every Red Zone girl loves to throw themselves at us FutureExecs. Every Connor University student is prime meat on the hoof if you want to get your dick wet. No offense, Georgia."

"None taken," Georgia said. "I prefer to remain disease free. Red Zoners give me hives."

I grimaced but quickly covered it up. Red Zones were the new slang term for non-corporate run cities and urban areas in America. As the name implied, they'd rapidly gone to hell due to the pulling out of corporate and government support. If you weren't in a Blue Zone—run directly by a megacorporation—or a Green Zone—where they were supporting the local government—then you might as well be living in an anarchy.

"You shouldn't be so down on Red Zoners," I muttered, giving a weak defense. "They were part of the rest of the country until just a couple of years ago."

"We're in a Blue Zone, Rob," Georgia said, shaking her head. "It might as well be Mars."

"Just the university," I muttered, thinking about the rest of Chicago being surprisingly still a mixture of Green and Red Zones despite Butterfly's headquarters being located here. "But yeah, I know what you mean."

Connor University was not quite Ivy League, but it was one of the best business schools in the country and had freely embraced the money of its corporate donors to become the place to be if you wanted to become a future Butterfly executive. It had the children of its current leadership, geniuses headhunted from across the country, and the lucky few who could just afford to bribe their way in.

Butterfly was the world's largest economic body in the middle of the twenty-first century and more people wanted to be part of it than to be president or a senator these days. The school looked like a picture from a magazine with its red brick buildings, clock tower, and immaculately trimmed grass.

4

The only things out of place were the holographic interfaces and armed guards posted at every street corner. Those were Monarch Security, a bunch of jackbooted thugs increasingly allowed police powers at any facility even remotely connected to my present employers. I'd learned to ignore them in the interests of preserving my scholarship and recent internship. God, I hated them.

"I do worry about your social life, though," Georgia said. "I could introduce you to some of my girlfriends if you like. They don't have herpes, unlike Trevor."

Trevor rolled his eyes.

"Like you ever complained."

"Aren't you two together?" I asked, looking between them.

"It's complicated," Georgia replied.

"It's destiny," Trevor said, smugly.

I hated that word. "I'm fine, really. I need to focus on my studies."

Honestly, the thought of dating one of the corporate hopefuls at Connor University didn't appeal to me either. It wasn't that all of them were narcissists or sociopaths, Georgia, for example, was one of the nicest women I'd ever met, but I couldn't exactly open myself up to anyone either. Never mind the time travel and past trauma, I couldn't talk about what I really thought of Butterfly or the other megacorporations. I considered what was happening to the world to be a tragedy and that the megacorps were a genuine force for evil in the world. There was no way that I could ever let that get out or I'd never have a chance to dismantle the power structures I was trying to gain influence over.

"Just don't let the pressure ruin your prospects of happiness," Georgia said, sincerely.

An advertising kiosk scanned us and immediately projected out a series of logos for Butterfly-based products. They might as well not have even bothered since Connor University was a community sealed off from the rest of Chicago. All products were produced by one of the company's subsidiaries and virtually everything else was contraband.

I remembered when I'd first arrived on campus and was introduced to the kind of futuristic luxury and simultaneous oppression that was everywhere. My old girlfriend, Anna, would have hated it here, but last I heard she'd joined the army. There was no sign of trouble on campus, though. Student demonstrations were forbidden, and everyone knew their place. With things like food riots and civil unrest popping up across the country, no one here wanted to screw up their shot at a better life.

"Speaking of pressure," Trevor added, "you think maybe you could show up when I get my interview for the Butterfly Placement Program? It's time for us to move up to our actual careers. I think you could help me with that, Rob."

Georgia rolled her eyes.

"What? Really?" I asked, genuinely confused. "Why me?"

"You're legit," Trevor said, sounding shocked. "A real up-and-comer. Everyone knows Colin Reilly paid for your scholarship."

He was talking about Colin Reilly, the richest man in the world, chairman and CEO of Butterfly. Trevor seemed to know a ridiculous amount about the man and was always speculating on the corporate politics. Some men followed football fanatically; Trevor followed corporate gossip. I knew he'd had his sights set on assuming a spot in the megacorporation's leadership ever since I met him. I admired his determination. He was the only man who wanted to lead as much as I did, though for presumably different reasons.

"If you think it'll help," I muttered, uncomfortable with the request.

I didn't comment on it often, but Trevor was a mystery to me. Unlike Georgia, who had a Monarch executive for a mother, Trevor had appeared from nowhere and I couldn't find out his background. I'd initially pegged him as a kind of genius who was here on merit but that was quickly disabused. He ignored his studies half the time and often took weeks off to go visit various Butterflies holdings across the globe where he got the royal welcome. Yet, despite acting like he didn't care half the time, his position here at Connor University seemed secure. My current theory was he'd inherited some massive Butterfly stock from a dead relative somewhere. Jane would have speculated he was a spy. I didn't discount that possibility either.

"Trevor, you worry too much," Georgia said, cheerfully. "You're going to be a junior Butterfly executive as soon as Monarch accepts your application. They prefer to promote people trained in the corporate side of things. You'll be filing papers in the Counterterrorism or Executive Solutions sections any day now."

"Yeah," Trevor said. "Maybe I'll be able contribute to taking down HOPE someday."

Georgia frowned. "Of course, you will. Someone needs to stop those terrorists."

"Yeah," I said, uncomfortable.

If only they knew that I was a former HOPE "terrorist." The organization I once belonged to had been officially designated by the federal government as a terrorist organization a few months ago. My former group had been in the news lately for getting more extreme and radical in their demonstrations, but with Butterfly controlling the media, it was hard to tell what was true and what was just propaganda. Granted, I'd been out of the loop for a while, but I couldn't imagine their tactics had gotten as violent as the news was saying.

"Well, I'm not taking things for granted," Trevor replied. "I haven't started because I have a lot on my mind."

"You shouldn't worry, Trevor. You're a shoo-in," Georgia said. "Everyone loves you. It's not who you know but how you win people over."

"Says the woman whose mother is the Monarch CSO," Trevor muttered, referring to the position of Chief Security Officer.

"Well, that doesn't hurt either," Georgia admitted.

"If you're thinking I have any sway, Trevor, you're wrong," I said. "I don't have any connections outside of you guys. I'm not part of your class."

Georgia giggled a bit. "I admit that some people are a better class than others. But you are part of that class now, Rob, or you wouldn't be here."

Oh, yay. Thank you, Georgia. A reminder I was now part of the parasites destroying the Earth. I smiled, faking sincerity. "You know just what it takes to make me feel better."

"What is given can be taken away. Remember that," Trevor said, sharing a private joke. "You can be riding on top of the world one day, master of all you survey, and the next rotting in a Monarch prison somewhere."

"Yeah," I said in response to Trevor's words while eyeing a pack of Monarch troops hassling a pizza boy from the outside. They looked like orange and black stormtroopers and I had to wonder who'd designed them to look like the baddies in a science fiction movie. Had they deliberately gone for that look, or had it just happened by accident? "Some things are easier to take than others. Like freedom."

I hadn't meant to say that aloud. Whoops.

"Oh, please," Georgia said, laughing off my concern. "When was the last time you, or any of us for that matter, were bothered by Monarch?"

"That's because we work for Butterfly," I replied, embarrassed by letting my cover slip. "Not everyone is so lucky."

"Don't be too sympathetic," Georgia said, rolling her eyes. "We're the job creators."

"There's the boot and the ant, man," Trevor said, smiling in a weirdly knowing way. "Remember which you want to be."

"I will," I replied. I could never forget that, and I wanted to make sure as few ants were stomped on as possible. That was years, possibly decades, of work in the making. Maybe it was even impossible and the moment I tried to improve things for everyone, I'd get fired, but it was better than the alternative.

"In the end we all have to fight for our place in society," Trevor said, sadly. "Even if it gets us killed."

Trevor's remark sounded like something Jane would say when she was training me to fight. The two of us had a complicated relationship, and that was putting things mildly. There weren't exactly self-help books on how to deal with your future daughter that was the same age as you.

I often wondered what might've happened if Jane and I had stayed together. She was there that day in Chicago and was offered the same scholarship from Colin Reilly, but Jane was never one for school.

I'd objected as I'd still been worried that the two surviving future assassins would return to finish the job: Esther and Cody. I still remembered those two terrifying cyborg super soldiers. Jane said she'd taken care of them, though, and not to worry. She wouldn't tell me why or how, but I trusted her…up until she left without saying goodbye.

God, I missed her.

"Come on, Rob," Georgia said, giving me a light, playful shove. "I expect more enthusiasm from Colin Reilly's favorite pet."

"Stop," I said, covering my mouth as if I were about to throw up. "Really."

Trevor and Georgia both stumbled forward, laughing.

"He's not my friend, even if I am his personal assistant," I said. Honestly, I was ninety percent sure Colin Reilly knew I'd been part of HOPE and there to sabotage his company when he gave me the scholarship. He'd said he knew my secret and while I didn't think he was referring to time travel, I knew he was smart enough to know I was part of HOPE. It meant his patronage of me was all just a weird head game to him or he enjoyed showing that every man had their price.

"Technically, you're the intern to his personal assistant," Trevor said, smirking. "His personal assistant has a private jet. You ride the automated tram here."

"It's more efficient," I muttered, knowing they knew I couldn't afford a car even with the scholarship money provided.

Trevor took a deep breath and steered the conversation in a more grounded direction. "Rob does have a point about Connor, though. I had to attend a lecture at Wells University last week and the Monarch presence on campus was not anywhere near the same as it is here. And our school is like half the size."

"That's because Connor is the future of Butterfly," Georgia replied. "They chose this school because of its proximity to headquarters."

Trevor looked confused. "I thought it was because Connor was considered the birthplace of HOPE. Christine Trainer went here before she became a terrorist. I wonder if they'll ever catch her."

"Maybe." Even three years into our friendship, I still wasn't comfortable talking about my past. Not that anyone would ever believe it if I tried. It didn't help I'd known Christine and even had a little crush on her. No one had seen her in years, though. "At least we don't have to worry about it anymore. The organization is all but wrapped up now according to the news."

"You didn't hear about what happened in the New Orleans Red Zone?" Trevor asked, referring to HOPE.

"No," Georgia said, curiously. "When was this?"

Trevor took out his infopad and pulled up a news article, handing it to us as he spoke.

"Yesterday. An oil tanker bound for Africa exploded before it left port. Butterfly said it was related to a HOPE cell down there."

After scanning the screen, Georgia tossed the infopad back to him. "I'm sure they did say that. Monarch would rather blame some imaginary boogeyman than look incompetent from an accident."

I kept my head down, reluctant to join the discussion as Trevor returned the infopad to his pocket. "What about all the other HOPE-related crimes that make the news? There's been a lot more of them lately."

"That's just propaganda," Georgia said, grimacing. "It makes Butterfly look better if there's some terrorist group out there causing havoc to bring them down."

I was surprised she'd say this but maybe the fact she was daughter to a Monarch board member and general made her able to express more freedom than most of us.

"And you know this how?" Trevor asked, curiously.

Georgia held out her hands, almost embarrassed that she had to provide such an obvious answer. "It's common sense. What is more likely? A brilliant Butterfly disinformation campaign or some hidden gang of liberals trying to fight the biggest megacorporation in the world?"

Her comments made me reluctantly recall nights back in Revered Tully's basement, plotting and planning with Anna and the others how best to resist our evil overlords. I thought those were complicated times back then. I've almost grown nostalgically envious of their simplicity.

"You really think HOPE is gone?" I asked Georgia, forcing myself to neutrally enter the debate.

"I wouldn't say gone," Georgia said, shrugging. "They're like roaches. You can never get rid of them entirely. But the movement isn't nearly as strong as it was a couple of years ago."

"Now *that* we can certainly agree on," I said, woefully nodding with my gaze to the ground.

We walked a few more steps in silence before Trevor chimed in with his own opinion. "I'm sorry, but you're both crazy. HOPE is still alive and well."

Georgia nodded with a condescending grin. "And I'm sure you're getting this from your weekly get-together with Christine Trainer, am I right?"

She had no idea. Christine could be dead, killed by future assassins like the other members of our team, or locked away in a Monarch prison somewhere, without a trial or due process. I still dreamed of Christine some nights. She'd been so beautiful and charismatic. If Christine had been the leader of HOPE in the dark future Jane had come from, the Scorpion would never have arisen. Now she was America's most wanted and no one knew where she'd gone.

"They've just changed, is all," said Trevor, seriously answering Georgia's sarcastic question. "Went underground. Less and less public protests and demonstrations. HOPE wants war and Butterfly drove them to it, too. Turned the group from a bunch of peaceful misfits into a violent army. So, don't delude yourself, Georgia. HOPE is all too real. And they mean business."

Georgia put a stern finger in Trevor's face. "If you say so Trevor. I still think their threat is vastly exaggerated."

As if on cue, a thunderous boom rang out through the calm spring air. It was loud enough to encompass the entire campus and startled everyone present, student and Monarch guard alike.

Fuck.

CHAPTER TWO

It took me a second to register the sound as an explosion and I stood frozen in place. It brought back all the terrible memories of the violence and death I'd just barely survived in high school. Was it Jane? No, it couldn't be Jane. She'd never attack a school.

"No," I muttered, aloud. "This place is supposed to be safe."

"What the hell was that?" Georgia asked for us all. There was a strange look of calmness in her face that made me wonder what she was thinking.

Trevor was much more stunned in his expression and pointed out to a thin trail of smoke rising in the distance. "It came from the campus security center. Come on!"

The Monarch troops all took off running in the smoke's direction. Trevor, Georgia, and I were the only students to follow them. It took a second to realize how strange it was to be running toward a terrorist attack and I was proud of my friends in that moment. They clearly wanted to help every bit as much as I did.

I ran across the campus faster than I'd ever run in my life, which was damn fast since I'd joined the Conner University track team. I wasn't the best but knew how to run like hell when the occasion called for it. Jane had taught me plenty about physical conditioning before she…well, abandoned me. I'd also been experimenting with parkour in case I ever had to make a quick exit from the top floor of the Butterfly building. I wasn't very good at it. Not yet, at least.

I ran past crowds of people running in the opposite direction, and leapt over multiple steps toward the Campus Security Center. There, I saw something which horrified me. The octagonal building was on fire with its second floor having exploded, leaving shards of glass scattered across the ground. There were dozens of students on the ground, injured and bleeding from where they'd been struck with debris or caught in the aftermath of the explosion.

"No!" I shouted, staring at the nightmarish sight before me. This couldn't be happening. I was supposed to get away from all the violence. We were supposed to be avoiding the Scorpion's war.

A lone Monarch private was standing there, dressed in orange and black camouflage with a plastisteel vest and a beret. His laser canon T-211 looked like a toy he was uselessly waving about. The soldier had a bewildered look on his face and there was no sign of the rest of the units who should have been tending to the victims. Instead, he didn't even have his infolink activated.

I walked up to him and grabbed him by the shoulders. "You need to call for help, get the local hospital and some medics down here!"

The Monarch soldier immediately grabbed me by the shirt and growled at me. "This is an active combat zone!"

"People are dying!" I snapped at him.

"I know! HOPE did this!" The Monarch soldier hissed, saying the name of the organization like he was cursing.

"HOPE can't...HOPE couldn't have done this." I was taken aback and didn't know how else to respond.

The Monarch soldier looked like he was about to slug me when Georgia and Trevor managed to catch up.

"This is a 17-55. Please initiate a Delta Protocol," Georgia said, looking around. She was oddly calm, and I admired her restraint during this tragedy. "Rob, I've got Monarch Reserve Officer's Medic training. I think I can help some of these people make it through this but I'm going to need your and Trevor's help."

The Monarch soldier looked at her, then nodded and tapped the Infolink on the side of his head, starting communications for a Delta Protocol—whatever that was.

"How did you do that?" I asked, looking at Georgia. "Also, you're not in the reserve. Do they even have medics in the MOTC?"

"You just have to speak their language," Georgia said, smiling sweetly. "Now go!"

I didn't need someone to tell me twice and headed into the burning Campus Security building. The sight which greeted me was enough to make me sick. The top floor had collapsed, crushing many of the students below.

I was no stranger to violence thanks to my clashes with Monarch and the New Hope assassins, but this was something else entirely. The broken bodies and horrific scale of destruction reminded me of the tales of war Jane used to tell me about. The very same tales that used to haunt my dreams. I was frozen in place and instantly transported back to those nightmares. A future that the Scorpion...that I created.

I saw before me the burning ruins of New Detroit under a dark, cloudy sky. Flames ravaged the rubble and debris scattered between whatever tenements were still standing, scarred and scorched brick buildings pock-marked with holes in their facades. Hundreds of corpses littered the ground and were dragged from the wreckage by citizen-laborers before being tossed aside like garbage. The ominous skyline was full of vertical-lift-off transports as the New Hope Army tanks led prisoners down the streets with their hands up high.

The terrible premonition had me paralyzed and was followed by a series of equally horrific flashes: visions of murder, execution, slavery, and destruction. I thought I was through having dreams of the Scorpion, the Scourge of Humanity, but I guessed they were never really gone. The nightmares were always there, burned into my memory, and could flood my mind at a moment's notice.

"Rob!" yelled Trevor, snapping me out of my stupor. "Help me here!"

He had his arm around a woman and was helping her to her feet. I nodded and joined him.

During a crash course in field medicine, Jane told me you usually weren't supposed to move the injured, but the area was unstable with rubble constantly shifting above our heads and beneath our feet. It was only a matter of time before it gave out completely.

Had HOPE really done this? Why? I'd thought the stories of them becoming a terrorist organization were insane. What did they hope to accomplish? God, that just sounded like I was making a bad joke. There was nothing funny about this, though. There had been a bunch of students my age inside.

I helped half a dozen individuals from the damaged Security Center. There were EMTs and Monarch medics but none of them were attempting to move people out of the building. Instead, there was a small number of camera crews getting footage of the injured and wounded. It made me sick, but I continued my efforts.

"I need to check upstairs!" I said, seeing Trevor helping to remove the last of the still living.

"What? You're crazy!" Trevor said, sounding both surprised and panicked. "Don't be a hero!"

"I'm anything but a hero," I said, laughing to myself.

I had a horrible sinking feeling in my chest that I hadn't managed to change the future as much as I'd wanted. I'd done my best to remove myself from the conflict, even taking up a position with Butterfly. I had hoped to be able to change things from the inside, make it so the company didn't become the monstrosity it was in the future, but that seemed like a far-off dream. What if by doing that, though, I'd made things worse? No, I had to think it was over and this was just the fallout. A bloody horrible fallout. I pressed those thoughts aside and focused on trying to find any remaining survivors.

Running up the damaged stairs, I covered my mouth as my eyes and lungs were assaulted by the horrible burning stench. There was the smell of death, fire, and burning carpet. The upstairs didn't have any sign of survivors and I knew I'd made a mistake in coming up here.

"Is anybody still alive!?" I called out.

There was no response.

"Dammit," I said, hearing the twisting of metal as I felt the ground beneath me start to shift.

That was when I heard a soft moan across the hall from the second-floor offices. Taking a deep breath, I ran across the damaged and burned floor past several small fires while keeping my arm over my mouth.

"I'm coming!" I gave a muffled shout.

I ended up in the only undamaged part of the building, an office floor lined with cubicles. The explosion must not have reached this far. Everything appeared dark and still except for a slight movement behind one of the desks. I approached it, coming around the end, and expected to find someone injured. Instead, a lightning-fast hand grabbed my shirt and pulled me to the ground.

An African American woman, beautiful, with long curly hair, held me against the floor. Her grip around my neck was tight, cutting off my air and blurring my vision. I could see just enough to make out her plain, gray hoodie. As I focused, though, a familiar face buried within the hood came into view. A face that I had once cared for deeply and probably still did.

"Anna?" I muttered, my voice harsh and raspy. I had to fight against the chokehold to speak.

Anna's face widened upon hearing her name, almost as if she had just recognized me as well. We had not seen each other since the night of the heist. Not since she walked out of the church basement after our fight. Judging by her wide-eyed expression of shock. Anna was just as surprised to see me as I was to see her. She released her grip from my neck and stood up slowly.

I gasped, choking for air, and then spoke as soon as my voice would allow. "What are you doing here?"

Anna immediately turned and started sprinting in the other direction.

"Wait!" I yelled out to her while scrambling to my feet. "Hold on!"

Anna was never much of an athlete, but she somehow sprinted through the cubicles like a track star. I tried to keep up with her as she weaved in and out of the aisles, sometimes putting my agility to work by hopping over desks and chairs.

The distance between us was closing. Just a few more steps and I could grab ahold of her hoodie.

Approaching the wall, Anna lowered her shoulder and plowed into a door leading to the stairwell. I lost sight of her for a second but was still right on her tail. I leapt into the stairwell, ready to give chase, and was met with a right hook that sent me spiraling to the floor.

I hit the ground with a thud and saw a galaxy of stars flash before my eyes, more confused than anything else about what just happened. In the end, I woke up on a stretcher and blinked as I saw Georgia standing over me.

"What's going on?" I asked, staring up.

Trevor was leaning over me.

"I had to pull you out from the second floor. What the hell were you thinking, man?"

I blinked and looked up. "I thought someone was there."

"Was there?" Trevor asked.

I thought about Anna. I remembered the beginning of our relationship, losing my virginity to her, and our attempt to break into the Butterfly headquarters at the end. What the hell was she doing here? Was she still a part of HOPE? Did she…could she have…set off that explosion? I now missed Jane more than ever and wished she were here to help me get through this.

"No," I answered Trevor, realizing it was best to keep things to myself until I knew more. "There was no one there."

Trevor looked at me suspiciously then shook his head. "This is proof HOPE is evil."

"I admit, I was wrong," Georgia said, looking over the mass of dead and dying students. There were at least seven bodies covered with a sheet and probably a half-dozen more still on the second floor. "HOPE is awful."

They were oddly subdued reactions to having their fellow students killed and a terrorist attack having been carried out right next to them. Then again, that was a quality of people who went to Connor. Everyone was very good at faking emotions, but everyone also seemed to be colder and more ruthless than other people, like they'd screened for those traits on their applications.

"Yes," I said, staring at the horrible burning remains of the Security Center. "The people who did this are monsters."

"I wonder if we knew anyone there?" Trevor asked.

"Unlikely," Georgia said. "Students that worked for Campus Security were typically doing it just to pad their resume. Anyone with real Monarch aspirations was already employed by Butterfly like us."

"Then what was the point of all this?" I asked, quickly changing things. "I mean, from HOPE's perspective. They must've had a plan."

"They're terrorists," Georgia said, sounding like she was reading a script. "They won't stop unless Monarch forces find them and make them."

Georgia meant kill them. That was when our infopads, gifts for our internship, all rang simultaneously. Georgia checked hers first. "They're calling us to the BBN Studio."

She was referring to the Butterfly Broadcasting Network, a national station. The local studio was inside Butterfly Headquarters where we worked, meaning we would have to take the local maglev train to get there.

"What?" I asked, confused. "We can't go in now. It's the middle of the day. We have classes."

"You know work comes before school for Butterfly employees. We need to get ahead of this," Georgia said, looking at the cameras. "You, Trevor, and I are about to be heroes."

Trevor smiled.

I felt disgusted.

CHAPTER THREE

The maglev train ride to Butterfly headquarters was weird as we were the only people in our car. Occasionally, a Monarch trooper would walk through the aisle, but we were kept separate from the rest of the hundreds of people who took the trams through downtown Chicago. People like me, normally. I used to have a car but it wasn't the right kind of "look" for a Butterfly executive-in-training so I'd sold it for extra textbook money. It was kind of eerie since we'd just come from a terrorist attack site, and we were now in a silent chamber with pretty train attendants constantly asking whether we needed anything.

I could tell Trevor was shook up by the events, but Georgia spent virtually the entire time on her tablet, typing out a speech and going through the camera footage of the event. I never thought Georgia was a psychopath before this, but her cold, callous handling of the death of at least a dozen fellow students reminded me of Colin Reilly.

"Are we really going to just go to work?" I asked, finally breaking the oppressive silence.

"Why not?" Georgia asked, confused.

"People died," I said, softly. "People who could have been us."

"Our job is to make sure they didn't die in vain," Georgia said, talking as if she was discussing the mail. "Whoever controls the narrative will be able to determine the future of the war."

My eyes widened. "War?"

"The war that is inevitably going to happen between the old world and the new one," Georgia said, tapping her tablet. "Look to your side."

"Ah, that war," Trevor said, suddenly interested in the conversation.

I turned my attention to the glass view of the city as Butterfly had made it. Most of Chicago had been demolished with much of its population relocated. Instead of old crumbling buildings with character, there were hundreds of gleaming skyscrapers which invoked a kind of classic sci-fi future but seemed subtly "off."

Butterfly did not act like a corporation anymore. It acted like a state and Chicago was its capital. This was where its headquarters were located and where it controlled its ever-growing empire. Millions of workers had been imported to replace the old population and they'd largely succeeded. Employees gave birth, raised their children, and would die in their employer's service.

It was a vision of the future that Colin Reilly and the other eleven megacorporation heads were peddling to the world. No more governments, no more bureaucracy, no more countries or borders. Religion was fine but only in small, sanitized amounts. A corporate-run world run for the purposes of the bottom line and shareholders. Ten years ago, it would have sounded crazy, but the US government was just a shell of its former self now. People wanted corporate rule and it was everywhere.

The Red Zone versus Blue Zone conflict was just one of the ways that Butterfly was feeding the conflict. Butterfly backed politicians that wanted to make sure the poor had no government assistance while dismantling every public utility they could until it owned everything. The Red Zones were then left to wither on the vine and flooded with drugs, guns, and rhetoric that it was the government who had abandoned them. Whenever things exploded—and it seemed they did every other week—the crackdowns were brutal—which only led to more unrest.

The maglev train even made it a point to pass over the Red Zone sections of Chicago and I could see several fires currently raging. The people who didn't want to live under corporate rule or couldn't afford to were packed together like ants in a hill. The areas had concrete walls constructed around them and checkpoints with guns that required people to produce IDs to move back and forth to their jobs in the other parts of the city—when they had them. No wonder Anna had radicalized to become a terrorist.

Anna.

"I get what you're saying," I said, sick to my stomach. "I do."

"Do you, Rob?" Trevor asked, surprising me.

"Yeah, of course," I said, defensively.

Trevor looked at me funny. "Because you've always been kind of unenthusiastic whenever HOPE gets brought up."

"What do you mean?" I asked, starting to panic.

Trevor made his palm perfectly straight and moved it below his waist. "This is Rob."

"Uh huh," I asked, already annoyed at his euphemism.

Trevor lifted his palm up to his forehead. "This is me. You need to get into the game, pal. Because this is a tragedy."

"No shit," I muttered, wondering what he was getting at. "I knew some of those guys. Peter Johnson and Kate Wilson are still among the missing."

"No, they're definitely dead," Georgia said, dryly, checking her infopad. "I've also checked the social media feeds. No way they wouldn't have updated by now. On the plus side, that means we'll never be subjected to Kate's InfoFeed page about faux-Red Zone wear. Fashionable poverty is a style I just can't get behind. I like looking rich."

I stared at Georgia in horror.

Trevor just ignored her. "But this is also an opportunity."

"What?" I turned to Trevor in horror, feeling like a ping pong ball.

Trevor pointed to me with enthusiasm. "Exactly! That's the look we need! We need to look traumatized! Perfect. Milking the devastated survivor thing is perfect for our long-term prospects."

I opened my mouth and closed it, unaware how to respond. It seemed that I'd clearly horrifically misjudged my friends. They were not only not any better than the other rich snobs at Connor, but they were also worse. Were they psychopaths or just opportunists? I couldn't say but it was now clear I was never going to fit in here.

I'd planned to keep my head down and move up through the ranks by acting like everyone else, but was that even possible anymore? If everyone else was a monster in the FutureExec programs, there was going to be a time when I couldn't hide anymore. What did that leave me as an option to oppose Butterfly? Violence? I'd seen Anna. I'd seen her kill a bunch of people and now I didn't know what to think. She was my first and, so far, only girlfriend.

Now she was a terrorist. A murderer who was willing to kill students like me by the dozens all so they could...I don't even know what. Kill future Butterfly leaders? Destroy a building? Make a statement? Cause general mayhem and chaos? It seemed I couldn't fight without becoming a monster, but what was the point of not being a monster if everyone you loved became one instead? I didn't have any answers.

Georgia nodded. "We could be in speaking engagements and shaking hands with executives over this for the next ten years."

"I hate those terrorists," Trevor said, his voice like steel. "I hate them for what they've done and what they represent. We're the future, not them."

Georgia shook her head. "Say you love our corporate granted freedom instead."

"I love America," Trevor said, shifting his pose dramatically. "I don't understand why they hate it."

"Good," Georgia said, cheerfully. It was an absurd reaction the same day as such a treachery. "I want to make these bastards pay but we need to express that sentiment only in private. We go high, they go low."

"Until we put them in the ground," Trevor said, smiling broadly. "I need to get in touch with my publicist."

"You have a publicist?" I asked.

"You don't?" Georgia asked, confused.

"Sure," I said, going along with the group. "They work with my makeup artist and biographer."

"I actually know a guy who has both of those," Trevor said. "Personally, I'm waiting until I'm at least thirty for the latter."

Georgia texted me her publicist's contact information. "I'll get you a meet. He's going to love you."

We pulled into the underground terminal of the Butterfly Building a few minutes later. It was a massive center with thousands of people using it daily. They all dressed nearly identically with blue vests over white shirts paired with blue pants. The executives could dress however they wanted but conformity was a necessity in the megacorporation's working class. Again, we were treated differently from the rest of the public as our car had its own cordoned-off section of the terminal. Walking inside, we took a private elevator up to the third floor where the BBN was headquartered.

"Are you sure we're necessary?" I asked, not wanting to talk about what I'd seen. "I'm sure they're going to have all the coverage they need."

"No, they're holding the story," Georgia said. "As far as the world is concerned, the event hasn't happened."

"What?" I asked, blinking. "Why?"

"Because we have to control the narrative," Georgia said, again. "I told you this."

"To say what?" I asked, wondering how she could even think about something like this right now. Our fellow students had just been caught in a terrorist attack, people were dead, and they were worried about how to spin this. I expected this from Butterfly's psychotic media department, but we were just students. Weren't we?

"The truth, Rob," Trevor said, putting his arm around me and giving my shoulder a squeeze. "That an evil terrorist attacked an innocent bunch of students and murdered them."

"Yeah…" I trailed off. "That is the truth, isn't it?"

Georgia and Trevor looked at me like I was an idiot child.

"You poor dear," Georgia said. "Sometimes it's so easy to see where you came from."

"You're lucky to have us as friends," Trevor said.

I was suddenly inclined to hate my friends. Well, maybe not so suddenly. I wished Jane were here. Sometimes, I imagined she faded away like Marty McFly's family in *Back to the Future*. We'd changed the future, but not as much as I'd hoped. Today's attack proved that.

"Yeah," I muttered, not even bothering to hide my sarcasm. "I count my blessings every day."

Georgia nodded as if not picking up on it.

Trevor just smiled.

We stepped off the elevator and into the BBN office. It was abuzz with hundreds of reporters, computer programmers, and office drones. This wasn't where we worked, but I'd been there before. The three of us were on the executive track and, even as assistants, seemed to have unearned authority. Business had changed with the rise of the megacorps as no one was forced to "pay their dues." Instead, you were trained for the job you were expected to have from the beginning. If you didn't work out, you were replaced by one of hundreds of others waiting to take your place.

Corporate feudalism was how one of my previous economics teachers, Mr. Barnes, had described it. He'd eventually disappeared. I didn't mean he was fired, I meant one day we'd come to class, and he had a replacement with his house having been sold and all of his possessions were missing. I hadn't even been able to find out anything on social media. Barnes' social media accounts had all been deleted. Scrubbed even. Monarch was barely hiding the kinds of things it did to protect Butterfly's reputation and stock prices these days. After all, who would question what happened in the Blue Zones if it kept them from being like the Red Zones?

"We have two subjects for interviews," Georgia said, looking over at one of the workers here. "They are the heroes of today."

"We're not heroes," I said, automatically. Because I wasn't. I was covering up for the fact I knew who'd killed all those students. I wasn't even sure why. It's not like I approved of what Anna had done. Was I really willing to go to bat for a mass murderer, even one who'd used to be my friend? I wasn't sure.

"So modest," Georgia said, smiling. "You're definitely one. We'll have you all over the live feeds by lunch. Rob Stone, corporate scholarship student, runs into burning building to save classmates from terrorist attack."

Her expression toward me was desirous, and for a moment I wondered if she was interested in me now. It was a surprising sentiment and I wondered how I was supposed to react to that. Georgia was beautiful enough, truly, and a supportive friend, but it was a bit like attracting the attention of a shark.

"Thank you. Lieutenant Colonel Boulder is preparing the release of the Monarch aftermath report. If you could go over and talk to him, it would be good," the worker said, looking petrified of Georgia. It was ridiculous as we were just assistants, but he reacted like we could have him killed. Maybe we could. I didn't know anymore.

"I see," Georgia said, sounding disappointed.

The worker leaned in. "Colin Reilly and his wife are visiting the headquarters today. They just had their first child. A boy. I understand they're going to be meeting with all the up-and-comers."

"I see. Thank you. Run along now." Georgia smiled as if the worker was a little dog yipping at her feet.

Trevor frowned. "A child, huh? That changes the future of Corporate America right there. I bet he'll be president someday."

Trevor was fascinated by the Reilly family and collected just about every single detail regarding Colin as well as his wife Anastasia. They were a sign of just how much history had changed. I learned from the book Jane brought with her from the future that in the original timeline, before we had altered it, Anastasia had been assassinated before she'd given birth. It had helped compel Colin to dissolve the puppet government in Washington DC and institute open corporate rule after blaming a conspiracy against him. It was possible, if she stayed alive, things wouldn't get quite as bad. At least, that was what I was hoping for. The butterfly effect. No pun intended.

"Don't worry, Trevor," Georgia said, cheerfully. "I'm sure their son won't show you up."

Trevor frowned. I didn't get the joke. Really, it seemed like they were often having two conversations around me. Maybe that was what happened when you dated someone long-term, whether they liked to label it or not.

"Heya, Rob, Gigi, Trevor!" A familiar voice spoke as a tall, broad-shouldered man with a goatee came up behind us. He was about my father's age and built like a brick wall.

"Hey, Phil," I said, uncomfortable.

"Are you guys alright?" Phil asked, displaying the first real concern I'd seen anyone display.

"We're fine," Trevor answered for us.

"Thank you for asking," Georgia said, politely.

I'd grown quite close with Phil Boulder since working at Butterfly. He was a hell of a guy. Tough as nails and a loyal Monarch employee to the core. But the man had a heart and wasn't afraid to show compassion when need be. Between my father and being in HOPE, it was easy to demonize all Monarch personnel as meathead psychopaths. Real easy since they put me in the hospital after the protest that got this all started.

Phil taught me otherwise. He reminded me that a megacorporation was just that. Mega. Not everyone who worked for Butterfly—or any of the megacorps for that matter—was evil. Some, in fact most, were just average citizens, happy to have a job that provided for their families. Some people just couldn't afford to be part of a revolution.

Still, I sometimes wondered how Phil managed to reconcile it all. He'd been a former member of the United States military before joining Monarch and was now actively working against his former country even if he didn't seem to acknowledge it. He had to know what Monarch was up to and yet, somehow, didn't seem like an asshole. Part of me admitted that it was his resemblance to my father—the better parts of him at least—that was influencing my opinion. I'd never gotten to reconcile with the abusive drunk before, well, he'd died saving me.

"I'm sorry about what happened," Phil said. "Did you know anyone there?"

I paused, then shook my head. "No, I didn't."

26

Trevor and Georgia looked at me strangely.

"You knew a couple," Trevor said, subtly suggesting I should milk that for sympathy.

I didn't want to have this conversation. "Not well, I mean."

Georgia raised an eyebrow. "We need you to get him prepped for interviews. That means makeup, vocals, retakes, and whatever it needs to show him off."

"Hey!" Trevor said, frowning.

"You too," Georgia said.

"No, I need to look exactly like I do now." I shook my head, speaking up. "I haven't washed my face or even my hands. They need to see what I look like as I tell people what happened."

I wanted, desperately, to keep this from being a disaster. HOPE had changed and become a terrorist organization, but I didn't want to rile people up either. The criminals needed to be punished for this and I was prepared to give a big speech over it. It was the first time I'd felt alive and vigorous in a long time, that I was going to be able to do something important. So, of course life crushed me immediately.

"That won't be necessary," a fat man with a clipboard said, walking nearby. "I've just gotten word from up top. They're going to be doing a speech by Colin Reilly on this instead."

"Oh," I said, staring at him. "I see."

Georgia patted me on the back. "Cheer up, Rob. We'll get 'em next time."

"Cheer up?" I asked, looking at her in shock. "After a *bombing*?"

"Poor choice of words." Georgia looked down.

Phil looked at me. "Rob, could I have a moment of your time?"

I blinked. "Um, sure."

Phil led me over to one of the offices belonging to a mid-level manager. The lights were off, and it seemed they were out for vacation (or worse). Phil closed the door behind us and took a deep breath. "Rob, there's something you need to know."

"Yeah?" I asked, now uncomfortable.

"This is the biggest terrorist attack HOPE has ever done."

"Yeah," I said, still thinking of Anna.

"But it's not going to be the last," Phil said.

"What?" I asked, doing a double take.

"There's a lot of chatter about HOPE having been training terrorist cells across the country. There is even talk US military personnel have been defecting to join their cause. It seems a lot of people aren't ready to accept Butterfly in charge of things."

I was about to say "good for them" but kept my mouth shut. My enthusiasm for resistance had taken a serious hit as one might imagine. "You really think it's going to come to war?"

"Yes," Phil said, taking a deep breath. "They've even got their own flag now. An arachnid."

"A spider?" I asked, knowing the answer but refusing to believe it.

"No, a scorpion."

I felt sick to my stomach. "No."

Phil reached for the back of his pants and pulled out a Strike-44 Pistol. My eyes widened, and I briefly debated grabbing it. Instead, I took a deep breath and watched as he held the weapon towards me. "You should take this."

I took the gun and blinked at it. "Uh, thanks."

I hadn't carried a gun in years even if I hadn't forgotten all of Jane's training.

"You need to keep yourself safe," Phil said, taking a deep breath. "You're a B-level target."

"A B-level target?" I asked, blinking. "Me? I'm just an assistant!"

"An intern to an assistant," Phil pointed out.

I frowned and rolled my eyes. "As people keep reminding me."

"Maybe," Phil said, frowning. "You came up in chatter and that's suspicious. I've seen a lot of things lately that have changed my view of how the world works. Nothing particularly relevant, just that HOPE's agents know you go to school at Conner and work here. I'm worried for you, man."

"Thank you," I said, looking at the gun like it was a live grenade. Reluctantly, I switched on the safety and put the gun in my pants underneath my shirt. "I'll keep the others safe."

Phil smiled but it was empty of mirth. "Yeah, I bet you could."

I didn't like the implications of that. Then again, Phil didn't know me as anyone but another privileged scholarship kid. He didn't know the kind of hell I'd endured getting here or the number of times people had tried to kill me. It was better that way since I was all on my own now. I didn't have Jane to rely on. Dammit. I took a deep breath.

"Phil?" I asked.

"Yes?" Phil asked, looking up.

"Do you think we're on the right side of this?" I regretted asking it immediately. It could get me in a lot of trouble.

Phil paused, his expression unreadable. "Until today? I wouldn't have been able to say so. I'm not a dummy. I know the megacorporations can be dangerous at times, and I've seen firsthand what Monarch is capable of. But with what HOPE is doing now? Killing civilians? Can you say we're not?"

"Sure. That makes sense, yeah," I answered, knowing Phil was looking for his own reassurances. It seemed he'd seen something that had caused him to question his loyalty to the company.

Phil gave me a squeeze on the shoulder. "You hang in there, kid."

I remembered that Phil had a nephew about my age who was currently fighting in the South America Wars. "Yeah, I will."

That was when Phil's infopad beeped, and he picked it up to read the resulting text. "Huh."

"What's wrong?" I asked, half expecting another terrorist attack to have occurred.

Phil looked like he'd seen a ghost. "Colin Reilly wants to speak with you."

I sucked in my next breath then blinked. "Yeah, I guess I should go speak with him then, huh?"

"Yeah," Phil replied, looking more scared of his boss than HOPE. I didn't blame him.

It was time to go meet with the devil.

CHAPTER FOUR

"So," Trevor said, pausing. "Phil just handed you a gun."

"Yes," I muttered, having hidden it in the back of my pants with my shirt covering it.

"You, a former radical student activist," Georgia said.

"Yes," I said before doing a double take. "Wait, what?"

"Please," Trevor said, showing I'd severely underestimated their ability to find out information about me. "And now you're going to meet with Colin Reilly, the man who is single handedly responsible for most of the world's current crises."

I was deeply confused. "Wait, what? Why are you saying this? How?"

Georgia shook her head. "What Trevor is asking, Rob, is—"

"Whether this is a test or is Phil literally the *worst* security guard in the history of the world," Trevor interrupted, turning it all into a joke.

"Probably both," Georgia said, dryly.

I had no idea how to respond.

The elevator doors opened to the fifty-sixth floor where all the social media managers for BBN worked, which was mainly a standard office space filled with cubicles, and private offices outlining the perimeter. The environment was buzzing with activity and about as crazy as I had ever seen it.

A symphony of ringing infopads went off one after the other all around the room, and the constant hum of chatter never let up for a minute. The atmosphere reminded me more of a Wall Street trading floor than a corporate workplace, and I was positive everyone present was focused on roughly the same task: damage control in the wake of HOPE's attack. Georgia and Trevor worked on this floor. I was just passing through.

By design, Colin Reilly's office was not the easiest place to get to. Even though we rode the building's main elevators as high as they would go, there were still several more floors above us. That was where upper management kept their spacious, luxurious offices. The only way to get there from inside the building was a separate, private elevator in the back of the floor we were on now. Only us peons who entered headquarters from the ground floor used it, though. Colin Reilly and the others got in from the roof, where their personal helicopters routinely landed on the building's dual helipads.

I stepped out of the elevator with Georgia and Trevor on either side of me. Despite the swarms of people darting through the cubicles, from where we were I had a clear line of sight to the executive elevator on the other side of the room. I started marching towards it with my two friends accompanying me.

"I wonder why the boss man called you up," Trevor thought out loud.

I shrugged. "He probably just wants me to get him coffee or something."

"Butterfly International's chief junior executive training facility was just hit by a majorly embarrassing attack. One to which you were witness, and I got footage of you going in to rescue survivors," Georgia said, her voice flat and lacking any sort of pitch. "I doubt he wants you to get him coffee."

I let out a light chuckle at how dramatic she could sometimes be. It was fake since I could not help but feel queasy at her describing the attack as "majorly embarrassing." It seemed the understatement of the decade.

"On the contrary. A coffee would be the perfect thing to start off a night of stress and world domination."

"You just can't take anything seriously, can you?" Georgia rolled her eyes.

"He takes everything seriously," Trevor said, smiling. There was something almost predatory in his smile.

"I need to go," Georgia said, checking her infopad. "I need to get down to make up to muss up my hair and add some artfully applied smudges."

"Yeah," I said, feeling more comfortable being horrified now. "God forbid you don't look your best for surviving a terrorist attack."

"Laugh it up, funny man," Georgia scolded with her back to us. "See if Colin Reilly is in the mood for your jokes."

Trevor and I both quietly watched her walk away. It was only once she disappeared within a moving wall of office workers that my friend finally broke the silence between us. "I think I love her. She's utterly insane, though."

"I know, right?" I shared his smile. "I think she's a product of the corporate environment, though."

"Aren't we all?" Trevor asked, knowingly. "It's why you're doing what you're doing."

"How much do you know?" I weakly asked, wondering if Trevor was going to "out" my past. Maybe even try to blackmail me, though I wasn't sure what he could get out of me that he didn't already have way more of already.

"More than you could possibly imagine," Trevor said.

"I doubt that," I said, thinking about time travel.

"We're all trying to change the future in our way," Trevor said.

That shut me up. I wanted to ask him if he knew but the chance was too great that he'd think I was a lunatic. Together we continued our path towards the private elevator in awkward silence.

"You gonna ride the train back with us?" Trevor asked, resuming our conversation.

"I have no idea," I replied, shrugging. "He might keep me here all night."

Trevor's chest bounced up and down as he snickered. "Jeez. If only they paid us overtime."

I let out a long sigh that was peppered with light laughter. "If only they paid us."

"You'll make the big bucks eventually," Trevor said, reassuringly. "If you aren't killed first."

"Right," I said, awkwardly. "That was a lot funnier before we just witnessed a bombing."

"Who said I was joking? Good luck up there," Trevor said, his voice briefly holding the sense of something more. Something intense.

Trevor headed towards one of the private offices while I turned my attention to the elevator, which was guarded by a single Monarch soldier. The man stationed here was usually dressed like normal building security with a button-down shirt and tie. Today he was decked out in full combat gear of a vest, assault rifle, and riot helmet. Everyone must have been on high alert because of the attack.

I flashed him my Butterfly ID on my way to the golden-colored elevator, but the guard shot his hand out, blocking me from walking past him. "No one's allowed up."

I held up my ID again, this time closer to his face so that he could obviously read what it said. "I'm Mr. Reilly's assistant."

"It says you're the intern to his assistant," the man corrected.

"Oh, for fucks…" I trailed off. This was one element of working for Butterfly I hated even more than the fact they were all a bunch of evil cyberpunk villains. Every single one of them felt like they needed to act like they were kings of their own personal fiefdom. They got shit on by their bosses, so they shit on their subordinates, until it became the Great Pyramid of Crap™.

"He's in the middle of a broadcast," the man sternly replied. "No visitors."

Almost at a loss for words, I tilted my head to look at him sideways. "I know, but he called for me."

"And I said he's in the middle of a—" He cut himself off by bringing his hand up to the side of his head as if he were listening to a radio in his helmet.

"Uh huh," I said, annoyed and crossing my arms.

"What is it? All right, copy," he said to someone on the other end of the line. The man waited a moment before speaking again. He stepped away from me, clearing a path to the elevator. "Go on ahead."

I briefly thought about giving the guy a piece of my mind but decided against it. Monarch grunts didn't usually respond well to criticism. Instead, I continued to the elevator and opened it using my ID. Hitting the button for Reilly's office inside the elevator was practically instinctive for me by now. Of course, it had to be on the top floor of the building. The floors below him belonged to the COO, the CFO, and other upper-management positions. I'd never been on any of them but couldn't imagine they were anything like Reilly's.

When the doors opened, they led to a reception area that would have been impressive as a lobby for any building. Bright light reflected hard off the shiny marble floor and a gentle stream of waterfalls trickled down the walls. There was an entire seating area of velvet couches set up on one side and a long granite counter positioned on the other. Despite being so large, only a single receptionist sat behind it. She was new and I didn't remember her name. Reilly's secretaries never lasted long before they were fired or quit in a dramatic exit of tears.

I approached the woman, Leslie I think her name was, and she greeted me before I even reached her. "Go in. They're expecting you. But be quiet."

Leslie motioned towards the unnecessarily large wooden doors that lead into Colin Reilly's office. Slowly and carefully, I pulled one side open just enough to slip my body through. It was designed so that those who were impressed by Colin's reception area were then floored by his office. Ornate carpeting covered the entire floor of the expansive room. Intricately trimmed wooden paneling was on the walls, all except the back one, which was a single pane of floor-to-ceiling glass. In front of the window sat Colin at his massive glass desk. With his shaved head and trademark goatee, the thuggish-looking CEO was focused in on a single cameraman filming him right in front of me.

A news crew of several producers, technicians, and makeup artists from the BBN were behind the cameraman and I discreetly slipped into the crowd as Colin delivered his address. "Peace. It's a word we've heard from these terrorists' time and time again. They claim to be 'peaceful' and strive to 'keep the peace.' But today proves without a doubt that peace was never their intention."

I noticed one of the producers in front of me held a tablet with a live feed of what the broadcast looked like to the audience. Colin's image slowly transitioned to footage of the attack. There were close-ups of mutilated bodies and blood-stained rubble. They censored nothing as Colin spoke over the carnage. "HOPE is what they call themselves. An acronym. But nobody cares what it stands for anymore. And that's kind of the point. These people have no ideals. No principles. They don't stand for anything. They stand against something, and that something is progress."

Colin paused, allowing the montage of the attack to fade back to him before continuing. "Who employed millions around this country when they had no place else to turn? Who bought up swaths of property, worthless to everyone else, and transformed whole decrepit neighborhoods into thriving communities? The answer isn't HOPE. They're nothing more than misguided obstructionists throwing tantrums instead of solving problems. No. It was the Butterfly Corporation that became the backbone of this country during its time of crisis. We were the ones to raise this great nation out of despair."

"And why?" he asked while standing from his seat. "Because of this."

Colin held his hand out to the side calling for his wife, smiling and holding up their newborn son, to enter the frame. I hadn't even seen her there, which was surprising given how stunning she looked. The woman was practically a super model. She was tall, skinny, and wore a tight, form-fitting dress. Her perfectly straight black hair draped over her shoulders and barely moved as she took her place by her husband's side.

"Family," Colin said, wrapping his arm around his wife. "The bedrock of the American Dream. Does HOPE believe in family? I don't know. What I do know is that they've torn many apart. At Butterfly we strive to build families up. And you know how we do it?"

I watched the broadcast on the tablet zoom in to a close-up of Colin's face for one final, definitive shot. "Through peace."

Colin held a smile as the feed transitioned back to a BBN news desk.

"Aaaaand we're clear," said the producer holding the tablet. "That's a wrap, people. Move out."

In an instant, the stagnant BBN crew turned into a weave of organized chaos. The makeup artists and cameramen packed up their equipment while several producers offered their CEO some generic praise.

"Perfect, Mr. Reilly."

"Nice work."

"Very well done, sir."

Colin ignored them all, catching sight of me standing still amidst the swarm. "Rob, over here."

I walked around his large, glass desk to approach the Reilly family as the patriarch greeted me. "What did you think?"

"Fantastic," I said, nodding my head.

Colin stared at me, raising an eyebrow in an identical fashion to Trevor. "Really? Because I thought it was crap."

I blinked. "Uh, um--"

"Every one of my speech writers took my idea for a heartfelt sincere address and dumbed it down," Colin said, lecturing me. "Then they dumbed it down more by passing it on for rewrites. Apparently, they don't think the average food-rationed Red Zone mouth-breather relates to someone who knows what the world's largest terrorist organization's acronym means."

"Oh um," I started to say. "Well, I--"

"And Butterfly is about family? Really?" Colin asked, throwing his hands out. "Like the terrorists don't love their kids. I swear, if I didn't actually have marketing research that this crap actually worked, I would have fired them all years ago."

I opened my mouth then closed it, unsure what to say. "Yeah."

Smooth, Rob.

Thankfully, Colin didn't seem to notice. "I'd like you to meet my wife, Anastasia. Anastasia, meet Rob. Rob is my assistant's assistant. My assistant is in Amsterdam right now, so Rob is my assistant."

"It's a pleasure, ma'am," I said with a slight nod.

The glowing, radiant smile she had on camera instantly dropped, replaced with a blank expression of obnoxious arrogance.

"Of course, it is," Anastasia said handing the baby over to her husband. There was a vague look of distaste on her face regarding the child.

Unlike most children, Colin and Anastasia's child had not been born the old-fashioned way. Instead, he was the product of a patented Butterfly process they were advertising to the world. Gene editing and therapies designed to make him superhumanly smart, strong, and beautiful had supposedly been used. So far, he just looked like a normal baby. The only distinctive things were his absurdly expressive eyebrows.

As soon as the newborn was in Colin's arms, Anastasia walked away and out of the office. I guess the supermodel looks came with the persona, too.

Colin lowered his gaze to her legs as she departed and shook his head. "I hate to see her go but I love to watch her leave."

I grimaced at Colin's blatant sexism. "You wanted something, sir?"

His focus turned to the neatly bundled child he cradled in his arms. "I want a lot of things but right now I'm introducing you to the family. And this little fella is Emmett."

It was bizarre to see Colin Reilly, a man I had known only as cruel and ruthless, melt into a big softy. The sight gave me hope, though. If Butterfly's leader was capable of kindness, then perhaps compassion wasn't that far off. Then again, maybe he was just a monster to everyone but his immediate family or this was just an act for the public. Those were possibilities too.

"Is he going to be my boss one day?" I asked, only half-jokingly.

Colin looked up at me with a smile. "Maybe you could be his."

The Colin Reilly I knew could've been baiting me, but his smile looked completely sincere.

"Thank you for thinking so, sir," I said, humbly nodding my head.

Colin rocked Emmett a few more times before signaling a woman, presumably a nanny, to approach him. As soon as the child was out of his arms, all warmth was gone and he was once more the depraved salesman who held most of the country by the throat.

"I heard you were walking by when it happened," Colin said to me while handing the baby over to her. "It must've been horrible seeing such destruction and carnage."

The nanny walked past me on her way towards the door and I shrugged in response to Colin's comment.

"Wrong place at the wrong time, I guess." I wasn't about to confess that I'd had to run across campus toward the bombing. That would require more explanation than I was prepared to give right now.

"Or was it the right one?" Colin asked with a smirk.

Understandably, I was always on edge around Colin. Especially at times just like now, when I couldn't quite gauge his expression. "I don't understand what you—"

Colin cut me off by leaning on his desk to watch the BBN news crew shuffling out of the room. "This is twice now that you've found yourself in the middle of HOPE's antics."

Uh-oh.

Colin knew something. I didn't know what, but he wouldn't be talking like this unless he had proof. Of what, though? His words from the day we met came back to me: "I know who you are." But that was years ago. I've been his trusted assistant since then and have only been loyal through my actions, even if my thoughts were somewhere else. HOPE was long behind me.

I opened my mouth without knowing what to say, hoping the words would come out on their own. Yeah, some genius charismatic leader I was turning out to be. "I…"

That was as far as I got, causing Colin to fill the conversation. "Also, twice you've proven yourself as an asset to this company in the face of such radicalism."

Phew. He was proud of me. Not suspicious, which allowed me to relax my shoulders and smile humbly. "I was only trying to help."

"Don't be so modest," Colin said, leaning off the desk and turning to me. "It's courage like that which shows I was right to grant you a scholarship and take you under my wing."

Without even trying, I found my smile growing wider on its own. Was I enjoying his praise? The thought made me gag since I knew this man had been involved in everything from bribery to murder. Supposedly, he'd started multiple wars to rebuild the countries after the fact. I didn't doubt it. "I appreciate that, Mr. Reilly."

"Not as much as I appreciate you." Colin opened his hands and motioned for me to sit in the massive leather office chair behind him.

My eyes widened, surprised by the gesture. I'd never seen anyone else sit in his chair before. It was practically his throne. The place where he ruled all of Butterfly. "Thank you, sir."

"You started in a dark place," Colin said, making yet another allusion to the fact that my past with HOPE was less hidden than I'd hoped. Dammit, that pun was unintentional.

"Yeah," I said, wondering where he was going with all this and wondering if he was going to reveal this fact to all his hangers-on.

"But we both know there's something more important than improving the world and high ideals," Colin said. "Something even better for motivating people to violence."

"Family?" I asked, wondering if that's where he was going with this.

"Money!" Colin said, cheerfully, reminding me he was less a Hitler or Scorpion and more a deranged used car salesman.

And no less dangerous for that.

"Oh. Right." Still in shock, I slowly walked over and sat down in the chair. "I don't know what to say to that."

Colin looked back over his shoulder and waited a few seconds for the last of the BBN crew to leave. The door shut behind them with a boom, a signal that we were now finally alone.

"How about the truth?" Colin finally asked in a flat, accusatory tone.

"What truth?" I pleaded, honestly perplexed. I was now on my guard, though, and wondered if I'd have to use my gun. Not that it would do any good. I'd be gunned down by Monarch soldiers before I reached the nearest elevator.

"The truth about why HOPE attacked Conners' Security Center today." Colin stared at me with cold, dead, and reptilian eyes.

I had no idea what he was searching for, so I gave the one answer I knew couldn't get me in trouble. "They're terrorists. They blew it up to kill people and cause mayhem."

Colin took a step forward to stand in front of the chair, towering over me. "Don't do that."

"Do what?" I said, confused and completely at his mercy.

"Don't tell me what you think I want to hear by reciting that crap those talking heads down at the BBN spew to the masses. HOPE is a lot of things. But random is not one of them. They attacked that building for a reason."

My memory brought me back to hours earlier when I was chasing Anna through the building. Why was she there? I didn't have an answer, so I technically didn't have to lie.

"I don't know why," I finally replied.

Unsatisfied by the response, Colin persisted. "But you were there. You must've seen something. Heard something. Someone you recognized."

"No," I answered quickly, pushing thoughts of Anna aside. "There was nothing. Just bodies and debris."

Colin swiftly leaned forward onto the chair's armrests, bringing his rigid scowl right up to my face. "Really? Just nothing? Nothing at all?"

"I haven't been involved with HOPE for a long time." I shook my head, just missing brushing our noses together. "I didn't—"

"Remember who you're talking to, son," he interrupted, with a dagger-like voice.

Colin Reilly was truly a terrifying man. His eyes were like weapons, they stared right through you, instilling nervous panic that was impossible to shake. In two years as his assistant, he had never pressed me like this before. What was his game? What did he know? I still had no idea.

I wasn't a stranger to fear. I had felt it enough while the Scorpion's assassins were after me, but Jane had taught me to harness that emotion and use it. Putting an act on for the CEO of Butterfly was practically what she trained me for. "Honest, Mr. Reilly. I have no idea."

Colin tilted his head to the side as if analyzing my features. He stayed there for a moment before pushing off the chair to stand up straight. "I believe you, Rob. I do."

"Thank you, sir," I said, forcing a gracious smile onto my face.

"Because if I didn't believe you, we wouldn't be having this conversation," Colin said, threateningly. "Remember, there're a lot worse things I can do to you than fire you."

It was ridiculous, really, the most powerful man in the world bothering to threaten an intern. Yet, one thing I'd learned about the power structure of Butterfly—hell, power in general—was that it was a drug to the people who wielded it. It didn't matter if they were threatening someone close in rank or far beneath them, some people got off on making other people squirm. I had to force down my sense of defiance and look terrified. Which wasn't hard because I honestly was. I just was able to control my fear, which someone like Colin would never understand.

I sucked in my breath. "Yessir."

Colin grabbed onto the back of the chair and swiveled it to the side, giving me the necessary room to stand up. "We've got a long night ahead of us with a lot of work to do. I hope you're ready."

"Always," I responded, quickly hopping out of the seat, and turning to face my boss.

"Good." He swiveled the chair back around and sat down, scooting himself back under his desk. "Now, do me a favor and get me a coffee. Espresso double latte or whatever you call the fancy shite with too much milk."

"Right away," I said, laughing inside at the request.

I scurried towards the door, grateful that I dodged a bullet. But I couldn't shake the feeling that Colin Reilly had another one for me waiting in the chamber.

CHAPTER FIVE

C olin Reilly was right. It *was* a long night.

    He didn't trust me with anything too important but the paperwork I did for him was still pretty informative about the state of Butterfly and its goals. I also picked up on things I suspected Colin believed I was too stupid or naive to. Things like the fact that Butterfly was doing far poorer than it appeared from the outside. Trying to drive the majority of America into corporate rule was costing a substantial sum of its resources and tanking the US economy in Red Zones hurt Butterfly's overall bottom line. If Colin's plans succeeded, they'd be the effective owner of the country but until then they were bleeding money—both US as well as Butterfly Dollars.

    There was also a project in Alaska that Colin was devoting massive amounts of funds to, hundreds of billions of dollars in fact, which seemed an annual drain on Butterfly resources. I didn't dare ask about it, but it piqued my interest, and I even learned a couple of code words associated with it: "Blue Cascade" and "Aurelia" among others. Unfortunately, I had no idea what to do with this information and it wasn't like I could report it to BBN. Most of the other major networks were also megacorp-friendly even if not Butterfly allied. Either way, it was almost midnight by the time we finished, and I was surprised how very little the terrorist attack had occupied our time together.

    I rode alone in Butterfly's private maglev, the same one I took on the way into the city. Trevor and Georgia had gone home after their interviews hours before. But unlike earlier, when the other cars were packed with passengers, the entire train was nearly empty. Heading home this late wasn't a common occurrence, but it did happen from time to time. CEOs didn't reach that level of success by getting off work early, and I didn't expect anything less being an assistant to one.

Okay, assistant to an assistant.

I didn't mind making the trek home by myself, though. It allowed me time to process the day's events, and on this day a bit of self-reflection was desperately needed. These moments reminded me that although I was a part of Butterfly, I would never become one of its drones. My mission was to change the company, not let it change me. It might've been a pointless endeavor, but this path was better than what I could become if I chose to do it HOPE's way.

By the time I reached the dorm back on campus I was ready to just collapse in bed and pass out. The halls, completely drenched in darkness, were still and quiet. Everyone was asleep.

As I approached my room, I noticed a small stream of light filtering out from under the door. It was the only light I'd encountered inside the entire building. My first thought was that my roommate was awake. His name was Billy Jones, and I spoke to him so little that it had taken me months to learn his last name. If he were still up then I assumed the door would be open, but it was shut tight. Checking it, it was locked too. Very strange. Maybe Billy had chosen to lock it due to the terrorist attack, which was a silly but understandable reaction.

I used my key and went inside only to find Billy asleep in bed with the light on. The room was small, like all dorms in the buildings. Billy kept his bed on one side and mine was on the other with only about eight feet or so between them. I didn't know my roommate well, but I lived with him long enough to know he'd never do something as bizarre as fall asleep with the light on.

That was when I felt a presence moving along the wall behind me. In an instant, Jane's training rushed back to me, and I moved to attack. My strike was countered before it had even begun as the intruder locked me up and slammed me against the wall. I wondered who could've predicted so perfectly what I was about to do, and then I realized it was because my opponent was the very person who taught me.

Jane had returned.

She let go of her hold as our eyes locked and a surprised smile spread wide across my face. If we had passed each other on the street, I might've not even recognized her. My future daughter still had her white hair, which was a dead giveaway, but it was up in a ponytail, something she would've never been caught dead wearing the last time I saw her. The rest of her outfit, a strappy top and yoga pants, had a sporty look as well. I wouldn't even begin to presume about what she'd been up to these past nearly four years, but it appeared as if she had grown quite comfortable in the present.

"Jane!" I shouted in a muffled voice. "You're back!"

"Obviously." Jane scrunched her forehead at me, looking more confused than excited. "Why are you whispering?"

I nodded my head in the direction of Billy sleeping peacefully in bed. "I don't want my roommate to hear us."

Jane uncaringly waved her hand at him. "Don't worry. He's not waking up."

Staring at Billy, I leaned in for a closer look to confirm that he was drooling wildly all over his pillow. It took me a moment to figure it out, but once I did, I turned back to Jane with a baffled expression. "You knocked my roommate unconscious?"

"Technically, no," Jane replied, shaking her head with an innocent smile. "He was already asleep when I drugged him."

And just like that, I realized how much I missed having this crazy assassin from the future in my life.

"Ah, that's my girl," I said, smiling proudly at her.

Jane didn't return the gesture. She coldly stared at me with a blank expression while waiting for my joy to simmer.

"You don't look happy to see me," I muttered as my smile faded. "Not that you ever look particularly happy, but something tells me this isn't meant to be a social reunion."

The corner of her mouth lifted ever so slightly, bringing life to her stoic face. "I am happy. I just…"

I couldn't tell if she struggled to find the words or simply to say them, so I finished the sentence for her. "You didn't know how I would react to seeing you after you abandoned me."

Her body stiffened as she defensively shouted. "I didn't!"

Jane caught herself from yelling, realizing that attacking me probably wasn't the best response. Her head lowered humbly instead in a rare show of remorse. "I'm sorry."

I could've just let things be. I was happy to have her back. But my pain had had years to fester, and I wasn't about to let her betrayal go that easily. "You never even said goodbye. Where did you go, Jane? Why did you leave?"

I didn't want to sound like a whiner—which I was failing at miserably—but it wasn't like the last four years had been champagne and roses. Constantly keeping everyone at arm's length, focusing constantly on trying to master the arcane systems Butterfly operated on, and lying to everyone all the time had worn me out. The fact I'd only had Jane to even confirm any of what I'd experienced was real only made it worse.

Her moment of weakness ended when she looked up at me with strong, protective eyes. "I did it to keep you safe."

I rolled my eyes. "As my bodyguard, I'm pretty sure you need to be around in order to do that."

Jane sighed and then walked past me to sit down at the edge of my bed. "I made a deal with the remaining New Hope assassins. I convinced Cody and Esther that if HOPE was gone then there was no chance the Scorpion could rise. Allowing his army to die out before it was born would be the same as killing him. But that also meant I had to leave you and let you find your own path free from any influence, including mine."

"And that worked?" I asked, skeptically.

"Are you alive?" Jane asked.

"Yes,' I replied, frowning.

"Then it worked," Jane said. "Remember, Cody and Esther used to be zealots in your service. They only wanted to kill you because things had gotten so bad in the future that there was no choice but to take drastic action."

"They killed my dad," I replied.

"That was Sabrina, and she was always kind of a bitch," Jane said, defensively. "Anyway, they decided they preferred living here in this time to going on a continuous killing spree until all traces of the Scorpion were gone."

"Except HOPE isn't dead," I replied. "It's also been radicalized."

"The giant smoking hole in the campus where you've been staying clued me in," Jane replied, showing she was still significantly harder than I would ever be. "I'm afraid Cody and Esther might see you as the source of it all."

If there was one thing Jane taught me that didn't have to do with fighting, it was how to properly analyze a situation. If she was concerned the assassins might've come to that conclusion, then she could've also believed it herself. "So, you came back to what? Make sure I was alright? Or was it to make sure I wasn't a part of it?"

Sensing I felt betrayed, Jane looked up at me from the bed with an uncharacteristically innocent smile and shrugged. "Couldn't it have been both?"

After spending the entire night with my boss, it seemed as if Colin Reilly had more faith in me than Jane did, and I let her know how I felt about that, too. "Seriously? After everything we've been through together you think I would start planning terrorist attacks?"

Jane didn't show a hint of shame, and, even now, she still stared at me, scrutinizing my reaction. "I had to make sure."

I had nothing to hide and walked forward to sit right next to her on the bed. "Well, I'm sure you'll be happy to learn I'm not a part of HOPE anymore. The exact opposite, in fact. I'm working with Butterfly."

Jane flashed a slight frown, which either came from concern or futility. "Still trying to bring them down from the inside?"

"Yeah," I corrected. "I want to change them into something better."

The frown returned to Jane's face and this time it stayed there. "Can't say I'm happy about that. It's dangerous being an outlier in an organization built on control."

I shrugged, indifferent to her concern. "It's been working for me so far."

"Do you really think so?" Jane asked.

I remembered Trevor and Georgia's reactions to the bombing and how they were already picking up on the fact I thought fundamentally *different* to them.

Faced with the fact the past four years might have been wasted, I chose to lie, "Absolutely."

Jane placed a hand on my shoulder, her frown morphing into one of the sincerest expressions I'd ever received from her. "Which is why I have faith that you'll one day succeed."

I would be lying if I said her confidence wasn't inspiring, but the uplifting feeling only lasted a moment before a rush of self-doubt took its place. "But not fast enough. I'm just an assistant right now and things are escalating quickly. HOPE is still becoming an army without me. They've even…"

I was rambling but still managed to catch myself before saying too much. I was afraid of how Jane would react, which she instantly picked up on. "What is it?"

There wasn't any point keeping the news to myself, so I swallowed deeply and just came right out with it. Phil's earlier words had rocked me to the core. "They've even taken up the scorpion as a symbol."

Jane literally didn't move. She had no response, verbal or otherwise. Her non-reaction surprised me until I realized what it meant which surprised me even more.

"You knew?" I asked.

"I've seen them flying it on flags," Jane said with the same deadpan expression.

"And that doesn't concern you?" I asked, still baffled that she wasn't going crazy over this.

"This time was way before I was born. But from what I understand, the scorpion was never a symbol of the New Hope Army. Only a moniker taken up by their leader."

Jane was never one to be indirect and I glared at her for beating around the bush. "You mean me?"

Jane ignored my clarification to reiterate her point. "Whatever HOPE is transforming into it's not the army the Scorpion led."

Still discouraged by the development, my chin drooped onto my chest. "Why does that matter if the end result is still the same?"

Even though I wasn't looking at her, I could still feel Jane's steady eyes peering through me. "Because I still believe in you and your ability to shape the future."

My head reflexively shook in response without even looking up at her. "If the world goes to war, Jane, then all this was for nothing."

Jane didn't say anything at first, almost as if she were gathering her thoughts and preparing a speech, which she eventually started after a long sigh. "If there's one thing I learned as a soldier it was that some wars are inevitable. Humanity has been fighting since the beginning. It's a cycle of violence no one can stop. All we can do is hope and pray that by the time it's over, the world is a better place because of it."

That wasn't exactly the pep talk I needed. I lifted my heavy head to look up at her. "Really?"

That was when I realized she had just paused, waiting for me to make eye contact before continuing. "Yes. But the Scorpion never learned this lesson until he was lying on his deathbed. Not you, though. You're aware of it now. Your choices have freed the planet from a terrible fate. Because of your actions, the future is opened to becoming something better. It might not seem like much, but take it from me, it's a victory and you should be proud of that."

I knew I missed Jane, but I didn't realize how much until this moment. She always knew, at least for the most part, exactly what to say, and I found myself grinning at her without even trying. "Thank you."

We both smiled for a moment, happy to just be back in each other's company, but Jane ended it when she stood from the bed and began walking towards the door. "It was good to see you."

"You're leaving?" I quickly hopped up to cut in front of her. "Just like that?"

Jane puffed out a slight annoyance that her exit had been blocked but composed herself enough to explain. "If Cody and Esther are honoring their end of the bargain then I have to honor mine."

Her body started moving again to resume her departure, but I quickly spoke to stop her. "I've been thinking about you a lot these past few years. I could really use your help and guidance."

"I came to this time to stop the Scorpion and that's what I did." Jane scowled at me, annoyed that I wasn't backing down.

I ignored her point and continued to press my own. "You told me you spared my life because you thought you could guide me down a better path. How can you do that if you're not here?"

"I see you're doing just fine without me." Jane walked around me to continue towards the door. I didn't physically stop her this time, but I wasn't done with the conversation.

"Is that it?" I asked sarcastically. "Or do you not want to be around me now that I know the truth?"

With Jane I could never be quite sure what would set her off, but I obviously struck a nerve because she immediately turned around with the most condescending glare, I'd ever seen from her. "Yeah. That's exactly right. I ran away from home because I'm afraid of all your potential dad jokes."

I scrunched my forehead as much as I could and waved a stern finger in her face. "Don't take that tone with me, young lady."

It was silly, stupid, and not really all that funny but I needed any levity I could get.

"That's it," Jane declared dramatically, throwing up her hands. "I'm leaving."

Jane reached for the door, and I had to hold in a chuckle while quickly grabbing her arm to pull it back.

"Wait. I'm sorry. I swear I won't do that again." I thought it was a good joke. "It's just we never got the chance to properly deal with…" Still struggling to find the right word, I eventually just waved my hand back and forth between us. "…this."

"What's there to deal with?" Jane's expression never changed. "Yes, genetically I'm your daughter. But you're not my father any more than that joker sleeping behind you."

"Billy isn't so bad," I said without turning around. "It's just he's the son of a pair of Monarch realtors so he's decided to major in pot. Really, I've had worse roommates. My previous one funded his curriculum with homemade cyberporn."

"I didn't take you for a prude, Dad," Jane said, deliberately making me uncomfortable.

"It was a bit of a shock when I found them in the middle of filming, on my bed," I replied, accenting the last part of the sentence. "I had to throw out my old action figures after I'd seen what they'd been used for."

Jane smirked.

"Fine," I conceded, eager to make my plea. "But what we went through couldn't have been easy for you. Your own father sent you to kill his younger self and you ended up becoming my friend. All that time we were living together, and you kept this enormous secret to yourself. It must have been eating you up inside."

Again, Jane showed no emotion and responded while turning her back to finish her exit. "Don't worry about me, Rob. I can take care of myself."

I really didn't want her to leave. We'd been apart for so long and I truly did miss her. But strangely enough, I wasn't sad by how we left things this time. I did, however, have one question. "How did you know not to call me Robbie?"

Jane smirked. "I've got bugs and cameras in your room. You're right that porn guy was a real freak. Some of it was pretty hot, though."

"I need to throw up now," I said, looking down at the ground. Looking up, I saw Jane was gone before I had a chance to say anything else. "Seriously, how the hell does she do that?"

It was hard having cyborg Batman as a daughter.

CHAPTER SIX

"*1*984 by George Orwell is a work that was made to critique Stalinism as practiced by the then-extant Soviet Union. This despite the fact George Orwell was a socialist himself," Professor Higgins said, addressing the class as he wore a tweed sweater and pair of khaki pants. He was a good-looking, middle-aged, black man with a shaved head and a welcoming demeanor that made him perfect for the many PSAs that Butterfly liked to show on all the campus holograms.

The classrooms of the advanced political science courses were a lot more laid back than other Connor University classes. We were all gathered around the room, some at desks, others sitting on couches. You only got to take these classes if you were guaranteed an executive position past graduation. Georgia and Trevor were present but not really paying attention.

I was struggling to listen to the professor, but my mind continually returned to Jane. I was still dealing with the fact she'd made a deal with the New Hope Army behind my back. It was hard to believe the people who'd murdered my father and traveled back in time to kill me would ever make such a deal. However, I was willing to believe just about anything Jane said. She was someone who had done so much for me. Yet, I was angry she'd abandoned me. Jane was my only family left.

Professor Higgins sat on the edge of his desk.

"One of the chief themes of *1984* is the willingness of individuals to compromise themselves in a dictatorial society. Winston hates the government of his nation and Big Brother but he's still part of the system that oppresses the public. He is interested in becoming a rebel, but his actions, small and large, only result in him becoming more compromised until the book's final dramatic moment."

"Do you think Winston is a coward?" Georgia asked, surprising me. I hadn't expected her to be paying attention.

"Obviously, he's a coward," Trevor said. "He betrayed the woman he loved."

"I'm not so sure," Georgia said, frowning. "I think he was afraid, yes, but the walls were closing in on him the entire time."

"Interesting," Professor Higgins said, looking over at me. "What do you think, Rob?"

I blinked, suddenly aware everyone was looking at me. My notebook was full of names, doodles, and random thoughts. "Pardon?"

"What do you think of Winston? Was he a coward or not for the way he chose—or didn't choose—to stand up to the government of Oceania?"

I tried to think of my answer but found myself troubled. "I don't know. I think it really boils down to what you think of heroism and resistance. Winston thought he was resisting the government, but he was just doing what he wanted. He began an affair with a beautiful woman and continued living his semi-comfortable life with the Outer Party. It was easier than trying to change his life. To make real change."

I was old enough and wise enough to understand how hypocritical that statement was. I'd chosen the easiest path possible with my own life, no matter what my justification. When faced with the evils of the Scorpion and Butterfly, I'd decided to just live a life of luxury as a scholarship student. Well, life of luxury was an overstatement since I didn't have much more than paid board and tuition, but it was a lot better than I'd had before.

Was I just running away from my problems? I'd done that before and it had gotten my father killed. The New Hope Army had tracked me back to our home and he paid the price because of it. I'd changed the world by choosing not to become the Scorpion, but now it was all seemingly coming to pass anyway. The specifics were different, but the generalities were the same. It was like the weight of history was a tidal wave and I was just one man standing in front of it. I could move a little of the water around, but it would eventually crush me. Or was I just telling myself that?

"Do you think our society has any similarities to the one in Oceania?" Georgia asked, making a shocking suggestion.

I agreed with her. The news was completely controlled by the megacorporations and didn't care if the truth was suppressed. Websites that reported the truth were drowned out by counterfactual reports. Everyone used the same search engine, Imago, and that always reported the spin the companies wanted. Private security firms had replaced the police departments and virtually everyone was watched twenty-four/seven via their infopads, televisions, or computers. It didn't matter if people ever had their data looked at, they were still constantly under surveillance.

Professor Higgins was not apparently ready to go that far, or he was scared to. "Oh, I don't know about that. In many ways, I would suggest that we're probably freer now than we were a few years ago."

"Interesting." Georgia gave him an enigmatic stare.

What was she playing at? I had to admit that as much time as Georgia and I had spent together, the two of us didn't really know each other at all. All I really knew about her was she was incredibly intelligent and able to play the corporate politics of Butterfly far better than actual executives.

"I think we should move on," Professor Higgins said, stuttering a bit before clenching his fist and coughing into it. "Does anyone have any objections to that? Let's move on to the next book, *Brave New World*. I'd like to offer a bold new interpretation: that the world Huxley proposed was a utopia rather than a dystopia."

I didn't get to comment before a soft alarm started sounding around the classroom. The glass doors to the room shut and locked. I'd never seen anything like it before, even when the terrorist attack went down. Then again, I hadn't been inside one of the classrooms when it had happened.

"Please remain calm," a drab, unpleasant voice spoke. "We are conducting an inspection and will resume normal operations after matters are settled. Please cooperate with the Monarch security operatives."

Oh crap. I couldn't help but wonder if they'd somehow connected me with Jane. I didn't know what she'd been up to, but something told me she was probably on one of Monarch's hit lists. It might not have been Jane. It might have been my connection to Anna. What if she was still hanging around campus? I dug my nails into my palms and wondered what was going to happen next.

The answer came seconds later when the doors opened and a squad of Monarch soldiers entered, fully armed, and carrying M60 rifles. Rifles, which were aimed at us. Everyone panicked but Georgia, Trevor, and me.

"Do not move!" the captain of the squad said, circling around the group and surveying each of us.

"What is the meaning of this?" Professor Higgins said, keeping his hands raised. "We've done nothing wrong."

He was rewarded with a rifle butt to the face. It sent him spiraling to the ground with a broken and bleeding nose.

"Shut up!" The captain shouted. "Up out of your seats and against the walls!"

The violence, once again, brought one of the many futures from my nightmares back to the surface. I was surrounded by New Hope soldiers as a Scorpion flag flew across the halls of an advanced military fortress. Pillars stood against the walls and bodies were lying across the ground by the hundreds. They didn't even bother to clean them up before forcing more prisoners up to execute.

This was not the ramshackle army of my earlier dreams, fighting over the ravaged ruins of a dying world. No, this was a cool, calm, and professional army of soldiers wielding technology I hadn't seen anything the likes of. There were magnetic planes rising off the ground before taking off like jets, spider-tanks, and everyone wielding personal magnetic railguns. It was like I'd stepped into a science fiction movie.

Was this the future as it was supposed to be? Or just another world given shape by my worst fears?

I never got to find out. A moment later I was put up against one of the walls and shot to death with a dozen other nameless prisoners.

"Gah!" I said, awakening from my daze.

"Don't move!" one of the soldiers said, keeping his gun in my face.

"Leave him alone," the captain said. He then turned to Georgia, looking at her with a contemptuous glare. "Student-31B5, you are under arrest for suspicion of violating the Rosencrantz Act."

"The what?" I asked, confused as hell as to what was going on. If Monarch was arresting them publicly like this, it had to be bad.

The captain stared at me before turning back to her. "Come with us quietly or we will make you come."

Georgia didn't seem surprised. Instead, she simply raised her hands and let them cuff her before letting them lead her out the door. Some of the Monarch soldiers looked like they wanted to beat her down with their batons, but they held off.

For now.

When the last of them was gone, I turned to Professor Higgins. "What the hell is the Rosencratz Act?"

I shouldn't have bothered since Professor Higgins was still on the ground, holding his nose. I ended up having to help him up. It was times like this that I tended to forget just how little your average person was prepared to be caught up in the horrors of the struggle against Butterfly.

Trevor surprised me by answering. "The Rosencratz Act is a new addition to the US legal code, designed specifically to protect the megacorporations. It allows their security to arrest and detain anyone for ties or even suspicion of ties to one of the groups on the Anti-Corporate Watchlist."

I processed what he was saying. "They think she's a part of HOPE? That's insane!"

"Now, now," Professor Higgins said, his bloodstained hand holding his nose. "I'm sure the Monarch PMC has its reasons for doing what they're doing. We should get back to class and—Oh wow, that's a lot of blood."

"I think you should go to the hospital," I said, looking at him.

Professor Higgins nodded. "I think that is an excellent idea, Rob. Class dismissed. Please, do your reading and writing. Also, I don't want anyone to refer to this incident in your reports on dystopianism. Don't mention anything about Monarch or Butterfly at all in fact."

"Right," I said, trying to hide my disgust. Higgins was a coward but at least he'd tried to talk to the troops carting Georgia away.

I'd just sat there, confused.

Trevor grabbed me by the shoulder and pulled me out of the classroom. I could already hear our other classmates talking smack about Georgia. They discussed how she was an ungrateful witch for turning against Butterfly, how she was a traitor, and how they'd never liked or trusted her.

"What the hell?" I asked. "I never thought Georgia was even remotely anti-corporate. Hell, I thought she was the next super executive."

At best, she was moderately pro-HOPE's goals but that wasn't something I was going to mention aloud where someone could hear.

"Maybe we didn't know her as well as we thought," Trevor muttered. There was something about his tone, though, that told me he wasn't telling me the whole story.

"What do you mean?" I asked.

Trevor looked at me with a strange expression, as if he was testing me. "She could've been putting on a mask for everyone. Georgia liked to act like Butterfly always knew what was best, but I could tell there were parts of the system that disgusted her. No matter how hard she tried to hide it."

"I never suspected," I said, blinking.

Trevor snorted. "Come on, man, you put on a mask, too."

"I do?" I blinked. "No, I mean, no I don't."

"Listen, I understand what you're doing," Trevor shook his head. "We've all seen things we don't want to admit are wrong. I'm just better at spotting the lies than most of us. I get why you do it. Why I do it. Why Georgia does it. It's either fall in or fall behind in this world and you must suck it up to avoid joining the latter."

I did a double take as I tried to process what Trevor was saying. In a way he was right. I had been putting on a mask the entire time I'd been studying here but hadn't given any thought that other students might be. Still, Trevor was wrong about why I did it. I wasn't doing it so I could be the exploiter rather than the exploited, and the fact he was made me worry about him. I was doing this to help the world. Wasn't I?

"We've got to go get her out," Trevor said, taking a deep breath.

"Wait, what?" I asked.

Trevor looked back at me. "Georgia might have some reservations about Butterfly, but come on, do you think she could be involved with terrorists? She was the person who sent us into that burning building to help survivors. Trust me, this must be a misunderstanding."

I wasn't so sure. Seeing Anna involved with the bombing had shaken me badly. If I didn't know my own ex-girlfriend well enough to know that she could be capable of becoming a monster, then did I really know anything at all? Then there was Jane and whatever she'd been up to this entire time. Plus, Georgia had reacted coldly and calmly to the bombing. Even exploitative. I didn't picture her as the kind of person who would blow up a building full of students, but I didn't know who the kind of person was to do such a thing.

"Yes," I said, deciding to go along with Trevor. I wanted to believe Georgia was innocent. "You're right. There's no way she could be guilty."

"Yeah, we have to prove her innocence," Trevor said.

"I'm not sure innocence is what matters," I said, cynically. "What matters is what the people with power think."

"Maybe we can convince them?" Trevor suggested.

"Maybe?" It occurred to me that this was perhaps a turning point of what comes next. My choice here could have a serious impact on the rest of my life. On the future as a whole. I was tired of following the path laid out for me by Jane. I wanted to make a difference.

If Georgia wasn't guilty, then she needed someone to intervene on her behalf or she would just become another statistic of Butterfly's tyranny. She'd end up locked away, beaten, and eventually forced to confess to whatever they wanted her to. Maybe her mother could get her out of it or maybe not. It was common for Butterfly loyalty to cleave families in half.

If Georgia were guilty, then maybe she could link me up to HOPE and I could find out what was going on with that organization. If they were becoming the terrorist organization from my dreams, then I needed to stop that from happening. I didn't know how I was going to do that, but I would do anything to find a way. No, not anything. I'd already killed once. Never again. Not if I had any choice in the matter. And I did. Didn't I?

"Then let's get going," Trevor said, putting his arm over my shoulder. "Let's try and flex some social networking magic to help her."

I wasn't sure if it would be that easy. Monarch was a close-knit private army that was increasingly the United States' answer to secret police. The notion they were able to arrest people and hold them indefinitely on their own initiative said everything that needed to be said about that. The fact they weren't actual police or military officials is part of the reason why they weren't subject to the same restrictions as the rest of the country's law enforcement. I wasn't sure if it would be possible to help Georgia, but we had to try.

"You got it," I said, putting on an optimistic smile. I had to wonder if the reason I'd been able to become the Scorpion was because I was so good at lying. Even so, it felt like Trevor was manipulating *me* more than the reverse.

"I wouldn't be too worried about her, anyway," Trevor replied. "I have a lot more friends in high places than you might imagine. People way more important than her mother, who probably reported her in the first place."

There was another hint of Trevor's weird level of influence for a college student again. He acted like he was concerned about his grades around me but other times, he implied he was already a board member. It made his attempts to cozy up to me all the weirder.

"Just not Colin Reilly."

"Yeah." Trevor grimaced, as if I'd stabbed him.

What was going on here?

CHAPTER SEVEN

Honestly, I had no idea how we were going to help Georgia. Regardless of how much of an iron thumb Monarch might have already had on the campus, they still did not mess around when it came to detaining someone. Especially a Butterfly executive assistant with a parent high up in the Monarch hierarchy. They must have had some reason to go after our friend. Our plan, we assumed, was to figure out what it was and prove it to be a mistake.

Luckily for us, the Butterfly board called an emergency meeting to address the crisis, and as their assistants—well assistants' assistants—it wasn't that hard for Trevor and me to find out about it. With all the top executives in one place it would be easy for us to plead Georgia's innocence. Mind you, it was entirely possible we'd end up getting ourselves implicated but I owed Georgia. Sociopathic social climber or not, she was my friend. Okay, that sounded better before I thought it out.

We arrived at the building shortly after nightfall and the place was like a ghost town. Unlike the last time we were in the underground train terminal, only the Monarch guards patrolling the area were in sight. Granted, the normal workday was over, but there still should have been the after-hours employees doing their jobs. Janitors cleaning up and engineers performing maintenance. There weren't any of them in the terminal.

Trevor and I stood on the platform and looked around dumbfounded for several seconds before I finally asked, "Where is everyone?"

Trevor shrugged while continuing to scan the barren terminal.

"I don't know. The execs must've sent everyone home after they called the meeting."

"That can't be good," I said as my throat tightened. I really meant it.

"Come on. Let's find out just how bad then." Trevor grimaced.

We walked side by side to our private elevator. There was usually an operator present that would take us up the building, but we still had access to it with our keycards. When the doors opened, Trevor and I were barely able to take two steps before Phil intercepted us.

"What are you two doing here?" Phil asked.

The building's security center must've caught us on their cameras and told him we were coming. I looked over Phil's shoulder to find two more Monarch guards stationed by the boardroom's entrance. The double doors were closed, indicating the meeting was probably already well underway. Besides the main boardroom, there were also two smaller conference rooms on either side of us. I half expected those to be occupied too. They didn't have any guards, though, indicating they were probably empty.

"Georgia was arrested," Trevor answered, caring less about our surroundings than I did. "They came right into our class and took her away."

I was expecting Phil to look surprised at the news. Instead, his face drooped into a morose expression. "I know. And as her friends this is the last place either of you should be."

"That is exactly why we *need* to be here," I replied, eager to defend Georgia's honor. "*Because* we're her friends."

"We want to prove to the board that she's innocent," Trevor added, giving the fakest smile possible.

It was unsettling.

Phil quickly glanced over his shoulder to make sure nobody was approaching and then turned back to us, clenching his teeth in frustration. "Believe me. I, as much as anyone, want to help Georgia. But there's a time and a place for that. Now is not it."

"But—" I started to protest.

Phil quickly cut me off. "No buts. Go home. Get some sleep and I'll reach out to you in the morning."

I didn't have to look over at Trevor to know he was making the exact same scowl that I was. We both stared Phil down, who somehow had the ability to simultaneously exude the rigid authority of a Monarch goon while maintaining the heaviness of genuine regret in his eyes.

Our brief standoff ended when a loud voice yelled from the boardroom entrance. "Oh, come now, Lieutenant Colonel Boulder. Surely you know Butterfly treats its employees better than that."

All three of us looked over to see Colin Reilly standing between the double doors. I hadn't even heard him open them.

"Especially those whom we executives trust with the important task of pouring our coffee and walking our dogs," Colin mocked, parting the two motionless Monarch troops to approach us.

I was caught off guard, unsure as to how to cautiously broach such a sensitive subject with such a dangerous man. Trevor didn't share my concerns.

"Why was Georgia arrested?" he asked bluntly. His sharp tone practically sounded like an accusation. "She's not a member of HOPE. She's more loyal to Butterfly than—"

Colin put his hand up upon reaching us, cutting off Trevor's rant. "Phil, would you please escort Mr. Monroe back to his train car."

"No. We came here for answers and—" Trevor was not happy.

"I'm *talking to Rob*," Colin said, cutting Trevor off. "You can get anything you want to know from him."

Trevor did not appear pleased. He looked to me, hoping for backup, but being hunted by assassins has taught me to be pragmatic. This was always an uphill battle for us, and now the Butterfly CEO was willing to give me an audience. I wished Trevor could be by my side. I really did. But this was better than nothing, and I was willing to take it.

"It's okay," I said to Trevor with a grateful nod. "I'll call you as soon as I know something."

Trevor sighed, releasing the anger in his face. He did flash me a subtle smile, though. Trevor nodded back and looked over to Phil, letting him know he was ready.

The two of them entered the elevator together and Colin waited until the doors were closed before giving his instructions. "Follow me."

Colin led me to one of the two conference rooms beside us, which was just as empty as I'd thought it would be. He shut the door and walked around the long, oval-shaped conference table.

The silence was uncomfortable, which forced me to engage in small talk. "I've never seen the building this quiet."

"We sent everyone home," Colin replied without looking at me. "It's board members, major executives, and primary stockholders only right now. Well, plus their entourages, but they hardly count."

"Why?" I asked.

Colin continued his path around the table, stopping to grab a remote controller off the other side of it. "Because a calm always comes before a storm."

I hated when he started talking in vague metaphors. It reminded me of a creepy Bond villain ominously referring to some secret evil plan.

"What storm?" I asked, half-afraid of the answer.

Colin held the remote up, aiming it at the plasma screen on the far side of the wall. "War, Rob. That's where we're headed."

"War? But I thought…" My voice trailed off after Colin clicked the remote, revealing a harrowing image on the screen. It was a black-and-white feed from a security camera inside a small, dark room. A dirty, uncomfortable room, too, with concrete walls and a floor that hadn't been cleaned in far too long. Random stains were all over it, some of which I assumed were blood. Especially because there was a single individual tied to a chair in the center of the room. She was beaten and bruised. Clearly a prisoner that had been recently interrogated. And by interrogated I meant tortured.

That wasn't what left me speechless, though. Sadly, my time with Jane had gotten me comfortable seeing such gratuitous violence. What had me in shock was the fact that I knew who the prisoner was.

"You recognize her?" Colin finally asked, responding to my silence.

"That's Christine Trainer," I said flatly and dryly, trying my best to hide the knot in my throat.

"And how do you know that?" asked Colin without missing a beat.

All my memories with Christine instantly flashed before my eyes. I remembered the first time we met, when she was my tour guide during my first visit to Connor University. I remembered when we marched to this very building, protesting Butterfly and its corruption. I also remembered when she volunteered to be a part of our heist back in Chicago. It was the last time I'd seen her. I guess she really did never make it out of that building. Monarch must've grabbed her and had been keeping her prisoner for the last nearly four years. Four years! *Oh, Christine...*I felt so guilty. I couldn't worry about that now, though. Colin asked me a question, and despite all my memories to the contrary, I easily found a plausible answer.

"She's the founder of HOPE. Anybody who has watched the news in the past four years knows who she is." Colin smirked, pausing for just a second to make my skin crawl.

"You're a hard worker, Rob," he finally said through his creepy smile. "I'll give you that. But you're not as good of a liar as you think you are."

Uh-oh. After all this time. After all the hours I spent by his side, Colin never once called me a liar. This couldn't be good.

I tried to hide my nervousness as I choked out an answer. "I—I'm sorry, sir, but—"

"You didn't honestly think that I'd allow a former member of HOPE close to me without knowing everything about him, did you?"

That was it. The cat was out of the bag. But then again, it was never in. Colin Reilly always knew about my past. The "I know who you are" he said to me after our failed heist proved it. So, oddly enough, I wasn't afraid that he had learned my secret, but I was curious. I needed to know the truth.

"Then why am I not the one tied to that chair?" I asked.

"I did say 'former member,' didn't I?" His smile remained as he answered.

I had plenty more questions, but this was all just too much to take in. I had to turn back to the video feed and look at Christine. She looked so miserable and in so much pain. I was already plotting in my head ways to help her, futile as it may have been.

"Do you consider her a friend?" asked Colin, with an unusually sympathetic tone.

There was no point lying, so I nodded while keeping my eyes on the screen. "I did."

"Does it hurt to see her like this?" Colin asked.

I nodded again, this time without saying a word.

"We had no choice, Rob. She's a terrorist leader." Colin gave an insincere smile.

I wanted to reach over and start punching Colin Reilly's smug thuggish face in. If I'd had the gun Phil had given me, I might have shot him, so I was glad I didn't. He knew Christine had been my friend and had saved this for a particularly dramatic moment. Had he had Christine this entire time? Had she been tortured for months? Years? What was the fucking point?

Power.

Power was the point. It was easy to see my entire plan was a chimera. Colin Reilly had never intended to let me become an executive. I'd just been his pet HOPE terrorist that he played with like a cat played with a mouse. Maybe he'd continue playing with me after tonight, but it was just as likely I'd get thrown into the same sort of cell Christine was presently occupying. Possibly Georgia too.

Bastard!

I turned to face Colin with my back straight and my eyes steely. The kind of confidence he paid attention to.

"Then put her on trial," I said.

"So that her little band of misguided misfits can make her a martyr?" he asked rhetorically, staring at me but pointing to the screen beside us. "I don't think so. She'll stay in the Chrysalis where she belongs."

I knew where Christine was now. It was kind of by chance I even had that information. As Colin Reilly's assistant, I'd had "access" to tons of classified documents. Not that I ever actively snooped around. I'd heard rumors of what Monarch did to spies accused of corporate espionage and I rather enjoyed keeping my digits attached to my body. But Colin and the other executives had me perform tasks from time to time that inevitably led to sensitive materials coming across my desk.

The Chrysalis was one such detail.

After crunching the numbers, the megacorporations deemed that the populations of America's so-called "flyover" states were draining too many resources. But the states still had value as farmland. So, a deal was struck with the government to completely automate the agriculture industry while evacuating most human beings that lived within former independent farmland. It had been the beginning of the resistance to the corporations. The largest of these agricultural zones just so happened to be the perfect place for Monarch to build their off-the-grid prison. Colin probably didn't even know I was aware the Chrysalis existed beyond using the name right now. Which was lucky for me. If he did, he probably wouldn't have mentioned where she was while showing me a video.

I did my best to hide my realization from my expression. "Why are you showing me this? I came here to talk about Georgia."

"So did I," Colin stated bluntly.

I was getting angry but showing it would have gotten me nowhere. This was a man who was used to being praised, pampered, and getting what he wanted. I had to be reserved and respectful if I was going to get anywhere with him. It was probably pointless but I had to try for Georgia's sake. "I'm sorry, Mr. Reilly, but I don't understand what—"

"Miss Trainer told us that a Butterfly executive assistant was a HOPE informant. My first thought, obviously, was you, but Georgia's zealotry for Butterfly put her under suspicion as well. It didn't take long for Monarch's internal investigators to find the evidence they needed."

There was always the chance he was lying. A man didn't become the CEO of a slimy company by not being a snake himself. But a part of me knew he was telling the truth. Colin was putting all his cards on the table. I was no threat to him. I'd assumed, stupidly, I could change things and decided to play the toady to work my way up. Colin must've known this. He probably knew it all along and basically told me as such. There was no longer any reason to deceive me. So, I knew he was being truthful. Georgia was a part of HOPE and there was nothing I could do for her. I couldn't look at Colin any longer and my eyes drifted to the floor.

"Chin up," he said, recognizing that I had given up on my friend. "They also ruled you out in the process. So, you, see? The system works."

The system disgusted me. It ran on fear and power. I couldn't fight it from the inside anymore, though. I debated grabbing the nearest hard object, a chair maybe, to beat him with it. My fury was barely contained, and I was stunned by my own desire for violence.

Colin didn't seem to notice as he walked behind his desk and continued his smug Lex Luthor monologue.

"But that system is being threatened by these animals…these savages who think a synchronized Kumbaya will make the world's problems go away. But people don't need to be coddled. They need to be shepherded and controlled. Society wouldn't exist otherwise. I've brought you on my team to show you—someone who used to be one of them—that HOPE will never achieve the peace they claim to fight for. All their actions will lead to is anarchy. That's why we need to stomp them out like the insects they are before—" His speech was sharply interrupted by an explosion that ripped through the room.

Huh, I did not see that coming.

CHAPTER EIGHT

The explosion was not a large one, and it bothered me that I had experienced enough terrorism in my life to know the difference. This was a homemade explosive device which probably used a demolition charge from a construction site. It detonated at the other end of the conference room, sending fragments of the heavy wooden table flying into the air as my ears were deafened by the sound.

I pushed Colin Reilly to the ground, trying to get him to safety despite the fact the immediate threat had passed. Also—and I hated that it even occurred to me—that it would have solved a lot of problems if he just died here. Colin Reilly was the evil heart of the New Freedom Party's finances as well as the head of America's largest megacorp. If he disappeared, then there would be people who would still try to forward their agenda, but no one to headline their agenda.

There was no one capable of carrying on Butterfly when Colin died either. All the executives underneath him were a pack of wolves that hated each other as much as they revered their chairman and CEO. With Colin dead, they would turn on each other and tear apart the corporate empire he'd built.

Or destroy the world.

Dammit, I couldn't take that kind of risk. As much as I wanted to personally beat him to death, we couldn't plunge the world into chaos.

"Are you alright?" I shouted, unwittingly yelling in his ear. The ringing in my ears hadn't stopped yet.

"You little traitor!" Colin shouted, looking at me with pure hatred in his eyes.

I blinked. "What?"

"You set me up!" Colin said, climbing to his feet faster than I could.

"No!" I said, blinking. "There must have been a bomb set under the boardroom tab—"

I didn't get to say anything else because he grabbed me by the shirt and lifted me a foot in the air before slamming me against the wall. Despite my impressions of the CEO as a middle-aged corporate suit, he was a lot more physically formidable than I gave him credit for.

"You know, I thought there might have been potential for you," Colin said, his voice gaining more of his Irish brogue than he let out on television. "That you might be a little smarter than your moronic band of economic terrorists but clearly I was wrong."

"I didn't do this!" I snapped, ready to punch him.

Colin proceeded to grab me by the throat with both hands and start to strangle me. He was far stronger than he looked, and I had to wonder if he was modified like Monarch's Special Forces. Unable to persuade him of my innocence, I pushed back and struggled to get his arms off me.

Seconds later, four Monarch soldiers wearing gas masks entered the room. The explosion had taken them a surprising amount of time to respond to. They were three very tall men and one slight but fit-looking woman. I hoped for a second, they would try to get Colin off me. That hope was dashed by the reaction of the lead soldier.

"Sir?" the captain asked.

Colin tossed me against the wall across the room and I slammed against it like a sack of potatoes hurled by a bodybuilder.

"Prep him for transport to the Chrysalis. We'll get everything he knows about this terror plot from him, by hook or by crook."

I stood up and stared at them. "You have no idea what you're doing."

"Use electricity charges," the Monarch captain said. "Maximum power."

"Yes, sir," the woman in the back said.

As they aimed their weapons at me, the woman fired into the backs of each of the three Monarch soldiers in front of her with electric rounds. All of them, including the captain, fell to the ground with blue-white electricity arcing across their bodies. Electricity shots didn't usually kill you but were far more effective than a Taser.

"What the hell?" Colin said, reaching into his pocket.

The woman proceeded to aim her gun at him and shot him in the face with another electricity charge. "Lights out, Your CEO-ship."

I blinked. "Lights out, your CEO-ship? Did you get that from a bad movie?"

The woman removed her mask, revealing Jane's face underneath.

"Yes. The new James Bond movie. I've been trying to catch up on this era's culture."

"Jane!?" I exclaimed in shock. "What the hell are you doing here?"

"Seeing if you needed any help, which you obviously did," she replied like it was the most obvious thing in the world. "Now come with me if you want to live."

I didn't need any further persuading as I got up off the ground. "I guess this means that I'm no longer going to be able to reform Butterfly from the inside."

"You guessed right," Jane said, lifting her pistol to Colin's unconscious body before switching to lethal rounds.

"No, wait!" I snapped, running up to her side. I grabbed the gun before she could fire it, though there was nothing preventing her from shooting him anyway.

"What? Why?" Jane asked, confused. "You realize he's an enormous pile of shit, right?"

I stared at her. "Believe me, I know. But you can't kill him. If you do, then we'll be hunted forever. Plus, it might cause a civil war."

"Oh, Robbie," Jane muttered.

"Rob," I corrected.

"You are too damned good," Jane said, kicking Colin instead. He made a grunting noise, which showed he was already starting to wake up.

"Let's move!" I snapped.

The two of us headed immediately out the door and into the hallway, where a large hole to the sky outside now stood where the boardroom had been only moments ago. The entire Butterfly board...killed in an instant by the explosion. It was now more important than ever that Colin stayed alive.

As I was busy surveying the destruction, two Monarch soldiers entered the hallway, drawing their weapons as they ran. Jane didn't hesitate to shoot at both of them, sending them fleeing down the halls. She could have killed them but was more interested in scaring them off.

"Those weren't stun rounds!" I shouted, stunned.

"You're right, they weren't," Jane said, pulling out an ARC-7 pistol from her pocket and handing it to me. "Do you remember how to use one of these?"

I took the gun and cocked a round in the chamber automatically. "Unfortunately."

"Good," Jane said.

Jane seemed like she was in her element, and I wasn't going to contradict her, but I couldn't help feeling disappointed. She'd managed to stop the rise of the Scorpion, but she was still fighting a war that she'd been born into. I'd hoped she might find some kind of peace, but it seemed it was her desire to continue fighting forever. That made me sad. It also wasn't something I could afford to think about now if I wanted to survive.

Running down the halls, Jane and I ducked down into the stairwell where a group of Monarch soldiers were heading up the stairs beneath us. Jane led me up the steps to the next level and we watched the Monarch soldiers pass down below us. None of them noticed us and disappeared through the door that shut behind them.

"Idiots," Jane said, immediately heading down the stairs.

"How did you even get in here?" I followed her as I took a deep breath.

"I made a deal," Jane said.

"A deal?" I asked, cautiously surprised.

"HOPE wanted to infiltrate the building," Jane said. "I approached them to offer my assistance."

"What?" I asked, stunned. "You made a deal with terrorists?"

"Freedom fighters," Jane muttered. "And I didn't have a choice, even if they are becoming more extreme than ever."

"You think?" I asked, shaking my head. "First the explosion at Connor U and now this?"

Jane shook her head. "I learned HOPE didn't blow up your school or the boardroom. At least…not that I'm aware of. By the way, I should mention it wasn't just Colin Reilly who was subject to bombing."

"Who else?" I asked, shocked.

Jane paused. "Well, you know it's almost a shame we're outlaws now because the possibility of advancement up the corporate ranks is looking really good with the board and a good fifty or sixty other executives dead from other explosions. Not counting their lawyers and assistants. Because, really, who would? Really, it's a shame HOPE didn't do this because it's a damn effective decapitation strike."

I was utterly shocked by her revelation. "If HOPE didn't set those bombs off, then who did?"

"I don't know." Jane shook her head. "But we have bigger things to worry about."

"Surviving?" I joked.

"Worse," Jane said, no humor in her voice. "Have you been having nightmares?"

Like usual, I was stunned by Jane's seemingly infinite insight. "How did you know about that?"

"Not good," Jane muttered.

"What do you mean not good?" I asked, wondering exactly what she knew that I didn't.

That was when we reached the bottom of the stairs, just a short flight across the lobby to victory, only for another squad of four Monarch soldiers to enter. Jane lifted her gun, but she was grabbed. What followed was a masterful display of martial arts as she managed to disable three of them with chops to their stomachs and a leg grip around one's neck that flipped him over. The fourth, however, just aimed at her head. So I shot him.

It was an automatic action I didn't have time to think about. I just aimed the gun at the Monarch soldier and pulled the trigger. I hadn't killed anyone since Gunner, the assassin whom I killed nearly two years ago. That was self-defense, though. It was kill or be killed. This wasn't the same thing. I did it to protect Jane, but still. It was murder, plain and simple, and the act momentarily stunned me.

Except then I noticed that he was thrashing on the ground with blue electricity moving around him.

"You didn't tell me it was an electrically charged gun!" I snapped, relieved but aware I'd been fully prepared to kill someone without thinking.

"You never asked," Jane said, bored.

The two of us didn't stand still, though, and headed into the lobby over the bodies of the disabled soldiers. What greeted us was not the largely empty location I'd hoped for. Instead, there was a group of almost a dozen elite Monarch Heavy Assault Troopers. They were dressed in orange balaclavas, plastisteel armor, black berets, and carrying assault rifles.

There were also RFX-8 attack drones hovering in the air and a bipedal automated tank that looked like the latest *Robocop* reboot's ED-209. I sometimes wondered if the lab boys down in Monarch's weapons development saw their job as to make as much science fiction into reality as possible. I suppose we were lucky there wasn't a bunch of robotic xenomorphs crawling through the vents.

We were surrounded.

I turned around to run back but, much to my disgust, I saw the soldiers we'd "outwitted" coming down the stairs behind us. Colin Reilly was behind them, looking furious. He had a pair of Monarch soldiers holding bullet-proof transparent riot shields in front of him. Apparently, he wanted to taunt me in person without putting himself in danger.

Asshole.

Jane turned to me. "Are you rethinking killing him? Because I'm sure I can take him out before we're gunned down."

"We should surrender," I said, dropping my gun on the ground.

"And end up like the rest of Monarch's prisoners? Vanished from the face of the Earth," Jane asked. "Do you really want that to be your fate? Give me death on my feet."

"With pleasure," Colin said, clearly hearing us despite the fact he was a good dozen feet away. "I'm afraid these individuals were killed escaping."

Jane smiled.

I didn't understand why, before she threw me to the ground as she hurled a grenade toward Colin Reilly and the other soldiers. They all hit the deck, one of them trying to cover Colin with his body to shield him from the explosion. Instead, the room filled with an opaque black smoke. Similar clouds of smoke filled the air as gunfire went in every direction.

"What's going on?" I asked, more confused than ever.

"We're escaping!" Jane said, pushing me to one side as the soldiers fired at the sound of my voice. "Now shut up!"

A second set of grenades were thrown as these emitted ear-piercing wails. Jane grabbed me and pushed me to the ground. We crawled on the ground as there was more random firing in every direction until we were past the soldiers, running to the lobby glass doors that mysteriously opened as we approached.

Waiting outside the building was a group of cleaning vans and gray suit-wearing janitorial staff who were holding machine guns. There were perhaps two dozen total. There were Monarch soldiers on the ground who hadn't been disabled. They'd been killed.

"HOPE," I said, taking in a deep breath. "You had this planned."

"More like I went along with it," Jane muttered. "Now do you want to live or not?"

I had no choice and ran into the nearest van, which had its door opened. The interior was gray, full of cleaning supplies and weapons. Jane quickly joined me as a pair of HOPE operatives closed the door behind me. They got into the front of the van as there was the sound of more gunfire and the vehicle started.

"We'll set off the IEMP after we're a sufficient distance from the HQ," the woman in the driver's seat, who I didn't recognize, said. "That should royally screw with Butterfly's day."

"IEMP?" I asked, knowing what she meant but still reeling.

"Improved Electromagnetic Pulse. The military has gotten around most of the protections for modern computers and HOPE just happened to have one of their weapons grade devices," Jane said. "It's not like in the movies, Robbie...I mean, Rob. It burns out computer circuits permanently. Everything in the computer hard drives will still be accessible but the machinery itself will be ruined. It'll also disguise the viruses we've uploaded to the system until they've spread further. Another way of slowing Butterfly down."

"That was the goal?" I asked, looking at Jane. "Set off a bomb and kill all those people just to cover your stupid IEMP?"

"We weren't involved in that!" the woman driving yelled back at us. "That was another group."

Jane frowned while gesturing to the front of the van.

"Told you. They had nothing to do with it. Planting the IEMP was just the price I had to pay to get you out of there. We just had the mother of all bad timing to do it with whoever else was planning their attack."

I was grateful for it too. Jane was not HOPE's biggest fan. That she subjected herself to working with them to protect me was huge. Still, the idea there was another group at work behind the terrorism I'd experienced made me wonder what the hell was really going on. Was it a HOPE splinter group? An entirely new group? Some rogue Butterfly faction? I wasn't used to this sort of insanity.

The driver clearly wasn't happy with us and kept her foot on the gas as she screamed. "Can one of you tell me what the hell happened in there?"

"Just keep driving," Jane said, annoyed. "We'll go over everything back at the base."

No matter how many times I've been down this road with Jane, her cool, collected demeanor always impressed me, but there was something else she said that bothered me more. "You mentioned something earlier about nightmares."

Jane's expression became unreadable as she lowered her voice so that only I could hear her.

"He's just a lab tech now, but there's a man out there that will grow up to become Doctor Charles Kepler, the person who will crack the secrets of time travel."

Jane looked to the front of the car, making sure no one was listening in before carrying on. "I was forced to read dozens of his books before coming here, and Kepler believes that when history suffers changes, people intimately tied to these changes will catch glimpses of what will be. They're called Fulcrums and merge with their other selves."

"That sounds ridiculous," I said, not hiding my opinion.

Jane shrugged. "I've had a lot of bad dreams since we saved the world. Can't be a coincidence."

"But...did we save it?" I asked, the question that was obviously on both of our minds.

Jane didn't have an answer.

CHAPTER NINE

For nearly twenty minutes, the van zoomed around without stopping or slowing down. At first, I thought we were headed outside the city, but with the crazy number of turns the driver was making I started to suspect she was just trying to make sure we weren't being followed. Or—the more likely scenario—we had lost whoever was already following us.

Besides the screeching tires and hum of the engine, the ride was pretty much silent. I had questions. A lot of them, actually. I'm sure Jane did, too. Nobody said a word though. The inevitable discussion would have to wait.

The van sped around the city until I felt a slight dip in the road. If I had to guess, I figured we were driving downward, probably into a garage of some sort. The van slowed as the sound of grinding gears echoed outside the doors. A moment later, those same doors opened and standing in front of us were two young adults, a Black male, and an Asian woman, both with the same hardened expression of conviction on their faces and automatic weapons strapped around their shoulders.

The driver of the van got out and the HOPE agents scooted past us to exit the van without saying a word. I looked to Jane for instructions, as I so often did in the past, but she said nothing and simply followed the agents out of the van. My options, at that point, were limited.

I exited the van as well and found myself in a medium-sized garage, probably a former automobile business of the kind that still existed in the Red Zones. I guessed we were in Chicago's and noted that was a downside of Butterfly's lack of influence there. I didn't know how we'd gotten past the checkpoints but, at this point, didn't really care. A thick metal door stood beside me, which more than likely produced the grinding sound I had heard earlier.

There were six other men and women positioned around the garage, all with the same expression and weapons as the two individuals who had opened the doors. They weren't wearing uniforms, but it was obvious they were trying to dress in similar attire. Each of them had on a different brand of grey jacket and pants. When combined with the dirty boots on their feet, the bunch of them were as ragtag a group of soldiers as ragtag could get. At least in appearance. They were all very disciplined and professional looking in demeanor. A far cry from the social activists I remembered mingling with when I was a part of the organization.

But not everything in the room was a new sight to me. Standing in the middle of the HOPE soldiers was Anna. She had both hands on her hips in a power pose so strong it made me nervous, though that might've just been the fact that she'd punched me the last time I saw her.

"Hey, Anna," I said, waving with an awkward smile. I wasn't sure how to begin a conversation with someone who was probably involved in a terrorist attack on a school, but to whom I now owed my life. That was not the sort of thing business negotiations training had prepared me for.

Anna started marching towards me without saying a word, and her strong, confident steps did not help calm my nerves.

"What—what are you doing?" I stammered.

Anna stopped directly in front of me and scanned my face with a blank expression. Before I had a chance to assess what was going on, Anna lunged her face forward and latched her lips onto mine. The unexpected kiss startled me, but after my brain had a chance to process it, I allowed myself to relax and grab ahold of Anna by her hips.

I brought her in close and enjoyed myself—genuinely enjoyed myself—for the first time in I didn't even know how long. In that moment, I just decided to believe she was innocent and pretend this entire nightmare of the past four years—hell, five—hadn't happened. The kiss brought me back to our days in high school. Simpler, quieter times, and even though I wasn't inside Anna's head, I think she felt the same way, too.

Our lips parted slowly, and she smiled before opening her eyes. The happy expression on Anna's face remained as she took a step back.

"Good to see you, Robbie," she said.

"It's Rob now," I corrected her, also with a smile.

Anna's joyful smile subtly morphed into a conceited smirk. "Of course, it is."

She then casually waved her hand in the air, a signal for all the armed HOPE soldiers to aim their weapons at Jane and me.

"Whoa now," I said, throwing my hands up in surprise. To say I was a little freaked out would be an understatement. "What's this all about?"

"We're being betrayed." Jane never flinched.

"Not exactly." Anna's voice sounded more chipper than you would expect from someone who had just ordered several guns aimed at an ex-boyfriend. "Threatened is more accurate."

"Threatened?" I repeated, not quite sure I heard her right. "Why?"

Anna placed her hands behind her back and started pacing around the garage. As much as I wished it didn't, I had to admit it was very supervillain-like of her. "I've had a lot of time to think about what happened to us, Rob. Where we went wrong. Where our bond fell apart."

"Was I too needy?" I asked, sarcastically. I should have been more understanding, given she'd just saved me, but I'd just had years of preparation and work shot to hell. There was no chance of reforming Butterfly from the inside now and the megacorp was acting worse than ever.

Anna stopped pacing and turned to face me dead on. "If I had to put a label on it, I would say it was your immature need to use humor as a coping mechanism."

"That's a joke, right?" I asked, less sarcastically.

"Of course," Anna replied with a slight smile. It wasn't a happy smile. More like a reassuring one meant to put me at ease as she moved her sharp gaze to Jane's direction. "What drove a stake in our relationship was her."

"Oh," I stammered, nervously. It seemed she thought Jane and I were an item. "We aren't...Jane and I don't...We never..."

"Are you looking for an apology?" Jane asked, interrupting me.

Ironically, she asked her question unapologetically, which I thought was kind of strange. While I was quick to rightfully deny Anna's assertion about Jane's and my relationship, Jane just didn't care. Instead, she was more focused on establishing dominance in the conversation. Personally, I just didn't want to get shot.

I honestly had no clue how Anna would react, but I relaxed when she simply shook her head instead of pushing back. "No. All I want is an explanation. Because the truth is whatever is going on between you two is bigger than me. I see that now. Our world is painted in black and white. There are two sides. HOPE and Butterfly. Good versus evil. Right against wrong."

Anna stopped and shifted her gaze back and forth between Jane and me to speak to me directly. "Through it all, Robbie, I could always count on you to have my back. To be my partner in the fight against corruption and injustice."

That was a very biased way of viewing things and didn't include the small detail of people trying to kill me. I hadn't told her about any of that, though. "You're being unfair."

"Then she came along," Anna growled, once again shooting daggers at Jane with a glare.

"Are you suggesting Jane made me take a job at Butterfly?" I asked, not quite sure what she was getting at.

"No," Anna replied. "Not at all. Things are way too complicated for that. So complicated, in fact, I don't even have a clue as to where to begin with you two."

Despite becoming a hardened revolutionary, it would seem Anna was being genuine in her curiosity. She really had no idea what was going on and was just fishing for the truth.

So, old habits died hard, and I reverted to my original excuse. "We're—"

As if reading my mind, Anna held up her hand and immediately caught me off guard. "If you say the word 'cousins', I'm going to order them to shoot you, which would be a shame because you are a way better kisser than I remember."

"Really?" I asked with a smile, ignoring the fact that she'd just threatened to kill me. The grin retreated when I caught sight of Jane staring at me like a parent embarrassed by their inappropriate kid.

"Sorry," I muttered to her.

Once she was satisfied with my shame, Jane transferred her focus back to Anna. "Are the guns really necessary? I did what you asked for to help rescue him. We're not your enemy."

"I know," Anna admitted, plainly. "Nice touch blowing up the building, by the way."

"I had nothing to do with that." Jane shook her head.

Again, Anna started pacing around the garage with her arms clasped behind her back. If I didn't know any better, I would assume whatever power she'd been given by her leadership role at HOPE had gone to her head.

"It's kind of genius, actually," Anna said, starting her monologue. "Taking out all the Butterfly board members when they're in the same room at the same time. You must've been planning this for years being Colin Reilly's little errand boy. Unless, of course, Colin ordered you to do it to eliminate his competition."

"I didn't kill Butterfly's board of directors!" I shouted at the ceiling, frustrated that everyone kept blaming me for something I didn't do— and almost died from, I might add.

Anna stopped marching and turned to us. "Well, I know we didn't."

"Really?" I said in the most obnoxiously sarcastic voice I could muster. "I'm not the one who set a bomb off at a school."

Anna's expression faltered ever so slightly. Not enough to give anything away, but enough to hint she was genuinely confused by my accusation. "I swear on Reverend Tully's life, I haven't set off any bombs. Would you be able to say the same? Oh, that's right? You two are just so keen on keeping secrets."

Anna was telling the truth. She had no reason to lie. But if she wasn't the bomber, then who was? It also occurred to me why they had guns pressed on me and Jane. Not only did they believe we were the ones who blew up the Butterfly board of directors, but they presumably thought I'd engineered the attack on Connor University as well. Anna thought I was some sort of criminal mastermind, which was both flattering and a bit disturbing.

There was a lot going on here I needed to figure out as well. HOPE apparently had access to military grade hardware, the gunmen here were acting like trained soldiers rather than armed civilians, and Anna was giving orders like an officer. Overshadowed by the assassination attempt or not, their attempt to cripple the Butterfly computer network was also a military strike rather than indiscriminate terrorism. Which told me that what was here in front of me was just a cover for something else.

But what?

"What's that supposed to mean?" Jane said, taking a step forward in anger.

All the gunmen trained on her tensed, but if Anna interpreted Jane's movement as a sign of aggression, she didn't show it.

Anna took a step forward, too, closing the gap between them. "You know exactly what it means."

"Hey! Ladies!" Wanting to diffuse the tension, I moved up beside them, careful not to make any sudden moves, which was probably for the best. As much as I wanted to calm the situation, getting between these two was the last place I wanted to be. "Think we can take it down a notch?"

Their stare down lasted a few seconds until Anna finally relented. "Fine. If neither of us killed all those Butterfly execs, then who did?"

Jane shook her head. "I don't know. But that's the least of our problems."

"Then what's more important?" Anna asked curiously.

I wasn't quite sure what Jane was referring to. It might've been her concern that I would get wrapped up in HOPE's crusade or maybe something about the visions I'd been having. Either way, I was willing to bet she wasn't about to share her thoughts with Anna.

"Can't tell you," Jane said, proving my suspicions right. "But you need to let Rob and me go so we can deal with this on our own."

"See?" Anna threw her arms up, clearly unhappy with Jane's response. "This is exactly why I don't trust either of you. So, while you might not be my enemy, you're certainly not my ally. Not while you're keeping secrets from me."

This was getting out of hand, and I had had enough of it.

"You want secrets?" I asked Anna, sharply. "Fine. How about the fact that Christine is still alive?"

The weapons aimed at us briefly faltered as my revelation struck a chord with every member of HOPE in the room, including Anna, whose face sunk in surprised disbelief. "Christine is…alive? How do you know that?"

Jane wasted no time on seizing the opportunity. She moved like lightning, knocking away the two rifles that were the nearest threats with a punch and a kick before sliding around Anna, grappling her in a headlock.

I had no idea Jane was going to do that, but I wasn't surprised by it. Seeing an opening and taking it is what she does. The remaining rifles were all on her now. None were aimed at me.

"Tell them to lower their weapons," Jane ordered Anna.

"Why?" Anna asked through gritted teeth. "Because this instills me with such confidence?"

"Stop!" I yelled to no one and everyone. "All of you! You want to know the truth, Anna, then clear the room."

Anna managed to chuckle despite Jane's firm grip around her neck. "You seriously think I'll let myself be left alone with you two after this?"

"Yes," I answered, staring right into her eyes. "Because the Anna I remember would do anything to get what she wanted."

Still continuing to hold Anna tightly, Jane looked at me with heavy eyes. "Rob…"

Jane's voice drifted off, almost as if she assumed I would know what she was thinking, which I did. For so long, my white-haired assassin-turned-bodyguard from the future fought hard to keep her true identity hidden. And I went along with it. Partly because I was scared. Partly because it was easier to believe Jane was right, which she was most of the time.

But I was tired of keeping secrets. Tired of hiding the truth, especially from the one person I wanted to be honest with from the beginning. I didn't know if there was much of a relationship between Anna and me left to salvage, but I was willing to at least make it right.

"Don't," I said to Jane, shaking my head to let her know there was no point in trying to persuade me. "We've done it your way long enough. It's time to try something new."

Jane thought for a moment—only a moment—before giving in and letting go of Anna completely. "Screw it. Not like things could get any worse."

"Stand down," Anna ordered the HOPE soldiers as soon as Jane's hands were off her.

Unhappy with the directive, one of the soldiers started to protest. "But—"

"Leave," Anna commanded, grilling the man with a stare so deathly that I was glad she'd never used it on me when we were dating.

Slowly—and I assumed reluctantly—the HOPE soldiers all left the garage, leaving just Anna, Jane, and me completely alone.

"Now…" Anna said, turning to us after the door slammed shut. "Tell me *everything*."

CHAPTER TEN

I was honestly surprised when Anna removed everyone from the room and left Jane and me alone. Well, alone with her. Then again, I supposed she didn't have much to fear from us. Neither Jane nor I was armed, and Anna was. Even if we managed to overpower her, what was the point? We'd still be two individuals in the middle of a paramilitary organization's headquarters.

Yeah, Anna had nothing to fear from us.

Nothing except the truth.

Anna pulled up a chair from the side of the room and sat down in it. "This had better be good, Robbie."

"Rob," I corrected for the second time.

"You don't get to be Rob here." Anna stared at me. "Not while I'm the one calling the shots."

That wasn't good. It meant she was treating this as an interrogation rather than a conversation between two friends. Then again, she did knock me out not too long ago, so I don't know why I would expect otherwise. Hell, I'd thought she was a terrorist attacking innocent college students so maybe I didn't have a leg to stand on to begin with. Especially since she apparently thought I was a terrorist too. Wow, it was almost comedic, except for the part where I'd probably spend the rest of my life in prison or get shot if I didn't persuade her otherwise.

"I understand," I said.

"Are you?" Jane asked.

"What?" Anna said, glaring at her.

"*Are* you in charge?" Jane clarified. "You're our age, and HOPE is a national organization with a lot more funding than it used to have. Those are military-grade weapons and there are many hardened soldiers among your people's ranks."

Anna stared.

"Jane…" I trailed off.

"We have friends now," Anna replied. "I'm more of a liaison for the movement rather than operational intelligence."

"Friends," I said, simply. "Who do you mean?"

"The US Government, mostly," Anna replied. "Or elements within it, at least. Senators, former members of the CIA, and even a Joint Chief. While most of the government has sold out to the megacorporations, there're still people who want to see a return to civilian control."

"Or at least non-corporate," Jane muttered, implying something I didn't understand.

"Maybe," Anna said, picking up on the implication in a way I hadn't. "My formal rank is lieutenant and I'm with US Army Intelligence. Of course, if anyone ever managed to capture me then the US would disavow all knowledge of our activities. Some real *Mission Impossible* bullshit. Now talk."

I contemplated the best way to phrase the next sentence to come out of my mouth before deciding to just blurt it out as plainly as possible. "Jane is from the future."

Anna got up from her chair and looked ready to advance. "Listen, Robbie, I am not—"

"Project: Aurelia," Jane said, simply.

Anna frowned.

"Project what?" I asked, more confused now than ever. I'd seen it among Colin Reilly's papers, of course, but had no idea where Jane had.

"It's the codename Butterfly uses for its time travel program," Jane explained. "Among other projects."

Anna frowned even more.

"What? This is a thing?" I asked, having never really given much thought to how Jane and the other assassins travelled to here from the future.

"It's nothing," Anna replied, unimpressed. "One of Colin Reilly's pet projects. Something he's put hundreds of billions of dollars into for almost no return. I mean…come on. Time travel? It's ridiculous. Any other CEO or chairman would have been fired over it, but it's the price of a cup of coffee for Butterfly these days. And its existence most certainly doesn't prove that she's from the future."

"You may be underestimating how much Colin Reilly has put the company in the red with it," I replied.

"I know you're thinking about hitting it," Jane remarked, ignoring my comment.

"Hitting it?" I repeated, wondering if I was hearing her right.

"Killing the scientists, stealing the data, confiscating the prototypes." Jane ran down the list as if it were the most natural thing in the world. "Aurelia is still years, maybe even decades away from anything tangible from what our people have heard. But that just means it's a relatively low-security project. Easy for us to take it as our own. It would also cripple Butterfly before they have enough technological weapons to fight the US military let alone an armed insurgency."

Anna then turned to Jane, genuinely shocked by what she had revealed. "But how could you know any of that?"

"I told you," I said, rolling my eyes. "She's from the future."

"Fine." Anna crossed her arms and sat back on her heels. "Let's say I believe you for a second. That Jane's ridiculous white hair is actually some kind of futuristic fashion statement and not just a cry for help. It doesn't explain how she knows about a top-secret Butterfly program and our plans to steal from it."

"She's a future member of HOPE," I revealed.

"By then it's been renamed the New Hope Army," Jane added. "But yes. Your attempts to secure Aurelia and continue its development are successful, which allowed me to eventually travel back to this time. However, it happens much too late to stop Butterfly from having most of the weapons developed by the project. Weapons they turn against the USA and use to cripple the government before launching a coup in the capital."

This was all new information for me. Jane had come back with a German language history book that had detailed Butterfly and the other megacorporations crippling the US government before instituting a fascist corporate-based replacement. However, the actual specifics had been pretty sketchy, and Aurelia certainly hadn't been mentioned. Jane had been holding out on me, possibly to keep me from wanting to go after it or informing someone.

Anna eyed both of us, clearly looking for more information. "And you came back to do what? Stop this? If so, you've taken a pretty roundabout way to do so."

I opened my mouth before the answer was fully formed and found it difficult to say the words. They choked in my throat. "She came...She came to..."

Anna grew frustrated by my stammered response. "To what, Robbie?"

"Not to stop the coup. To stop me," I said.

"Kill him," Jane corrected instantly, annoyed that I sugar-coated the situation. "I was sent to kill him in order to stop him from killing billions."

Anna nodded condescendingly and her eyes widened as she followed along with our unbelievable story.

"And yet you didn't," she noted, looking between the two of us with a smug expression. "Why?"

At least it wasn't a flat-out rejection. Still, it was clear we weren't convincing her. It was a crazy tale, and I still had a hard time coming to grips with it myself.

Jane looked at me then turned to Anna. "He's my father. He's also the person who gave me the mission."

Anna laughed.

"What?" I asked, blinking.

"Your father? Really?" Anna asked. "That's ridiculous. He sent his own daughter back in time to kill himself?"

"Yes," Jane said, not finding it in the least bit funny. "He was a...complicated man. And not the kind of person to disobey. I was raised to revere him as our leader, our absolute leader, but I saw the flaws in the Scorpion as a father. In the end, those impulses were contradictory."

"There were others like Jane that were trying to kill me. Jane saved me from them," I said, desperate for her to believe me. It felt like a great weight was lifted off my shoulders to share it with someone other than Jane.

Anna's gaze drifted to the ceiling, as if she were connecting the dots in her head.

"So, on the day of the heist…it was these time-travelling killers you fought off in the basement."

I nodded but then lowered my head as a wave of guilt rushed over me. "That wasn't the only time we ran into them."

"What do you mean?" Anna scrunched her brow, curious at my remark.

"They killed Rob's father," Jane replied. "And others, too. All because they were hunting us. Hunting him."

"And you chose to let him live?" Anna asked. "Robbie. The person who would grow up to become this…Scorpion?"

"That name means something to you." I noticed her hesitation to say the word.

"We started putting a scorpion on our flag," Anna said. "At first it was kind of a joke. Something that could eat a butterfly. But in reality, it's a name we use for an absolute order. We're controlled by a council now but there's been talk that we need a leader."

"So," I said, as I tensed up, "the Scorpion isn't really gone?"

"He's gone." Jane looked at me. "Believe me. No other Scorpion is capable of destroying the world."

"Destroying the world?" Anna interrupted. "We're trying to save it."

I shook my head. "It doesn't end up working out like that. The megacorporations don't go down without a fight and the Earth is scorched in the process."

"So, you want to just give up?" Anna asked quietly.

"No," I said, sucking in my breath. "I wanted to figure out another way to stop Butterfly. It's why I went to work for them. I figured I could change the company from the inside."

Jane, rather than Anna, looked at me sideways. "How has that worked out for you?"

I tried to defend myself. "At least I was trying something new!"

Anna looked between us. "Kiss her."

"Wait, what?" I asked, blinking. "Didn't you hear what we said?"

"Yes, and I want to see if it's true. Kiss her!"

I looked at her in revulsion. "I can't."

Not the least bit ashamed, Jane reached over with her arms outstretched. I bolted from her like I was struck by lightning.

Jane turned back to Anna. "Are you satisfied?"

"Yes, yes I am." Anna frowned.

"What?" I asked, confused.

"You reacted with genuine horror," Anna said, shaking her head. "Somehow, you at least believe her to be your daughter."

"And you wanted to test me that way?" I was furious as well as embarrassed.

"It worked," Jane said, dryly. "As disgusting as I found the prospect. Sorry, Dad."

I rolled my eyes. "You guys are both insane."

"Okay. I'll play along for now." Anna started walking around the room in a circle. "Why haven't you returned home to see if all this worked out the way you wanted?"

"My assignment was always meant to be a one-way trip," Jane said, taking a deep breath. "Time travel only works to the past because the future doesn't exist yet. It's always being rewritten. At least that's the way its inventor, Dr. Kepler, explained it."

Anna stopped. "But you came from the future. You must know how all this is going to turn out."

"No," Jane said, frowning. "I know how it was supposed to originally go in my timeline. However, every little change we've made has had repercussions for the future. Not just the big changes like Rob being the Scorpion, but people never meeting, businesses being delayed, or children not being born. These are all droplets in an ocean, but they can become a tidal wave of changes. For instance, the only reason my team and I could go back in time in the first place is because HOPE attacked Project: Aurelia and took all those prototypes."

The butterfly effect. Never had a scientific name been more ironic. A part of me wondered if there was a connection but I doubted it. What were the chances of someone like Colin Reilly purposefully building his corporate empire just to create something like time travel? Ridiculous.

Wasn't it?

Anna stared. "I'm sure the security at Aurelia, along with everything at Butterfly, is going to go through the roof after the attempt on Colin Reilly's life. Plus, from what you've told me here, stealing that data might be off the table."

"That's a very bad idea," I said, interjecting. "I can think of no one worse than Colin Reilly getting the ability to time travel."

"Perhaps the Scorpion," Jane muttered.

"This is insane." Anna rubbed her temple.

"You think it's insane hearing it? Try living it," I replied. "Ever since Jane came into my life, it's been nothing but trying to avoid being killed and having the apocalypse weigh down on me."

Jane looked down. I could tell my words had hurt her deeply.

"I'm sorry," she said. "I know you wish I'd never come into your life."

"No, that's not what I meant." I realized how badly I'd phrased things. Jane had to know that I didn't mean I resented her coming into my life, but it sure sounded like it did. "I would be dead if not for you, Jane. Don't ever think I'm not grateful for all that you've done. I don't know what the future holds but the fact we have a chance of changing the world is all because of you."

Anna took a deep breath then reluctantly sat back down. "That's very sweet of you, Robbie, but I'm going to need you to shut up so I can think for a second."

I was about to give her a piece of my mind when I saw Jane standing perfectly still, her eyes locked onto Anna as she stared at the floor in deep thought. As much as I hated being told off by my ex-girlfriend, if Jane thought it wise to give Anna a moment to gather her thoughts, then that was probably the right move.

After what seemed like an eternity of Jane and I standing awkwardly around, Anna finally spoke her thoughts out loud. "All the members of the Butterfly board are dead because of an explosion that conveniently spared its CEO."

"Colin Reilly had nothing to do with it," Jane noted.

"Oh, yeah?" Anna asked, looking up at her. "How do you know this?"

"I was there," I stated. "He was just as surprised as I was."

Anna rolled her eyes to look at me. "So, you say."

"When are you going to start believing me?" I asked, annoyed by her skepticism.

"Fine." Anna waved at me while sitting back in her chair. "Strangely enough, I do."

I blinked. "You do?"

"All of it," Anna said, sighing. "Not just because of the Marty McFly kiss either. I've been having...dreams. Dreams of things to come. A lot of it feels like what you're describing."

"Fulcrum." I stared at her.

Anna didn't respond to me but continued with her own speech. "But regardless of if Colin Reilly caused their deaths or not, he's going to make a move to solidify his power in the next few hours. Which means Project: Aurelia is going to get a security upgrade. Something we wouldn't normally care that much about because it's a fringe science, long shot of a pet project. Except now we've just learned that it works, and we have to steal it from Butterfly in order to save the world. Am I on the right track so far?"

"Yeah," I said, looking to Jane for support. "I think that just about covers it."

Jane didn't even glance at me. She continued to stare stone-cold serious at Anna. "What are you thinking?"

Anna took a deep breath, her gaze slowly shifting back and forth between both of us, and then soberly stood from her seat. "I think it's time you told me how you know Christine is still alive."

CHAPTER ELEVEN

I told Anna everything that happened earlier in the evening, including that Colin Reilly showed me a video of Christine being held hostage somewhere. And not just anywhere. I recognized the place, too.

My story lasted a good fifteen minutes. I expected Anna to interrupt with a few questions, but she never said a thing the entire time I was speaking. She just stood there, nodding, and listening intently to every word.

Even when I was done, she just kept on bobbing her head up and down, as if her neck were stuck in a rhythm she couldn't get out of. Anna had this blank stare about her, too, like she was lost in some faraway thought that no amount of yelling at her or shaking her shoulders could bring her back from.

"Follow me," she said out of nowhere and turned towards the door.

She used her fist to knock some sequenced code that seemed totally random to me. A moment later, the metal door swung open, and Anna stepped through it.

I hesitated to follow. Jane did not. I went after her instead. Trailing behind my ex-bodyguard seemed a lot easier than trailing behind my ex-girlfriend.

Anna took us through a series of concrete hallways reminiscent of an underground bunker. Lair seemed like a more appropriate word, but I tried not to use any language that might associate HOPE with a

James Bond villain. Not that I was convinced they weren't the bad guys, but I knew for sure that Butterfly wasn't MI6 in this analogy.

Eventually the halls opened to a space that made the Bond villain comparison more appropriate. It looked like a large training center with troops stationed in every corner of the room. There was a shooting range on one side with a mini-obstacle course on the other. Men and women in uniform and combat gear hurried all around us on business in some form or another.

We walked past this area, never venturing into it. Anna didn't look over at any of the action, obviously having seen it many times before. Neither did Jane, who had probably been around facilities like this one all her life. I was willing to bet this was a resort compared to the training grounds she was used to in the future.

I had never seen anything like it, though. Not while I was awake, at least. I suspected Anna walked us past it purely for my benefit. She wanted to prove to me that HOPE was no longer a ragtag group of liberal activists. That since I left the movement, they had really become a full-on militarized resistance. Except I didn't need any convincing. I already had the blood on my hands that told me exactly who they were.

After exiting the training area, the three of us entered another concrete hallway, where Anna broke the silence between us as we walked. "You probably haven't heard from Christine since the day of the heist, have you?"

The way Anna phrased the question concerned me. Almost like she knew something that I didn't, which put me at a disadvantage.

"Something tells me that you have," Jane remarked, also picking up on Anna's subtext.

Anna looked down as she walked, shamefully shaking her head. "I was so mad when I left you two that night in the basement of the church two years ago. I was storming across the parking lot when Christine stopped me. She told me how she got away from the Monarch thugs chasing her and came back to the church to regroup with the rest of us. I filled her in on everything that happened. That the heist failed, you two were deemed heroes by Colin Reilly himself, and Reverend Tully was…"

Anna stopped and turned around to face us. Her face looked pained, weighted, and droopy. It was the first sign of vulnerability I'd seen from her since I got here, and I expected as much. Reverend Tully's horrible death was still a sore spot for me, too. Even after all these years.

The expression quickly faded, though, as Anna puffed out her chest, appearing more resolute and determined than ever. "Christine and I agreed right then and there that drastic action needed to be taken. In many ways, that was the night HOPE began its new direction."

Anna entered a door beside her, and again, I waited for Jane to head on in first before I followed behind. It was a small mess hall of some sorts. Not nearly big enough for all those people we saw in the training area, but large enough that it reminded me of the one I had in middle school. Bland and basic with several tables and a long counter for setting up food. There was only a single basket on there now, probably because the room was empty, and Anna directly walked over to it. She picked up two apples from the basket and tossed them at Jane and me before sitting at the center table.

"Eat," Anna ordered. "You must be hungry."

I stood in front of the table, staring down at the apple in my hand. It instantly reminded me of Snow White, and I had a gruesome flash of me writhing on the floor with foam spraying out of my mouth.

I looked to Jane, as I did so often in times like these, and was put at ease as she took a bite from it and sat down across from Anna. Only then did I take a bite myself.

"Can you do anything without her telling you it's okay?" Anna scoffed and rolled her eyes at my hesitation.

"After the number of times she's saved my life?" I sat down as I chewed. "No, I can't."

"You were telling us about your leader," Jane grumbled, eager to continue the conversation.

"Right," Anna said, taking a moment to gather her thoughts. "Christine had been the face of the movement since the beginning, but she'd become too toxic to be in public. We agreed she would be more effective behind the scenes, managing HOPE from within. She cut off all contact with non-members, which, after that day, meant you, Robbie."

After everything we'd been through together, the fact that Christine could just cut me off like that left me heartbroken. She'd been my mentor. My friend. At times, I thought, maybe even something more. I'd understood HOPE meant everything to her, I had just hoped that I meant something, too.

I was too angry to speak, but Jane, always the focused soldier, kept the story going. "That doesn't explain how she wound up in Monarch custody."

"We had a deep cover spy working at a Butterfly science lab," Anna explained. "Super-classified stuff. Only Christine knew the source's identity, but she never returned from a meet with him a couple of months ago."

A couple of months ago? And here I thought Christine had been in a Monarch prison for almost four years. But it made sense. How else could she know that Georgia was an informant?

"How do you know if it's a him?" Jane asked.

The odd question puzzled Anna. "Excuse me?"

"The source," Jane clarified. "You said you don't know who it is, so how do you know if it's a him?"

Anna still looked perplexed, but this time I didn't think it had anything to do with being confused. "I guess I don't. But if the intel Christine was supposed to retrieve was science related…"

My animosity towards Christine softened enough for me to finish the sentence. "It could be about Project: Aurelia."

Even though she led us down this path, Anna was quick to dispel the assertion. "Could be. Or it could be about drug trials, cybernetic enhancements, gene mutations, or any of the million other cutting-edge research and technologies Butterfly has its hands in."

As soon as Anna finished talking, I was struck by another vision. It wasn't an image, though. It was a bright-blue beam that tore through my head like a bolt of lightning, and I had to squeeze my eyes shut to fight off the pain.

"You okay, Rob?" Jane asked. She sounded legitimately worried.

The flash was sudden and left me feeling like death, but whatever it was, I couldn't worry about it now. I had to push the blue light out of my mind and deal with the matter at hand. I didn't know if it was because I was a Fulcrum or whether because today had been full of ninety different tragedies all hitting me at once.

"I'll be fine," I said with a wave. "And I think this is worth a shot. Especially if it means freeing Christine."

I still had mixed feelings about the prospect, though. I spent several years not knowing if Christine were alive or dead, not knowing if I should mourn or abandon everything and search for her. She might've needed my help. I had no way of being sure.

I wasn't going to lie. That fact that she was not only alive but also actively avoiding me was hurtful. I wanted to free her because she was my friend, but a part of me wanted to see her just to let her know how I felt. But I was scared. I'd seen what the years had done to Anna. Who knew what effect they'd had on Christine. Especially after spending months in Monarch captivity. There was a real chance she was no longer the friend I remembered.

I kept all that to myself, though, and Anna nodded, assuming my intentions were above board. "I agree. Now...did you say you knew where she was being held?"

"I do," I replied. "It's called the Chrysalis. A detention facility in Kansas or Nebraska or one of those barren plains states nobody lives in anymore."

"You're sure?" Anna leered at me, skeptical of my intel. "I heard those places are nothing but corn and robots."

I flashed her a confident smirk. "I'm sure. Where else would you send somebody you don't want found?"

"Sounds like a fortress," Anna noted after I finished describing the Chrysalis to her.

"Can't be easy to break into."

"It won't be," I confirmed.

Looking down at the table, Anna frowned and shook her head. "My troops can handle a lot, but this..." She looked up and it was the first time I saw a lack of confidence in her eyes. "It seems like a suicide mission."

"Your troops," I said, shaking my head. "You've come a long way."

"We all have." Anna nodded.

Jane turned to me. "We'll need help."

She stared as if she were waiting for me to respond, but I didn't know how. I had no idea what she was talking about. We needed help? What kind of help? Who did we know that could possibly...then it dawned on me.

I turned away from her and crossed my arms, staring at the wall ahead like a child giving the silent treatment. "No."

"We need them," Jane stated.

"They won't help us." I shook my head.

"Then make them understand," Jane said, her voice hardened and firm like there wasn't even a discussion to be had.

"I don't trust them," I snapped, standing up and walking away from the table. "We'll just have to find another way."

One of the two women at the table stood up, and without even looking, I knew Jane was the one who remained in her seat.

"There is no other way, and you know it," Jane said to my back.

Jane had this way of arguing that always drove me crazy. Although she often used reason and logic to prove a point, many times she didn't have to. She simply stated what needed to be done with such conviction that her words had to be true. As if each sentence was a scientific law that couldn't be broken.

Still, I thought about possible alternatives. Ways we could accomplish our mission that didn't result in all of us dying or in a cell alongside Christine.

There weren't any.

"Fine," I conceded, dropping my chin onto my chest.

"Who are you two talking about?" I could sense Anna standing by the table, her confused gaze shifting back and forth between us.

I turned around and took a deep breath before answering.

"She wants to recruit the assassins that tried to kill me."

I knew the idea was crazy, but I didn't realize it was downright insane until I actually said it out loud.

CHAPTER TWELVE

I sat in the back of the Red Admiral Motors SUV. It was a crimson vehicle produced by yet another subsidiary of the Butterfly Corporation. I used to wonder how many executives sat around desks all day, thinking up vaguely butterfly-related names for subsidiaries as well as their products. The thing was, I now knew the answer and it was, "a lot of them and they all get paid very well for it."

Anna drove while Jane sat in the passenger seat. Anna didn't bring along any of her HOPE goons and I was grateful for that. Still, I wasn't happy about where we were going, who we were looking for, or what we might have to do to convince them to come along.

"So, you want to seek out the people from the future you came with," Anna said, staring forward.

"Yes," Jane said, wearing a pair of sunglasses as if that would keep her from being recognized by the police.

"People you came with in order to kill Rob," Anna asked.

"Yes," I said, answering for her. "People that I'd hoped were all dead."

"We didn't get them all that day," Jane replied, frowning. "We managed to eliminate some of my team but there were two survivors."

"So, what will keep them from trying to kill you again?" Anna asked, glancing at me in the rearview mirror.

"That's an argument I'd like to hear," I said, crossing my arms.

"Don't be a child, Robbie," Jane replied, ducking the question.

"Rob," I corrected for the umpteenth time.

"Then act like a Rob," Jane said. "They'll honor the deal I made with them if we stick to the terms. Besides, we don't have a choice. We need operatives capable of dealing with soldiers of this time."

"We have the soldiers of HOPE," Anna said, slightly offended. "They have experience fighting Monarch."

"Yes, but soldiers of the future are a different league," Jane said. "They're superhuman in their capacity for killing. The fighting techniques, training, and tactics drilled into us over a generation of war meant the difference between victory or death even against incredible odds. Plus, their implant technology is still a couple of generations ahead of anything the US military has."

"You're exaggerating," Anna replied.

"Jane never exaggerates," I said.

She wasn't, either. I still vividly remembered the fights Jane had with Monarch's soldiers. She'd utterly wiped the floor with them. I also remembered when she did battle with her compatriots from the future. It had been like something out of a movie, my eyes barely able to keep up with their speed and power. I didn't know if they were just pushed to the limit of human ability or there was something else at work, but Jane was right that regular soldiers just couldn't keep up.

Still, I was apprehensive about this plan. It wasn't that Jane was wrong. If we could get the future soldiers to help us against Monarch, then we would have a huge advantage. The problem was that I didn't think there was any way to get them to do anything but gun me down the moment they saw us. Jane had blown past my objections and seemed determined to recruit them.

"So, what is the strategy to get them to side with us?" Anna asked, lowering her voice.

"To ask them," Jane said.

"Really?" Anna asked, pulling the car to one side of the highway. "That's it?"

"Yes," Jane said. "They will accept my reasoning and help us against Monarch."

"We're going to need more than that, Jane." I stared at her.

Jane sighed. "The past is dead, or more, precisely, the future. The world we came from no longer exists. Things were already changing years ago, but now the differences are so vast, fate is impossible to determine along this timeline."

"And that helps us, how?" I asked.

"They know better than anybody that Butterfly is entirely capable of dominating the world," Jane said, disgusted. "The Scorpion thought that if he was killed—you were killed, Rob—that the war would be averted. However, Colin Reilly continues to push the governments and people to the brink in his quest for more power. HOPE continues to exist even without you, and it's become obvious that war is inevitable."

"War is happening now," Anna corrected. "It's small scale, but there's battles every day and soon it—"

"Yes, yes," Jane said, interrupting. "The point is that their reason for wanting to kill Rob is no longer valid."

"That's your argument? 'Sorry, the time for killing me—the Scorpion—is passed?'" I asked, acknowledging it was at least a little plausible. "These guys are fanatics. I mean, you're family. That's why you didn't want to kill me."

"They will obey you," Jane said. "Because they're also your family."

I stared at her. "Jane, you're not making sense."

"Do I need to turn this car around?" Anna asked, looking between us. "Because this seems like something we need to work out before we rely on these guys to help rescue Christine."

"These soldiers are the elite of the Scorpion's army." Jane frowned, a serious expression on her face. "His most loyal and fanatical followers. There was a reason we were chosen to go back in time to kill you. It wasn't because we hated the Scorpion. Quite the opposite. We were chosen because we were willing to follow his last command. Which was to undo what he'd done."

I hadn't heard that part of the story before. It certainly put a new perspective on why the assassins from the future were all New Hope Army members.

"That's crazy," Anna said.

"Yes," Jane answered. "It is."

"And these are the people you want to recruit," Anna said.

"Yes," Jane replied. "Because we've lived here in this world, this place, long enough to think of it as our home. Fighting Monarch is in our blood. It's all we've known. They will not refuse us if we ask for their assistance with it."

"And they're your friends," I said, realizing what she was getting at. "Despite the fact you were willing to kill them all for me."

I had never given much thought to how the conflict between the future soldiers and Jane must have affected her. She spoke with such disgust and loathing of the Scorpion's abuse that it never occurred to me that, like it or not, they were the only people she could call family. The Scorpion had raised her to be a weapon, and while it was irrational for me to feel guilty about that, that didn't mean I didn't.

"Yes," Jane said. "This is my last chance to make amends with my former squad mates."

"Won't they be angry you killed their friends?" Anna asked.

"Yes," Jane replied. "But they will also accept it. I think."

"You *think*?" I said, adding emphasis on the second word.

Jane nodded. "Infighting was not unknown among the New Hope Army in my time. We resolved it with duels. Death was a constant companion in the future, and we all grew numb to it. I don't think they'll hold it against me the way you would if I were to kill Anna."

"Wait, what?" Anna asked, doing a double take.

"Huh?" I asked.

"See?" Jane said, pointing to the road. "We should get back on our journey."

Anna reluctantly pulled the car back on the road and we continued onward to the hideout of the future soldiers. I tried not to think of Cody and Esther as the last time I'd seen them, it had been the former holding a scary ax, and the second had a bleeding heart tattooed right on her face. They came off as complete psychopaths and I wasn't sure they wouldn't come at me the moment they saw me. I had to trust Jane, even if I didn't exactly take comfort from the idea that she was missing these people.

The car eventually reached a location I didn't expect: the suburbs of Butterfly Economic Development Zone #23. It was row after row of identical two-story houses designed for families that worked for the megacorps, bought their products, and voted for the politicians who supported them. It was only when you realized that anyone who didn't serve their interests was quietly "disappeared" that you started to question just how much paradise cost.

"They live in the suburbs?" Anna asked. "Which house is theirs? Are we looking for a yard filled with skulls and body parts?"

Jane rolled her eyes. "Knowing how to infiltrate society and pretending to be a part of it was one of the most basic skills any Elite Scorpion Guard soldier learns. We blend in, disappear, and become part of the community until we strike."

I remembered how effortlessly Jane lied to my late father to get herself accepted into our household. She'd also managed to fake records, a Social Security number, and more to get herself accepted into my school. Given that she'd managed to stay off Butterfly's radar the entire time I was studying to be one of their executives, I supposed she was every bit as good as she was implying. I just found it hard to believe the other soldiers were equally talented.

"Elite Scorpion Guard?" Anna asked. "Were you trying to sound like a comic book villain or was that just by accident?"

"Oh, the irony," I muttered, thinking about how her organization looked like something out of a movie.

"What?" Anna asked.

"Nothing," I said.

We came to the end of the street and saw a house much nicer than the others. It was a small mansion with two very nice cars in the driveway, an immaculately cared-for lawn, and solar panels. It certainly didn't look like the home of a pair of murderous supersoldiers, but, as Jane said, maybe that was the point.

I looked over at Jane. "So, uh, do I just go up to their door and knock?"

That was when Esther knocked on my window, looking amused rather than murderous. She was just as cute as I remembered with her short red hair and the stabbed and bleeding-heart tattoo on her cheek. Time had matured her a bit. She was still our age, but a woman rather than a child soldier. She wore a summer dress with a floral print and held a tiny pistol aimed directly at me through the glass.

Jane rolled down her window. "We need to talk."

Esther smiled at me, then looked at Jane. "Wow. Crazy running into you two here."

"I agree, but the world has changed," I said, looking right into her eyes and hoping the window between us would protect me. "Butterfly is closer to taking over the world than ever."

Esther opened the door and slid into the back of the vehicle with her gun aimed at my chest.

"You tried to destroy the corporations before. You missed the mark a bit and destroyed the world instead."

"Yes," I said, still staring at her. "I did. I ruined the world and failed to save humanity. However, that doesn't have to be the case this time around."

I knew that if I broke eye contact with her, she'd kill me and then Jane would kill her. This entire trip would have been a massive waste of time and, you know, I'd be dead. I could tell there was something about my voice that spoke to her, though. It frightened me to think I'd become more like the Scorpion as the years had passed.

"What changed?" Esther said.

"I've spent the past few years working for Butterfly. I've learned the ins and outs of their empire. I know how to strike at it without destroying the world," I said. Only half of that was the truth, but I needed her to believe I had a plan. As Jane said, the future soldiers were fanatical followers of the Scorpion. I could use that.

"I see," Esther said, being the first to break eye contact as her gaze drifted to the floor.

I looked to the front of the car, where Anna seemed ready to pull out her own gun and shoot. I raised my hand, which was dangerous since I was technically still her prisoner. Jane, however, just nodded as if she knew I could pull this off.

"I need your help," I said, holding out my hand. "I need you to help me fight the corporations."

"When you're right, you're right," Esther confessed, still staring at the floor. "This war has only gotten worse without you. It seems killing you wouldn't have necessarily made things better, but I'm eager to try killing other people instead."

She then looked up, lowering the scarf to reveal the tattooed heart on her cheek, stabbed and bleeding ink down her neck. "You'll still have to convince Cody, though."

"I can do that," I said.

"Perhaps not." Esther smiled. "He speaks five languages. None of them are English."

"Then how the hell am I supposed to convince him?" I glared at her.

"Not my problem," Esther said with an indifferent shrug. "And I won't work against him. You were our leader once, Scorpion, but you're not yet that man."

"And if I don't want to be?" I asked, looking at her. "If I want to be someone better?"

Jane's eyes widened.

"Then you will have to prove it," Esther said, opening the door.

I followed her out onto the lawn and hoped that I wasn't about to be shot. Then I remembered that, with this duo, they'd be more likely to stab me to death or kill me with their bare hands. Jane stepped out of the car to follow us. Anna did as well.

"If you want us to shoot her, I'm all for it," Anna said loud enough for everyone to hear.

Esther continued walking towards the house. She didn't turn around, but I could see the corners of her mouth curl into a smile.

"You wouldn't even be able to get your gun out of its holster, sweetie."

"You'd be surprised," Anna replied. I turned around to see the cold, dead look in her eyes piercing Esther's back.

Yikes. I was surrounded by three dangerous women right now. I had to push that aside, though. It was time for me to impress a man who learned the art of war before he could walk. I had to be steady. There was no room for error. Christine's fate—maybe even the fate of the world—depended on it.

The front door opened before we reached it and Cody stepped outside. He looked exactly as I remembered him, and just as scary, too. He was a short, middle-aged Asian man with the physique of an Olympic athlete in his prime. He wore a polo shirt, slacks, and a menacing scowl so rigid it appeared carved from rock.

"Ah, crap," I muttered. The words just slipped out. I was really hoping to have said them just in my head.

"Having second thoughts, Scorpion?" Esther asked from beside me.

"No," I said, refusing to look away from Cody's stony gaze. "Does he understand me at least?"

"He can," Esther acknowledged. "Doesn't mean he wants to, though."

Well, that was helpful.

Without looking at any of the women, Cody retreated into the house. He left the door open, which I assumed was an invitation. I followed him inside and entered a carpeted living room that was as boring as the landscaping. Cody stopped in the middle of the room and turned, ready to receive me. Esther, Anna, and Jane stood just inside the door. One of them shut it. I couldn't tell which. I was too nervous to pay much attention.

"Cody," I started, "I know you made a deal with Jane to spare my life and I appreciate you sticking to it. I have, too. I've stayed away from HOPE and even took a job inside Butterfly to keep myself from becoming the Scorpion. But that hasn't mattered. You've seen what's going on out there. Butterfly continues to grow, and HOPE continues to oppose them."

I could see Anna squirm a little out of the corner of my eye. Her awkwardness was understandable. Cody and Esther essentially traveled back in time to stop her organization from growing. She probably felt that she was in just as much danger as I was, but we couldn't hold anything back. If we were to recruit their help, we had to put all our cards on the table.

"This is Anna," I said, looking over to her. "She's with HOPE and we're planning a raid on a Monarch facility we hope will give us a chance to—"

My words were cut off by Cody's quick fist jabbing me in the nose. I didn't even see him throw a punch, but the blow hit me like a brick wall, rocking my head back in pain. My first sight through blurry vision was Anna reaching for her gun, but Jane was quick to stop her. She knew what I knew. That if Cody wanted me dead, I'd already be dead. He could wrap his hands around my neck and snap it in a second. There was no stopping him. But he didn't. Whatever reason he had for punching me, it wasn't him trying to kill me, and despite my reluctance to get hit, it was better to leave it alone.

I wiped the reflexive tears building in my eyes, took a deep breath, and continued my pitch.

"Butterfly is evil. But we can't fight them head on. You know where that path leads. But there's another way. We have a plan to—"

Cody cut me off again with a one-two punch to my jaw and ribs. His strikes were swift and precise, like daggers stabbing through my flesh. I doubled over to fight off the pain.

"We need your help," I continued through gritted teeth. "This facility is like a fortress. Without you and Esther we won't be able to—"

This time I saw Cody wind up and deliver a hard elbow to the side of my head with enough force to drop me to the floor. Anna couldn't restrain herself anymore. She took a step forward to help me up, but I held out my hand to halt her from coming any closer. This was just how it had to be.

I pushed up to my hands and knees, still struggling to push the pain aside as I spoke. "How long have you been hiding here? Aren't you eager to get back in the fight? Aren't you eager to—"

Cody interrupted me with a hard kick to my stomach. The attack knocked me to my back and Cody followed it up with a barrage of punches all over my body. I brought my hands up to shield my face, but it didn't matter. The blows struck everywhere. My shoulder. My chest. My arms. And yes, even my face. It felt like a swarm of bees relentlessly stinging me all over.

When Cody finally let up, I could feel the bruises already starting to form and the blood pooling in my mouth. I thought about spitting it out and chose to swallow it instead.

Cody turned his back to me and walked away. Pushing through the soreness that was spreading throughout my body, I forced myself to my feet and watched as he approached the massive Viking battle ax leaning against the wall.

"I'm not going to beg," I declared with my head held high. "But if you ever believed in the Scorpion's dream to bring down Butterfly, then—"

In one fluid motion, Cody grabbed ahold of the ax's handle and swung it down over my head. It only took an instant, but I could feel the heavy weight of the blade bearing down on top of me, and somehow Cody managed to stop the sharp edge less than an inch from my face.

I didn't flinch.

Cody held the ax in place for a few more seconds before lowering it and taking its place. He brought his nose directly in front of my own and our eyes were locked. I tried to hold my breath to hide the fear pounding in my chest. Cody didn't seem to be breathing either, but I doubt it was from him being afraid.

Finally, after what seemed like an eternity, he muttered a single word in a language I couldn't understand and walked away, dragging the ax behind him.

I exhaled.

"Congratulations," Esther said with a smile. "You have our help."

I continued to watch Cody as he disappeared around a corner, heading deeper into the house.

"What did he say?"

"He said your name," Esther replied. "He called you Scorpion."

CHAPTER THIRTEEN

It turned out that getting Esther and Cody in on the plan was the easy part. Deciding what that plan would be was another matter entirely.

"You want to what?" I asked.

"Attack them head on," Esther said, as she walked around the garage of the abandoned gas station that was a couple hours outside of the Chrysalis facility.

The eastern half of Wyoming had been almost entirely evacuated due to the near meltdown of a nuclear power plant that was blamed on the incompetence of the Federal Government. This happened about ten years ago and was one of the major incidents that had led to the Corporate Reform Act which gave Butterfly authority equal to a US state. According to conspiracy theorists, it had been supposedly rigged by Butterfly. I didn't know if that was true, but I certainly didn't discount it anymore.

One certain thing was that the radiation levels had been wildly exaggerated since Butterfly and other megacorps had moved into a lot of automated facilities while leaving the towns around them to rust. It gave us a good place to rest and plan, even if we had to dodge a bunch of surveillance drones getting in.

"That's suicide," I said, looking over at the HOPE soldiers that were lingering about the empty room. Anna had contacted them and there were about a dozen present to back us up. They were hardened military men who didn't look happy to be taking orders from college kids but still respected Anna as their commander. I felt, well, ridiculous around them and hated that I was being forced to argue the finer points of tactics in their presence.

"Is it?" Esther asked. "They have prepared themselves for infiltration and have much of the region covered in drones, surveillance beacons, and patrols."

"That doesn't mean they won't be ready for something larger," Jane replied. "Monarch is the biggest private military in the world."

"Tanks, laser cannons, personal rocket launchers, plus a few anti-security bots the size of houses," Anna said. "You know. The usual."

"That's only if they can activate their defenses," Esther said. "The corporate soldiers of Monarch are untrained amateurs chosen for their willingness to kill and torture civilians rather than fight. They are untested in real combat. Eventually, the Great Civil War will cause them to harden, but now they are vulnerable to chaos."

The Great Civil War was the conflict between the New Hope Army and the megacorporations. It was a war that destroyed almost the entirety of the world. A war I thought I had prevented. Everything I encountered indicated I'd only delayed it, and possibly made things worse.

"Wars are won in the planning stage," Jane said, at ease with the psychopaths beside us. "We need to make sure every element of the attack is meticulously prepared for. Also, the soldiers of Monarch are still mostly ex-United States military. They've only just now begun recruiting civilians directly, ones whose loyalty and sadism can be counted on."

"No plan survives first contact with the enemy," Esther responded. "Especially if their first contact with us is our killing them."

Cody stood nearby, sharpening his ax. I didn't know if the warrior intended to use the anachronistic weapon in combat or if he was just trying to intimidate everyone present. If it was the latter, it was working.

"Do you even have a way to fight all these people or is your plan just 'attack, attack, attack'?" I asked.

Esther gave an evil smile. "Hehehe."

"What?" I asked.

"You're right, I think we should go with your idea," Esther said. "Which is…?"

"We infiltrate the facility," Anna said, dryly. She seemed bored, rather than horrified by our new allies. "We have some trucks left over from the cleaning services that Monarch used. We use them and our fake IDs that haven't been compromised. Then we strike."

"The same plan you used to infiltrate Butterfly's local headquarters," Esther said, her voice contemptuous. "Brilliant."

I didn't like that strategy any better. It was still going to result in us getting into a fight with much nastier people than our own. I had every confidence in the HOPE soldiers around me. I could tell just how seasoned they were with a single look. I also knew how dangerous Esther, Jane, and Cody were. However, if I could give us any advantage against the Butterfly forces then I would consider that a good deal.

"It's better—" Anna started to say.

"I accept your plan," Esther said, shrugging. "So does Cody. Let's just get on with it."

I didn't trust Esther's sudden change of heart and exchanged a look with Jane. She shrugged.

"Alright then," I said, looking at her. "I guess we should get going then. Do we have enough time to conduct the attack tonight?"

"If we go now, yes," Jane replied. "We should strike early. After Colin Reilly's brush with death, their defenses are likely to go up. Indeed, the only reason why the Chrysalis is unlikely to be even more secure is that it takes time for Monarch to mobilize. It's not a national military, yet."

I wasn't happy about being rushed, but I was the odd man out here. I'd spent the past few years learning how to manage a corporation, not how to command armies.

I walked through the metal door to the right and out into the parking lot behind the gas station. Laramie, Wyoming, was a ghost town with most of its buildings having succumbed to decay and weather. Wild dogs wandered through the area and there were rats everywhere. It was a sign of how little the corporations cared for anything other than the bottom line. The town's former population was broken up among hundreds of refugee camps filled with those who failed to toe the line in the new regime. Stripped of all their possessions, most of them had ended up either homeless or dead within a few years.

Anna had been correct in that she'd managed to get four more cleaning-service vans, the kind that did weekly check-ups at the Chrysalis facility. Our one advantage was that the megacorporations still thought like corporations rather than soldiers. They subcontracted out to whoever was cheapest rather than keep their own in-house people. I suspected that wasn't going to last, though, if HOPE kept using it as a means of getting their soldiers in.

"Let's hope it works one more time," I muttered.

Preparations didn't take long. Jane, Anna, Cody, Esther, and I, along with two HOPE troopers, were in one van while three more followed behind us. They were cold, hard, and unhappy-looking military men in their twenties who didn't seem pleased by our presence. Jane, Anna, and I sat along one side of the van while the New Hope assassins and a HOPE trooper sat on the other. The second trooper was driving.

For the most part, the nighttime trip was made in silence. We all just stared at each other, nobody too eager to start a conversation. It looked like Esther wanted to. Her foot anxiously tapped on the floor for what I could've sworn was an hour straight, but she kept her mouth shut. We all did. Until our journey only had twenty minutes left and Anna felt the need for a little pep talk.

"We're getting close now," she said rather anticlimactically. "Stay sharp, remember your roles, and everything will go according to plan."

"You got it, boss." Esther shot out her arm, giving Anna a sarcastic thumbs-up.

The tense atmosphere returned to the van, but only for a couple seconds. Anna immediately shifted her focus to Cody and used the opportunity to probe a topic that had clearly been on her mind.

"So, he can understand English but not speak it," Anna said, looking at Cody but clearly speaking to Esther. "How does that work?"

Esther shrugged, barely interested in the question. "He figured if everyone else spoke English then he didn't need to."

"What if he wants to let people know what he's thinking?" Anna asked as a follow up.

"He uses his ax." Esther's face didn't move as she responded.

Anna's eyes opened wide, clearly taken aback by the answer. "Oh."

The tense yet silent atmosphere returned once more, but only for a second. For whatever reason, Esther turned her peculiarly curious focus in my direction. "You look like you have a question, too, Little Scorpion."

"Don't call me that," I shot back at her with a firm glare that I immediately regretted.

I expected Esther to match my intense stare with one of her own, but she didn't. Instead, she leaned forward and beamed at me with a patronizing smile that strained her cheeks.

"But you're just so gosh darn cute," Esther said in a high-pitched voice, barely moving her lips.

For some reason, the less threatening that Esther appeared the more scared I was of her. She was clearly teasing me, trying to get a reaction one way or the other. Why, I had no idea. Did she want to start a fight? Intimidate me? Or was she just that crazy?

Regardless of the answer, I thought it best to leave it alone and address the question that had been on my mind. "You never asked what happens after this?"

"After what?" Esther curiously squinted.

"This," I said, gesturing to everything around us. "You argued with Anna about the mission, but you didn't once bring up what might happen if we succeed."

"Assuming we aren't captured or killed in a hail of gunfire?" Esther asked.

The brief image of Jane, Anna, and me lined up for a Monarch firing squad silenced me. Instead, I nodded succinctly.

"I haven't thought that far ahead," Esther said, flippantly.

"Really? I find that hard to believe." Her answer didn't convince me, especially at how difficult it was to get her to agree to this plan.

"Why don't you ask Jane?" Esther shot back, still leaning forward, and staring at the white-haired girl seated beside me. "She's the one with contingency plans for her contingency plans."

Jane didn't reply. She didn't even move. She just continued to sit calm and idle with her back against the van. The only sign that she was even paying attention was her steely gaze fixed in Esther's direction.

Esther smiled, very amused by Jane's non-reaction. "Don't worry, princess. Your silence is answer enough. The Scorpion always told us to watch out for the quiet ones. She's probably sitting there with this whole thing already plotted out in her head."

"Uh huh," I said.

Esther paused a moment before sucking in a breath of air and relaxing back into her seat. "Me? I'm more of a fly-by-the-seat-of-my-pants kind of girl. Shoot first and ask questions later. Life's a bit more fun in the chaos. Don't you agree, Anna Banana?"

"Don't call me that," Anna stated, plainly.

"Is there an echo in here or something?" Esther dramatically looked around the van.

"You're insane," Anna said, just as directly as her previous statement.

"Probably," Esther remarked casually before slipping her arms through the loose harness behind her. "But at least I never forget to buckle up. You should do the same."

Esther continued to smile, but her grin morphed ever so slightly. It wasn't just her usual maniacal disposition. There was a hint of cockiness behind it, as if she held a secret hidden behind the smirk.

The expression should've worried me more than it did. I was more confused than anything else, but that changed when the driver called back to us. "We're approaching the facility but...umm. We have a problem."

"What is it?" Anna asked.

I peered past the HOPE driver to the windshield in front of him. Outside the van was a single road cutting through a long, flat stretch of grass under a sky of darkness. The only blemish along the horizon was a single compound lit up in the distance. The driver seemed unconcerned where he was going, though, more focused on the steering wheel in his hands. "The van," he said. "I—I can't slow it down."

Anna got up from her seat to crouch alongside him. "What do you mean?"

The driver slammed his foot on the pedals. "The gas is stuck, and the brakes don't work."

"That would be my fault," Esther responded, casually drawing everyone's attention.

"What are you talking about?" Anna demanded, equally worried and annoyed.

"Monarch already knows we're coming," Esther explained with a shrug, "so why go through the hassle of trying to sneak in."

It was the same point she'd made a hundred times before we left, only now she said it as a matter of fact rather than a persuasive argument. Probably because she no longer needed to convince Anna of its importance.

"You agreed on the plan," Anna bemoaned, the worry in her voice starting to take hold.

Esther grimaced and nonchalantly waved off Anna's concern. "Yeah. I just did that to shut you up. Sorry."

Anna glared at her a moment before frantically turning back to the driver. "Take the key out."

The driver instantly grabbed the key and pulled it straight out of the ignition. Nothing happened. The van continued to speed ahead.

"Thought of that, too," Esther quipped.

Anna's face turned back to us slowly, her eyes growing wide in panic as she fully realized what was about to happen. Esther beamed at her with a smile.

"So just sit back and relax..." Esther paused to yank down on the harness, pulling the straps taut and securing her shoulders to the seat. "...and hold on for dear life."

Esther's words set off a chain reaction in the van. Anna immediately darted for her seat and slipped into her harness. I didn't need to sit down, so I tightened my harness just as fast. The same went for the HOPE trooper seated across from me. Jane adjusted her harness, as well, but she was slow and careful, obviously taking her time. She didn't seem that concerned, and it was only now that I realized Cody hadn't moved at all. He'd been strapped in for the entire ride.

"Brace for impact!" the driver yelled.

I leaned forward as much as the harness allowed to catch a quick glimpse through the windshield, but the van crashed into the gate at full speed before I saw anything.

The screeching roar of metal on metal echoed through the vehicle as everyone violently jolted in their seats. It felt like someone had grabbed hold of my head and shook it as hard as they could, scrambling my brain into mush. I knew only a few seconds had passed, but the chaotic moment seemed to linger for an eternity. That was when the van crashed into something else and came to an abrupt halt.

CHAPTER FOURTEEN

It was utter chaos and I cursed under my breath like a foul-mouthed sailor while wondering what kind of idiot I was to have ever trusted Esther.

"Get down," Esther said, chuckling as she shoved my head under the seat while everyone else ducked.

Gunfire poured onto the vehicle as Monarch troopers moved around us and fired into its side. Much to my surprise, we weren't instantly filleted by hundreds of armor-piercing rounds. Instead, the walls of the cleaning van seemed to be able to take the attack like it was nothing while the windows held up for several seconds before finally shattering above our heads. Apparently, the vehicles we were traveling in had been reinforced with armor and were just disguised as typical cleaning vehicles.

"You goddamn lunatic!" Jane hissed, losing her cool for one of the few times since I'd known her.

"Hush," Esther said, pulling out a handful of egg-sized balls then tossing them out the shattered windows. "Cover your ears."

I did so, as my suspicion about what they were was immediately confirmed. The explosions were small and contained but could still be heard through my hands. The gunfire was now farther away, and I had no doubt the people around us were dead. I removed my hands from my ears and stared at her like she was a lunatic, which I'm pretty sure she was.

"There. Distraction done," Esther said, showing far more confidence than probably should have been warranted.

"Distraction?" I shouted at her, confused as well as horrified.

"Yes," Esther said. "I coached it with little Anna's toy soldiers. We would go through the front and draw out the soldiers while the others took position to turn the area around us into a killing field. Already, they're picking off Monarch's alarmed rookies and making a bloody mess of things."

"You gave orders to my soldiers?" Anna asked, angrier than I'd seen her since the beginning of this ill-fated adventure.

"They're not really your soldiers, are they?" Esther smiled. "If they were then they wouldn't have listened to me."

I peered out through the broken windows of the vehicle and what I saw turned my stomach. We'd smashed into the courtyard of the Monarch facility and into the side of the central concrete building. It was about four stories tall and completely lacking in distinct features. Surrounding the facility was a long, two-story wall of concrete covered in spotlights, guard posts, and a tower at each of its four corners. It looked halfway between a castle and a prison camp.

Surrounding the van was nothing short of carnage, both from Esther's micro-grenades and a bunch of fallen bodies. I hesitated and ultimately stopped myself from putting the scene into words. Up in the towers and on the walls were shadows shooting silenced rifles and cutting down Monarch's soldiers left and right. The spotlights that were all converged on us had allowed our side to gun down the people who'd come to execute us. It was exactly as Esther had planned, which didn't make her willingness to throw our plan to the wind any more appreciated.

"This is crazy," I muttered.

"This is war," Jane said, grabbing me by the arm. "We must adapt to this. Are you ready to fight?"

I looked to her and was about to question what she thought I was here to do in the first place before she slipped a Monarch-811 pistol with a built-in silencer into my hands. I stared at the weapon and my mind briefly slipped into another place.

Hallways…

Bodies…

Blood…

A girl on the ground of a cell…

They were more dreams of the future, but it wasn't the distant future or a future that had changed. Instead, it was something so close to the present that it might as well be the present. I was going to have to kill people, and only now with the gun in my hand did it really dawn on me what that was going to mean. Jane was right to ask if I was ready. The answer was no. I most certainly was not. But I lied and nodded. "Yes. Yes, I am."

Esther stared at me, and I felt like she could see right through my false bravado. "One…two…"

Esther's timing could not have been better as the spotlights around us went out one by one. The HOPE soldiers had managed to do a lot of damage to the perimeter, but I could see reinforcements arriving out of bunkers to the back of the fortress. The darkness was only a small advantage, though, and we were still outnumbered five to one.

"I'll cover you," Jane said, taking my hand. "We need to get inside."

"I know the plan," I said, forcing open the door and heading into the darkness.

Even as I did, I couldn't help but think about how much of my courage was forced. I wasn't a soldier. I was a college student majoring in business and political science. Yet here I was on a half-brained scheme to rescue a friend I hadn't seen since I was in high school. All because of time travel. My life hadn't been the same since a white-haired girl from the future had saved me in an alleyway.

Jane and Esther fired into the darkness repeatedly, aiming as if they could see perfectly. Anna aimed where they did and followed them without difficulty. I had no idea where Cody was as I fired a few shots randomly into the dark as I struggled to keep up with them. I wondered if any of my shots hit anyone and felt sick at the possibility that I might be killing someone. I'd been willing to use violence before in self-defense, but this felt different somehow.

"We should have brought night vision goggles," Anna muttered.

"Be quiet," Esther hissed. "The entrance to the underground level of the prison is nearby. We've been here before."

"You have?" I asked, realizing she should have mentioned that.

"In the future," Esther replied.

I heard the whizzing of bullets around me as we ascended the front steps of the central concrete building toward the bright lights of the interior offices. I covered my mouth with my free hand in disgust as I saw a Monarch soldier sliced in half on the ground in front of the door. He was followed by a second, third, and fourth as we entered the building through shattered glass doors.

The Chrysalis' interior didn't look that much different than other examples of Monarch brutalist architecture. There were featureless gray walls, a pair of desks and metal detectors by the doors, a huge Monarch seal painted on the floor, and a set of elevators at the end of the main room. There were also a dozen corpses spread about like it was the lobby scene of *The Matrix*: Monarch soldiers, regular security guards, and several figures dressed like ordinary office drones. They'd been slashed to pieces and there was no sign we'd suffered any casualties in return.

Jane looked down at the corpses. "It seems Cody went on ahead."

"Is he actually using a battle ax instead of a gun?" I asked, stunned. "That's *insane*."

"No," Esther said. "He uses a gun then a battle ax."

I stared at her. "That doesn't make it any less crazy."

"It's what you brought us here for," Esther said, proudly.

Esther was right. You couldn't make a deal with the Devil and be upset with how he behaved. *God, what have I done?*

Jane fired a couple of times behind us and I turned around to see she'd taken down two more Monarch troopers. "The battle is not going well."

Anna turned to her. "How can you tell?"

"I just can," Jane said. "Monarch will overwhelm our men in the next several minutes."

"Yes," Esther replied. "The cannon fodder exists to divert Monarch from our goal. Don't worry. I have ways of making sure no one leaves this place alive. Except us of course."

"Those people trusted me—" Anna stared daggers at Esther.

"They knew what they were getting into," Jane said, surprising me by coming to Esther's defense. "A victory here means the survival of their leader. It was a risk they were willing to take."

I shook my head and started down the front hall toward the elevators. I looked around for some sign of Cody and wondered how he'd disappeared. I was continuously amazed with the seemingly superhuman powers of the future soldiers. Human augmentation on our military was only in its infancy but a major part of the Scorpion's army.

Having reached the elevators, I looked for a button to press for the underground level and was frustrated there wasn't one.

Jane came up to me with an ID card she raised in front of the elevator as a red laser ran over it and caused the elevator in front of us to ping. The doors then slid open to reveal Cody standing there, apparently waiting for us. He was holding his battle ax like a Viking, a big smile on his face.

Jane grabbed me and dragged me into the elevator as Esther followed. Anna stood her ground and fired behind us, only for Jane to reach out and pull her in even as a group of additional Monarch soldiers came into view.

"Stop them! They can't be allowed to reach the prison level!" the Monarch squad's captain shouted.

That was when Cody hurled a grenade at their feet, which landed right between them. He waved goodbye just as the doors closed. There was a sound of a loud explosion as the elevator began to descend into the depths of the Earth.

"You're a sick man. You know that, right?" I stared at him.

Cody just continued smiling.

I was a terrorist now, at least the way the government and Butterfly would define it. After they fired me, of course. I'd led an attack on one of their facilities and was responsible for numerous deaths, corporate goons or not. The fact that I was trying to protect the United States from falling prey to a fascist megacorporation hell-bent on taking it over and eliminating freedom didn't matter. That had been the Scorpion's justification and it resulted in him destroying the world.

"Damn," I whispered.

The elevator traveled for what seemed to be a really long time and I wondered if there was any way we were going to get out of this alive. Jane predicted our backup was going to get killed and, while we may have inflicted heavy casualties, that didn't mean much if there were more Monarch soldiers down here.

To say Esther and Cody were untrustworthy was also a bit like saying water was wet. I fully expected them to turn on me the moment there wasn't someone else for them to kill. I couldn't turn on them first, though, because our only way of getting out of here would probably be over a lot more Monarch bodies. Great. I was already starting to think tactically. The one thing I never wanted to do.

That was when the doors opened to the underground level of the fortress. It was a panopticon design, which meant it was layers of circles filled with prison cells descending into the darkness with balconies surrounding each. I knew of the Chrysalis's existence, but this was far bigger than I'd imagined and contained possibly hundreds of prisoners with room for thousands.

"All the people they've taken," Anna asked in horror, "is this where they go?"

"Detention of political prisoners," I said, whistling. "This is a place full of people who are too important to be killed. Activists, freedom fighters, dissenting politicians, and even the occasional corporate executive who wasn't a complete bastard."

"You knew?" Anna looked at me in disgust.

"I knew...," I replied, consciously choosing to look somewhere—anywhere—else, "...things as Colin's assistant. But I had no idea it was happening on a scale this massive."

A part of me felt sick reexamining just how inured I'd become to Butterfly's atrocities while going to Conner. I'd known people had been arrested, carted off to God knows where, and it had just seemed normal.

Jane looked around, too. "It doesn't look like it's up to full operational capacity yet. Which is a good thing because we're going to have to leave behind everyone who isn't Christine."

I hated that but couldn't disagree with her. There wasn't any way we could escape with more than a handful of prisoners and I wasn't even sure that was possible. The way we had come from was now swarming with Monarch soldiers.

"There's a train at the bottom that leads to a station many miles away," Esther replied. "We can take it with at least a few more prisoners if we seize control."

"How do you know that?" I snapped, wondering why there were no alarms going off down here or guards coming to assault us yet.

"We hit this place in the future," Esther said, dryly. "Didn't I mention that?"

Anna looked at me. "Great job recruiting her, Robbie."

"Rob," I said, dryly. "I'm not a teenager anymore."

"None of us are," Anna replied.

I headed over to a nearby computer terminal built into the side of the wall. It required an ID card the same way the elevator had but Jane handed hers over. Inside was a crude interface that showed the place wasn't yet completed. It did, however, list a catalog of prisoners. Just bar codes, though. No names.

Dammit.

So far there was no sign of Monarch soldiers or guards down here, at least coming for us. Cody had killed all the personnel upstairs, so it was possible they didn't realize we'd come down. That would rapidly change, though, especially if they finished off the remainder of our allies. I didn't know any of HOPE's soldiers' names, but I already felt great guilt for sacrificing their lives. It was going to be worth it if it got me Christine back, though.

"Check the category of prisoners," Esther said, looking over my shoulder. "You want triple-R classification."

"What's that?" I asked, searching the computer.

125

"Really, really restricted," Esther joked. At least, I assumed she was joking.

It took me a minute or two, but I found two prisoners with that classification. They were both on the bottom floor. "I have their locations."

"Good," Jane said. "Because we have some more trouble."

"What's that?" I said, looking back at her.

"Cody and Esther have decided to go on ahead," Jane said.

I could hear the gunfire, shouts, and more than a few screams. "This was a terrible idea, wasn't it?"

Anna ran past her with Jane following. "Only if it fails!"

I ran to catch up, wondering what kind of rabbit hole I'd jumped down.

CHAPTER FIFTEEN

Despite the sophisticated architecture in the rest of the building, the Chrysalis's bottom level resembled a dungeon, literally. The place looked like a gulag of some third-world country. Every inch of wall was constructed of pockmarked cinder blocks coated in grime. The hallways were lit with cheap light bulbs dangling from wires overhead. Even the doors were archaic, locked with plain old deadbolts rather than any sophisticated security system.

Walking through the hall, I expected to find bodies, blood, and gore everywhere. Cody and Esther had been leaving a trail of screams and agony in their wake, but there was no evidence of carnage here. Probably because they led the action away from us to the far side of the building, which was smart. That left just Jane, Anna, and me to free Christine without a hint of resistance.

There weren't nearly as many cells here in this cramped corridor as there were above us, and, according to the computer, only two of them were occupied. Cells numbered five and six. There was no way of knowing which one Christine was in. Not that it would be hard to find out. All we had to do was open the door and look inside.

We came across cell number five first and I scrambled to open the door. Anna practically pushed me aside to get in first. I tried to rush in after her but was surprised when she stopped short. She had barely entered the room.

"No," she muttered under her breath.

It was half whimper-half cry, and I had to squeeze past her to see what she was looking at. I didn't have an audible response when it finally came into view. Not like she did. But I had no control over the air escaping my lungs in a gasp.

Anna and I stood side by side, staring at a lifeless female figure propped against the wall. The cell was exactly like the hallway: a dungeon. And the way the girl looked only added to that feeling. Her head hung low, hiding her face from us behind a dirty mop of matted hair. She was skinny and underfed, and wore a very generic prison uniform. At one point it had probably been white, but now it was just a random mess of dirty browns and blacks.

Time seemed to stand still for a moment as Anna and I both waited for the other to move. I eventually relented first. Not because I thought I was braver than her. In fact, it was because I was too scared of standing still and waiting for Monarch to realize where we were.

I approached the body slowly, wishing that every step I was taking was somewhere else and not getting closer to what could very well be my dead friend. I bent down even slower and reached out towards the girl's slumped head.

"Is that…?" Anna asked, dreadfully.

She didn't finish the question. Nor did I want her to. I knew what she meant and breathed easy after brushing the girl's hair aside, revealing a face I didn't recognize. Strangely enough, it was the face I'd had a vision of only minutes earlier.

"It's not Christine," I confirmed.

Anna let out a sigh so loud I could hear it from the other side of the room.

It was a relief, but it was also tragic. Someone was dead. A young girl maybe fifteen or sixteen years old. Who was she? How did she get here? Or the more pressing question…how could they do this to her? She looked tortured, starved, and beaten. Was this what our world had come to? Is this what we could expect from our future? I stood and looked back to Anna, hoping she could provide some answers. "You know her?"

Anna shook her head. "She must've been the source Christine was meeting to inform her about the—"

Her explanation was cut off by a shriek. "No!"

It belted out from behind Anna, and although I recognized the voice, it wasn't until Jane stumbled into the cell that I believed it came from her. She had a horrific look on her face, and one I had never seen from her before. I couldn't quite put my finger on it. Depression? Dismay? Despair? Whatever it was shook me to my core. Jane had always been a source of strength for me. Right or wrong, she was always an unshakable bedrock. A force of nature with ice water in her veins. All that was gone in an instant.

She tore across the cell, practically diving to the floor. "No. No. No."

"What is going on?" I asked, weakly.

Jane cradled the poor girl in her arms as her quivering body rocked back and forth. She wasn't crying or sobbing, but she couldn't stop moving, almost as if her body were expelling an emotion it wasn't used to experiencing.

"She's not supposed to be here," Jane muttered under her breath. "It wasn't supposed to happen like this."

I didn't know what to do. I just stood there, watching my friend…my daughter…painfully mourn someone I never even knew.

"Who was she?" I asked softly.

"No one," Jane replied with her head down. "Not yet, anyway."

"What're you…?" My question drifted off when Jane rolled to the side, giving me another view of the girl's face. Having just looked at Jane I was struck by the resemblance. Obviously, the girl was a couple years younger and didn't have white hair, but if I didn't know any better, I could've sworn they were sisters. Or maybe even…

Then it dawned on me. I was looking at Jane's mother. As strange, bizarre, and seemingly impossible as that was, I knew it to be true. It was the only possible explanation for her reaction.

"Jane, I'm…" I struggled to formulate an emotion, much less eject the words from my mouth. "I'm so sorry. I had no idea."

"How could you?" She almost choked on the question. "You didn't even know her."

The question was half accusatory. As if the girl's death were somehow my fault. Jane was smarter than that, though. She knew that wasn't true. She was just lashing out and understandably so. "That doesn't mean…"

I tried to sympathize with her, to somehow rationalize this impossible situation. Jane didn't care, though. She stood from the girl's side, cutting me off.

"Come on," Jane ordered coldly while walking back towards the door. "We have a mission to finish."

And just like that…it was over.

A girl I'd never met, who I would apparently marry in the future, lay dead before me. After mourning her briefly, her unborn daughter just walked out of the room, leaving me alone with a cocktail of crazy emotions I couldn't even begin to process.

But that was Jane in a nutshell. Constantly surrounded by insanity yet continuing to carry on with relentless conviction. She really was a product of her environment. A warrior born from a time of survival and tragedy. Or maybe she was just the daughter of the Scorpion and carrying on after death was in her blood.

Either way, I was willing to follow her to the ends of the Earth. Right now, that just meant following her out of this room.

Anna gave me a confused frown as I walked past her, which I didn't even acknowledge. Whatever happened here was between Jane and me, but we weren't ready to discuss it. Now was neither the time nor the place, so I just pushed the image of the dead girl from my mind—the unnamed mother of my future child—and continued to the next cell.

I opened the door the same way as the last one and my depression instantly vanished upon spotting Christine. This cell was much darker than the last. Only a slim light shined on the back wall, spotlighting Christine strung up like Jane's mother. Except Christine was clearly alive with duct tape over her mouth. She looked right at us, her eyes wide and panicky.

I jogged towards her, but Anna blew past me in an all-out sprint. Jane entered the room last, just as Anna ripped the tape from Christine's mouth.

"It's a trap!" were the first words out of her lips.

I nearly jumped when the door slammed shut and a series of bright LEDs hidden in the ceiling flooded the cell with light, illuminating a squadron of armed Monarch commandoes that had been standing in the shadows along the walls.

"I didn't want to believe it was true," a voice lamented.

It sounded oddly sad for a Monarch trooper, but everything made sense when I turned and saw Phil standing in the corner of the room, the only one of them not in a helmet and holding a weapon.

"I heard you were part of the raiding party," he went on, disappointed, "but I had to see it with my own eyes."

"Phil, this is not what it looks like." I held my arms out, showcasing my innocence.

It felt natural to say, but I realized the statement was stupid as soon as I said it.

So stupid Phil didn't even acknowledge it. He just kept on staring at me with a confused glare. "HOPE? Really?"

Anna took a hard step towards him ready to brawl. "Listen, fascist…"

I shot her a cold look that stopped her in her tracks, probably because she was surprised by it. I'd never looked at Anna like that before. Never with such commanding authority. Not even while we were dating. I loved her. I respected her. But when it came to Phil, a man who I knew was a decent human being despite his profession, Anna needed to just shut the hell up.

I turned back to Phil and spoke as reasonably as I could. "Christine Trainer is my friend. That's all this is. Me helping a friend."

Phil was having none of it. He looked angry and pointed straight up to the cell's dungeon ceiling. "Tell that to all my men those two psychopaths are ripping apart up there."

My eyes shifted over to Jane. Hers did to me, as well. Even without speaking we knew what the other was thinking. But she shook her head, a subtle movement only I noticed. She was telling me there were too many of them. That she couldn't see an option to fight her way through this.

"C'mon, Rob!" Phil shouted, frustrated by my silence. "Say something!"

I looked at him, annoyed. I probably shouldn't have, but what else was I going to do? A guy I genuinely liked had set a trap for me, and the worst part of all, I kind of felt bad about letting him down.

"What do you want me to say?" I shot back at him. "That I'm sorry? Cause I'm not."

I expected him to yell again. To scream and call me HOPE scum. He simply frowned and shook his head, instead. "What happened to you, Rob? You were a good kid with a bright future at Butterfly."

"I hated working at Butterfly," I replied.

"How could you say that?" Phil asked, looking genuinely hurt by my response. "You were an executive assistant positioned for a leadership position in the company."

"Yeah!" I shouted, as if the answer were obvious. "So I could change it!"

"Now I know why you call your group HOPE," a voice taunted from the hallway.

Even muffled through the door I could recognize the voice as clear as day. I didn't want to hear it or even believe it was him. Of all people, he was the last person I wanted to see right now. But sure enough, when the door opened, he was there. Colin Reilly, in the flesh.

"Because hope is all you people have," Colin mocked us with a big smile on his face.

CHAPTER SIXTEEN

The air felt stale and tense. Nobody said a word. The Monarch troopers weren't going to say anything. They were pretty much just tin soldiers. And there wasn't anything for us to say either. They had us. Pleading or negotiating was pointless. Honestly, though, I was just pissed off at Colin's theatrics. The guy seemed to think he was a Bond villain and acted like it.

"How long did you spend rehearsing that line, Colin?" I asked, unimpressed with my former boss.

Colin ignored me and turned to Phil. "Take everyone out of here. I need to talk with my former assistant in private."

Phil's face grew long. He appeared genuinely surprised, if not downright concerned by his boss's command. "But, sir—"

"You heard me," Colin cut him off, sternly.

Phil swallowed his objection and nodded. For all the decency inside him, he was still just a Monarch employee serving Butterfly's whim. To resist meant putting his very livelihood at risk. I didn't fault Phil for choosing the easy path, but then again, nothing about our lives these days was easy.

Phil motioned to the armed Monarch commandoes, who escorted Christine, Anna, and Jane out of the room. Jane kept her eyes on me as she exited the cell, her gaze just as hardened as ever. It was an inspiring sight, and admittedly, one that I'd gotten used to. Jane didn't waver often, if ever. I'm sure she didn't think for a second the fight was over, but she didn't know how, and certainly not when. She knew we were getting out of this somehow, and I believed her.

After Jane disappeared into the hallway, Phil brought up the rear. He was the last one to leave the room but stopped just before doing so and turned around with a heavy frown of clear disappointment.

"I was looking forward to having you as a boss one day, kid," Phil said to me and then walking into the hall. "Now I'll just have to attend your funeral."

I liked Phil but sometimes, I really just wanted to flip him off. "See you there."

Colin Reilly barely waited for him to be out of the way before slamming the cell door shut, sealing the three of us inside. Christine just watched us from where she was imprisoned, seemingly either drugged or unwilling to speak after so much abuse. Colin paused a moment while still facing the door, and when the Butterfly CEO finally spoke, he did so with his back to me. "You must really think I'm stupid, don't you?"

I shrugged and looked at him.

"I feel like any response I give to that would be both right and wrong at the same time." I paused. "But yes, yes I do."

Colin spun around on his heels, quickly and somewhat aggressively. Not aggressive at me, though. More like he was just irritated by the situation. He even had the same disappointed wrinkle in his brow that Phil had had. Colin had really seen better days. He still wore the same suit from when he'd almost been killed by Jane back at Butterfly HQ. He also smelled of cigarette smoke and I wondered if the stress of the day made him fall back into the habit. There'd been a big article about him quitting last year despite the fact it was the least notable thing about him. There was a twitchiness to him as well, a sign that recent events had gotten to him.

I wasn't afraid of Colin anymore. He was far from the seemingly invincible villain I'd built him up to be over the years. Yeah, he'd apparently given himself a bunch of enhancements that he'd been able to throw me around like a rag doll but I'd faced worse than him. I might not be able to kill him, didn't want to kill anybody, but any idea he was some master genius had been obliterated with the fact he had been taken so utterly off guard by the terrorists who'd almost killed us both.

"Come on, Stone," he scolded. "You really think I had no idea you were snooping around my office? Every single room in headquarters is bugged, with three different offices designed to monitor the information. Nothing happens in that building without me knowing."

I had always wondered how easy it was to get a peek at almost anything the CEO had his hands in. Then again, I wasn't surprised he was spying on his employees. Butterfly was a snake pit and every single one of its workers was trained to bite at the other. It was a wonder they had accomplished anything.

"You didn't see anything I didn't want you to see," Colin bragged. "Including this place."

Colin was merely handing me the puzzle pieces, allowing me to put the big picture together myself.

"You wanted us to come here," I said. "It was a trap all along."

Surprisingly, Colin shook his head, dispelling my theory. "On the contrary. Some executives might consider their assistant's nosy curiosity a liability. I see it as ambition. Nobody rises in this world without a little cutthroat spirit in their blood. You weren't spying on me. You were looking for an edge up on your peers. A way to climb the corporate ladder...or so I thought."

Colin really had believed in me as his assistant, which was a strange notion. I hated the guy and wanted to learn from him to topple him. In some ways he must've known that, but instead of pushing me away, Colin accepted the challenge. He saw my heart as an ideological battleground. If he could win me over then he could win over anybody. Obviously, he couldn't. But Colin didn't know that. Instead, he thought I betrayed him, which sucked considering that I hadn't. To betray someone, you needed to be loyal to them in the first place.

"I already told you," I pleaded. "I had nothing to do with that bomb in your office."

"Yes." He glared at me with a condescending smirk. "And my surveillance team ruled you out as a member of HOPE. Yet here we are."

Ironically enough, it was his loss of trust in me that led me down this path in the first place, but it was pointless arguing about that now. What's done was done. It was time to move on. Besides, a part of me got a small thrill from the fact I could finally tell Colin what a callous, small-minded snake he was. I would hold off insults until I had more information, though.

"What do you want from me?" I asked, coldly.

Colin paused and took a deep breath. It was a mannerism I'd seen from him many times before. He was preparing for a lecture. "When we first met, HOPE was nothing more than a nuisance. A pesky little itch that needed to be scratched occasionally. Except I became distracted by other endeavors and ignored it. Now that itch is a rash and will continue to spread if I don't stop it."

He didn't say anything surprising. Well, other than the way he said it. "That was a rather…colorful analogy."

Ignoring my glib remark, Colin continued his pitch. "Right now, these terrorists are nothing more than a bunch of disjointed cells. But they're getting stronger and more organized. Thanks to your girlfriend, who is a particularly hard bug to squash."

"She's not my girlfriend," I replied through gritted teeth. The comment pissed me off more than it probably should have. Maybe that was kind of the point. Colin acted like he knew me, but he didn't. He thought I was some sort of terrorist living undercover and was acting like he was so smart for figuring it out. Except he only "figured it out" after a bomb had gone off in his office. He was completely wrong, anyway. About me and the fact that HOPE was disorganized with no government support. Man, these were strange times.

Colin didn't gloat on the fact that he got a rise out of me, though. He ignored my anger to carry on with his speech. "You arrived here with her and must've come from somewhere. A base or hideout back in Chicago. I want to know where it is."

"I don't know." The answer was easy.

Colin spat out a reply so quick I could've sworn he was going to say it regardless of my response. "You're lying."

I wasn't. Anna was careful to make sure Jane and I had no idea where we were while going to and coming from her base of operations. Honestly, her paranoia said a lot more about her than it did about me, but she was right for keeping us in the dark. I could make some basic guesses about where we'd been, but I had no reason to cooperate, and Colin was a fool to think that I would.

I wasn't exactly being interrogated. Not yet, anyway. But I wasn't afraid. Mainly because he wanted an answer I didn't have. "You told me before that I wasn't as good of a liar as I thought I was, so I couldn't hide the truth even if I wanted to."

Colin smirked. I'm not sure if he believed me or not. I think the point, though, was that he didn't much care. My fate was sealed either way.

Colin glared then twisted his gaze into a smug sneer. "Don't worry. You saw how we got the information on Georgia from Christine. It won't be difficult to do the same to you."

Colin turned to exit the room. That was when I realized Christine's cell was about to become my own. It was a bleak moment and made this entire mission seem more like a fool's errand. I'd brought everyone here on the same kind of quest that the Scorpion inspired others to undertake in his name. Except he had survived, and I'd led them to their doom. It was the only time in my life I ever wished I was more like my future self than the weak fool I'd proven to be.

As Colin reached to open the door, I decided to charge. I was sure I couldn't take him. He was superhuman and I wasn't. It was as simple as that. There was also the fact his online bio said he used to be a Navy SEAL and a football player for the University of Alabama. I gave that about a 50% chance of being true. But it didn't matter. This was my last and probably only opportunity to get out of here. I had to take it…even though I never got the chance to see if it would be successful.

As soon as Colin opened the door, he was hit with a wave of blue-white electricity that pushed him back into the room. I froze, startled and unsure as to what the hell had just happened. Standing in the doorway was a Monarch trooper that instantly reminded me of when

Jane saved me after the explosion. Had she done it again? I couldn't believe it. Probably because it wasn't true.

When Jane saved me before, her electric rounds were set to disable not torture. This time Colin was on the floor, fully awake but writhing in pain. The blast hadn't knocked him out, it had electrocuted him. It was at seventy-five percent charge, which was not lethal but meant to torture an individual before execution.

After Jane saved me, she'd wanted to kill Colin. I stopped her, but she was fully prepared to do it...with a gun. A plain old bullet to the head. That was Jane's style. Quick and efficient. But electrocuting him? It didn't make sense. Until the Monarch trooper removed his helmet and revealed the face of a friend underneath it.

"Trevor..." I muttered. "What the hell?"

CHAPTER SEVENTEEN

T revor's name left my lips as a confused sigh. I half expected him to smile at me. He didn't. I had no clue why he was here. Trevor was my best friend and the only person in the world I knew who wasn't involved in all this future war business. He was the bedrock of my normality and now he was wearing a Monarch trooper's suit. He wasn't a soldier; he was a young executive-in-training like myself. Well, like I used to be. What the hell was going on?

"Hello, Robert," Trevor said. "We do meet in the strangest places."

Besides dispassionate, his greeting was bizarre, considering the only people to use my full name were teachers on the first day of school. I felt like I was in a comic book and a super-villain had just unmasked himself. It didn't quite feel real, and it just added to the surrealness as Colin writhed on the floor beside us. The charge ended only after thirty seconds of continued torture. It couldn't have happened to a nicer guy.

"Robert?" I repeated, dubiously. I tried to ignore the smell of burning flesh and business suit in the air.

"I know," Trevor remarked. "Too soon for that. But it'll grow on you."

"What? What?" Colin repeated, staring up at Trevor. "You're HOPE, too?"

"Don't be an idiot," Trevor said, utterly disdainful of the world's most powerful man.

"Guards, guards!" Colin tried to shout and failed, his voice so soft and weak that it barely carried above a whisper. Events had taken out his enhancements and he was now weak as a kitten. I could also smell that he'd soiled himself. "My guards—"

"*My* guards," Trevor corrected him. "Once you're dead, of course."

Colin looked terrified as the implications of what was going on sank in. I didn't blame him.

I stared at the weapon in Trevor's hands and the stony look upon his face and realized this wasn't turning out the way I'd hoped. "Something tells me you're not here for a rescue."

I finally got a reaction out of him in the form of an amused, although sarcastic, chuckle.

"Wow," Trevor said turning his attention to Colin still rocking back and forth on the dirty cell floor. "Is that why you hired him? His excellent powers of deduction?"

Colin looked up with a vengeful sneer. "You're both traitorous, scum."

"Oh, shut up." Trevor put on a half-smirk and shook his head.

Trevor shot Colin again with the electric gun, except this time he didn't stop at a quick blast. Trevor held down the trigger, jolting the CEO with a continuous stream of electricity at maximum power for another thirty seconds. Colin screamed as the current ran up and down his seizing body in what looked to be excruciating pain.

"Trevor, stop!" I shouted over Colin's shrieks and the hum of the gun.

I wasn't sure if Trevor would listen, but he did. He just didn't look happy about it. "Stop being such a wuss, Rob. You have no idea how long I've been waiting to do this. Since childhood, really. After everything Colin's done to you—to both of us—give me one good reason why I shouldn't fry this coward to a crisp?"

When confronted with this same problem with Jane, I'd had a clear response. It was simple. Obvious, even. But Jane was a pragmatic soldier. I could reason with her. Trevor looked like a wild animal, someone who enjoyed electrocuting a helpless human being. It was a far cry from the person I had befriended over the last couple years.

"I don't know," I admitted, feeling like a fool for even trying.

"I guess you really were always weak," Trevor said in response to my silence.

It was an oddly phrased comment. Colin Reilly must've picked up on it, too.

"Who…who are you?" he groaned weakly in a hoarse voice. "What are you?"

Trevor crouched down beside Colin's face with a creepy grin. The role reversal was a strange thing to watch. Trevor always treated our (former) boss with respect, but now Trevor was the one in charge. I could believe there was something personal there but couldn't think of anything Colin had personally done to Trevor or his family. Hell, Trevor's background was incredibly bland and uninteresting. It only occurred to me in that moment that it was probably fake. Trevor confirmed it with his next words.

"What's wrong, Grandpa?" Trevor taunted. "Not used to being the one in the dark? It's funny because you were the most ignorant one among us. In the game of four-dimensional chess that we've all been playing, you weren't even a pawn."

The way Trevor said it with mocking confidence told me he was not using the word "Grandpa" as a figure of speech. He meant it literally. I didn't know how it happened, but Trevor was another traveler from the future and Colin Reilly's actual grandson. We weren't just dealing with *Terminator* and *Terminator 2* now. We were in full-on *The Sarah Connor Chronicles* reboot territory.

"Grandpa?" Colin repeated, his puzzled voice rough and raspy.

He probably felt the same way I did, and Trevor only welcomed the confusion. His smile grew wider, and he eyed Colin down, almost like he was savoring the moment.

"Don't you recognize the family resemblance?" Trevor asked. "Don't worry, I'm not here to complain about a lack of baseball games and positive reinforcement. I hate you for much bigger reasons. I'm here to save the family legacy and change the world. We were meant to be Caesars and you let us be Pompeys thanks to this Brutus."

It was a hard thing for me to fathom, but not impossible. Colin, on the other hand, looked downright bewildered, and his face looked pained as it tried to come to terms with the revelation. Or maybe he was just still in pain from the electrocution. It was hard to tell.

"That's...preposterous," Colin murmured, looking half-dead. The second jolt had come close to killing him outright. "You're mad, both of you."

Trevor remained crouched, refusing to break eye contact with the weakened man before him. "Is it? You ordered Butterfly scientists to develop a means of time travel. Did you never think they would succeed?"

Oddly, the puzzlement in Colin's face softened. He seemed to understand and even accept what Trevor was saying. More than that, he looked disappointed by it. Like if you discovered a new car in your driveway, only to find out that it had been delivered to your house by mistake.

"I only did that so Aurelia could be brought back to me," Colin explained, his face full of wistfulness that I'd never thought him capable of. "So that I could utilize it now...in the present."

I had no idea what he was talking about, but Trevor seemed to. He stood up calmly and leveled the weapon at Colin's head. "Yeah, well...plans change. See you in hell."

Trevor fired again and this time it was clear he wasn't going to let up. A seemingly never-ending stream of electricity flowed into Colin's body. I remembered the man as an intimidating, almost unstoppable force. Now he was just a helpless victim, convulsing in pain and screaming in agony.

I despised the man, but he didn't deserve this. No one did. I couldn't stop it, though. Trevor would have just as quickly turned the weapon on me. There was nothing I could do but stand there and watch until Colin's twitching stopped, and his cries went silent. He was gone. The electrical current stopped after a few seconds but not because Trevor took his finger off the trigger. The gun's battery must've run dry.

Maybe I was just deluding myself, because as I looked at his body, I couldn't help but imagine the world would be a better place now that Colin Reilly was gone. It was an ugly side of myself that I didn't want to admit existed but couldn't deny.

"I'm sorry," I said, only half telling the truth.

Colin couldn't hear me. He was already dead. His eyes were wide open and staring at the sky in shock. If there was a soul—something I believed in most days—it had left him and gone to whatever hell awaited men like him. Still, I couldn't help but acknowledge someone I'd known had passed.

"All used up," Trevor said, examining his weapon like a broken toy. "Here ya go, buddy."

He tossed the gun at me, and I caught it on reflex. I didn't know why, but it certainly evened the odds. I couldn't shoot him with it, but it was still something I could use in a fight. I raised the weapon and prepared to charge, but Trevor was a step ahead of me and drew a gun—a regular one this time—from the back of his armor.

"Uh-uh-uh," he said, aiming the gun at my head. "Don't think about it, hero."

That was when I realized why he made me catch the gun. He was framing me for Colin's murder. But it still wasn't adding up.

"What are you doing, Trevor?" I asked. "Why are you—"

I stopped from finishing the question, mainly because I was trying to think of the answer myself. If he was indeed from the future, then he knew what I would become. Him framing me could prevent that. It was as good a theory as any.

"You're doing this because I'll be the Scorpion," I stated. "It all comes back to that, doesn't it?"

Trevor let loose a hearty laugh. He found my statement genuinely amusing. "It's hard to make a peace deal with yourself."

I had no idea what that meant, and his reaction annoyed me to no end. "I don't understand."

Trevor shook his head as if he were in on a joke that would be too difficult to explain. Not that he needed to. His work here was done, and he still held the upper hand. He'd killed the most powerful man in the world and altered the future of humanity.

Yes, the Scorpion eventually killed Colin Reilly, but not for another decade. This, combined with the assassination of the board, meant there was now a massive power vacuum at Butterfly.

History may or may not proceed as it was "supposed to" — whatever that meant—but it would do so with all-new players. Any information I might have possessed about the future from Jane was useless now. We were in a whole new temporal ballgame.

"Please," I pleaded as he turned his back to exit the cell. "Tell me. You owe me that much."

I tried to appeal to our friendship. The move had the desired effect. It stopped Trevor from leaving. But for the opposite reasons than I'd expected.

Trevor spun around to face me, offended by my insinuation. "Owe you? I don't owe you a damn thing."

"We were friends," I said, softly, while remembering the years we spent together. I should have realized everything I knew about my friend and our relationship had been a lie. That he'd only been pretending to be someone who cared about me.

Trevor obviously didn't think too fondly of our time together. He laughed, but it was an angry laugh filled with resentment and anger. "Friends? That's funny. Considering you were going to turn your back on me the second you got what you wanted."

I shook my head. The thought had never crossed my mind. "I would never betray you."

"Really?" Trevor wasn't convinced. "What did you think would happen when you took control of Butterfly, huh? When you rose through the ranks and shifted company policy from global domination to world peace?"

I honestly didn't have an answer. All I knew was that I wanted to change Butterfly for the better. I knew I could achieve it, too, but I had never contemplated what that would entail along the way.

"I'll tell you what'll happen," Trevor said, using my silence as an invitation to go on. "There'll be a purge. Anyone loyal to Colin Reilly and the old guard would be tossed aside. Either locked up or blacklisted from ever working in a corporation again. You filled it with your goons, idealists, and cronies. People who supported and aided HOPE when they should have been working to establish a new world order. The country isn't collapsing because of Butterfly and the megacorps. It's because of the government's weakness. The people need someone to rule them. It could have been us."

Oh hell. He wasn't just a greedy corporate goon. He was a fascist, too. "And how do you know that?"

"Because I lived through it," Trevor stated, dryly. "I saw society collapse under the peace-loving ways of a government that let the populace run wild. You thought you were saving the world, but you left us to rot when Butterfly's power could have led us to the stars. Where *I* could have led us."

There was no arguing with him there, just as there was no arguing with Jane about the future she left behind. They both came from a world shaped by my actions that each of them traveled back in time to prevent. Jane for the better. Trevor for the worse. Except I'm sure he didn't see it that way.

"Wait, I succeeded in reforming Butterfly?" I asked, confused as to what he was saying. He was from a second timeline? A new future?

"That's right," Trevor said, again using my silence as a reason to monologue. "You succeed, Rob. You pull off a corporate takeover of my family's company and make peace with the New Hope Army. You even shake hands with the Scorpion at the negotiating table. Right before that anarchist stabs us in the back."

The last bit shocked me and clarified his earlier comment about making a peace deal with myself. "I don't become the—?"

I should have pieced it together earlier, but it was a titanic shift in my worldview. Trevor wasn't from Jane's future. He was from the future created by succeeding in my plans. A second timeline. Weirdly, *Back to the Future Part II* of all things popped into my head. Marty and company successfully changed the future for the better in the first movie but the bully, Biff, went back in time after that and turned their hometown into a hellscape of crime. It was ridiculous what your mind went to when things like this happened.

Trevor didn't realize the significance of what I said, though, and talked right over me to continue with his rant. "But peace with terrorists is for fools. HOPE doesn't stand *for* anything. They're only against something. You can't build a future without vision. Without purpose."

He then raised a gloved hand and clenched it, as if crushing the opposition in his palm. "That's where Butterfly's real strength lies, in its ability to fight for a world it strives to create. We don't have to rule the world directly, but we can control the people who do rule the world. Let the government continue to exist. We'll just have a steady stream of puppets to deliver our decrees and rubber-stamp our legislation."

It was a supervillain speech and made me realize what my former friend was capable of. "It was you who set off that bomb in the board room, wasn't it?"

Trevor nodded unabashedly. "With the executives dead, it paves the way for assistants like us to fill their shoes. Except for you, of course, having just murdered the CEO and all."

My blood ran cold as Trevor began chuckling. "Oh, how badly I wanted to end you and Grandpa Colin the moment I got here, but I couldn't. It's taken years to set this plan in motion. I had to eliminate future rivals and put pawns in place to take over. Now everything is set, and nothing can stop my rise."

His proud response disgusted me. "You killed all those people for what? A promotion?"

"What can I say, Rob?" he said with a casual shrug and indifferent grimace. "You and I both want to take control of Butterfly and lead it in a new direction. I'm just a little more proactive about it."

Trevor turned to exit the cell, leaving me to my fate. This was it. I was going to be blamed for Colin's murder. Most likely executed for it.

I started to picture myself hanging from the gallows or staring down a firing squad. Both thoughts, however, were interrupted by a loud boom that demolished the wall behind me.

CHAPTER EIGHTEEN

"Son of a—" I shouted, hitting the ground as the explosion temporarily deafened me.

A cloud of concrete dust filled the air as I was left on the ground next to a stunned Trevor and a now-deceased Colin Reilly. The door to the hall—no doubt full of Monarch troopers—was open while someone else was willing to blow us all up. If I weren't so utterly stunned by the shockwave of the blast, I would have laughed at the absurdity.

This was, in simple terms, an utterly insane situation and I was someone who'd long since come to terms with the fact that I was destined to grow up to become a psychotic warlord. Except, I wasn't anymore, was I? That was something that shifted the foundation of every single assumption I'd made and action I'd taken for years.

If I wasn't going to become the Scorpion, if I didn't have my fate set in stone, then I no longer had to feel the immense guilt I'd suffered for crimes I had yet to commit. Someone else was going to be the worst dictator of the twenty-first century and I'd apparently been able to make peace with them. It was a triumphant moment I would have loved to celebrate if not for the fact that someone was trying to kill me.

Again.

"Dammit!" Trevor shouted, aiming at the hole in the wall. "Stay back!"

That was when Cody and Esther stepped through the dust. Esther was carrying an enormous assault rifle and wearing ammo belts like she was a poster for a sci-fi movie, while Cody just held his axe like a modern-day Viking.

"We're here," Esther said. "Miss us?"

Trevor took one look at the pair before throwing his gun on the ground and running out the door. "The HOPE terrorists are here! They killed Mr. Reilly!"

"Bastard!" I shouted behind him while grabbing the gun on the ground. I took a few pot shots after him, knowing I wouldn't hit anything. I felt the sting of Trevor's betrayal and was surprised at how angry it made me. I also felt a little hypocritical because I'd been working at Butterfly with an ulterior motive for years. The difference, though, was that I strove for world peace. Trevor only wanted world domination.

Looking back to the assassins, I noticed Cody's eyes kept shifting back and forth between Colin's dead body and me. It didn't take a mind reader to figure out what he was thinking.

"It wasn't me," I uttered, awkwardly. "I didn't..."

Cody chimed in with a succinct Japanese sentence that I assumed by his annoyed expression meant, "We don't care."

Still, not completely understanding the madman with an ax looming over me didn't put my nerves at ease.

"Relax," Esther interjected. "We heard everything."

Except I couldn't relax as she didn't specify what "everything" was. That could've meant anything, and for a psychopath like Esther, there's no way to predict how she would interpret my conversation with Trevor.

Hell, *I* was unsure how to interpret my conversation with Trevor. For years, I'd been friends with another time-traveler, this time from a place where I'd saved the world—sort of—through peaceful reform. It was kind of flattering to believe I was able to make such a remarkable difference no matter what timeline I was in. But it was also terrifying. Because Trevor had decided to destroy that timeline and, like Jane, had succeeded. Were we just doomed from now on to have time travelers screwing with the present? Could the future even happen now? Or would it constantly get overwritten by whoever was disgruntled and had access to the technology? It was a sobering thought, and I wasn't sure there was an answer to it.

Fuck.

"Now would be a good time to get up and make use of this giant hole we made in the wall," Esther added, dryly.

"You don't have to tell me twice," I said, running to their side.

Behind me, I could hear Esther firing her assault rifle repeatedly while Cody hurled a grenade at the Monarch troopers coming in to engage us.

"Just how many guys do they have?" I asked, heading into a service tunnel they'd blown a hole into that was separate from the main walkways.

The tunnel was made of concrete and floor grating with bare light bulbs sporadically illuminating the way forward. I didn't know the direction I was supposed to be running, so I let Cody take the lead. He moved in front of us and jogged like he wasn't expending energy at all. He gave me a bright smile and I shook my head, wondering why I'd ever allied with these lunatics.

"A lot more," Esther said, following me. "Colin Reilly brought an entire division of Monarch troopers to reinforce his position here. All our team is either captured or dead. Thankfully, that Trevor guy did us a favor. Killing Colin means that it doesn't matter when we blow this place. A dead CEO isn't something they'll recover from easily. Especially with the rest of the board dead."

It scared me how casually she threw around plans of massive destruction. "Wait, blow this place up?"

"The prison is powered by a micro-fusion reactor of the kind that made Butterfly Energy its first trillion dollars," Esther said. "They're child's play to sabotage for a kilometer-sized explosion in the future. We decided to leave Monarch a little present, a much bigger one than we thought."

"You can't do that!" I said, horrified. "There are innocent people imprisoned here."

I could hear gunfire through the walls, which told me that there was a lot of it going on.

"They're executing them," Esther replied, as if discussing the weather. "All of them. And without central leadership, Monarch will probably destroy the place anyway. We're still in the time period that Butterfly is trying to hide its crimes."

I felt immense guilt for bringing this doom down to all these prisoners. They probably never would have escaped Butterfly anyway, but that didn't mean that what was happening wasn't my fault. "How long do we have to escape?"

"Escape?" Esther asked, as if it was a strange idea.

"Yes, escape! With the others! We need to rescue Jane, Christine, and Anna!" I snapped. "You're going to get us out of here with them and we're not going to be here when this whole place blows up!"

Cody stuck his arm in front of me and stopped, knocking me to the ground as I slammed into it. He looked down and, for a moment, I was afraid he was going to bring his ax onto my head like Jason Voorhees or some other horror movie serial killer. Esther raised her hand and shook her head, stopping behind me.

"You're not our boss," Esther said, looking down. "And now we know you never will be."

That answered that question. The assassins heard Trevor state that I was no longer at risk of becoming the Scorpion. But that revelation came with a double-edged sword. On the plus side, I was no longer their target to kill. But that also meant it would be harder to get them to listen to me.

"You're right," I said, looking up. "I won't become the Scorpion you remember. Jane was successful in averting your future. But that doesn't mean your fight has to end. Trevor will take over Butterfly and see to it that the war you came from still comes to pass. If you ever believed in me, Scorpion or not, then you understand what's at stake."

I was furious and sick of having to deal with these two super-powered psychopaths. I didn't know what kind of drugs or body modifications the New Hope Army had given them to make them able to do the things they could do, but I was finished with their attitude. They'd done nothing but sabotage this mission and play mind games since we'd joined forces. I didn't care if I lived or died right now. I was just through with their insanity.

"Now are you going to help me or not?" I snapped at them. "If you don't want to, then stay here and die with everyone else. I'll just have to rescue the others myself!"

It was an insane claim and one without a chance of being true. I probably couldn't escape on my own, let alone rescue everyone else. But it seemed to affect the pair. It didn't result in them looking guilty per se, but it did result in them feeling something. Confusion, maybe? Concern? I didn't recognize the emotion.

Cody said something incomprehensible. Whatever it was though, Esther understood and didn't look so happy.

"Dammit," Esther muttered. "You're right."

I couldn't tell if she was talking to me or her partner. Either way, Cody extended a hand to help me up.

I reluctantly took it and jumped to my feet. "So, you'll help me find the others?"

"Sure," Esther said. "You're in charge. For now."

Cody nodded.

Wow, I felt so relieved. Almost as if two great white sharks were talking to a seal.

"How long do we have until this place goes boom?" I asked.

"Thirty minutes, give or take," Esther said. "Core meltdowns are not an exact science. Once people realize what's going to happen, though, they'll attempt to evacuate. That could potentially cut off our only escape route."

"Which is?" I asked.

There was no way in hell we could go back the way we came, especially if they were bringing down an army of Monarch troopers.

"We can still take the train below us," Esther replied. "The station down there is lightly guarded or should be, at least. They're securing the prison floor by floor from the top down. That is if they're still following protocol."

"And if they aren't?" I asked.

"Then we all die," Esther said with a smile. "What's the plan?"

"Fair enough," I said. "Let's get our friends back. From there, we'll head to the train station and hope not to die."

"That's not a plan, that's a goal," Esther said.

"How about just kill everyone who stands in our way?" I suggested.

Esther's eyebrows perked up. "Now we're talking."

I hated giving that kind of order, but I wasn't under any assumption that I could stop these two from committing murder. We were reaching a crisis point where there were no easy answers. The clock was also ticking. It didn't matter if I was in charge or they were if the entirety of the compound blew up around us. "I don't suppose there's any way of shutting down the reactor?"

Esther smiled. "Now, that would just be silly of us to have left that to chance, wouldn't it?"

She pushed me through a service door while Cody followed, the three of us narrowly escaping a Monarch squadron as we found ourselves in the general prison area. We were at the bottom of the facility, with fenced-in cages, break rooms, security centers, and other things vital to the administration of the facility. There were a few Monarch personnel on the ground, murdered by gunshots and ax blows. Esther and Cody had already been this way, it seemed.

Cody bent the door hatch behind us with his bare hands. He then spoke in perfect English, "Good luck."

"Thanks," I said.

It was a strange feeling walking through what was essentially a warzone. Since Jane had come into my life, I'd encountered more violence than I ever wanted to and nearly died on several occasions. But never had I actually been in what I considered combat. Now that had changed, too.

My whole reason for fighting the Scorpion was to prevent death, and now I was in some way responsible for everyone who died here tonight. All the prisoners, guards, and soldiers who perished here were people whose blood was on my hands. I could suppress my horror for such a prospect, but only for so long. Even if I never became the Scorpion, I'd become what I'd never wanted to be: a warrior.

"Your girlfriends and traitorous daughter are this way," Esther said, gesturing through an x-ray machine and security scanner.

"How do you know that?" I asked, not sure I trusted anything that came out of her mouth. I also didn't rise to the bait of her "girlfriends" comment.

Esther reached up to her ear and pulled out an earpiece. It was one of the standard Monarch communication devices: an M-17 infolink. I could hear the various Monarch personnel and Trevor speaking through it.

"Fair enough." I slipped it in my ear and listened for their reports as well as troop movements.

Esther smirked. "Thankfully, the only prisoners being kept alive are on their way to the train station. That includes Jane, Christine, and your girlfriend. In a few years, this place would have been home to forty thousand prisoners, including the President of the United States. You should be proud of the fact you've shut it down."

"Really?" I asked, sarcastically. "Should I be?"

"No," Esther scoffed. "We're the ones who did all the legwork."

I shook my head and headed forward in front of the others. If I was going to lead, I had to do it from the front. Besides, if they were going to stab me in the back, then they could do it at any time.

"One more thing," I said, gesturing with my gun.

"Yes, oh fearless leader?" Esther asked.

I really disliked these two. "No killing unless I order it."

"Sure," Esther said, reluctantly. "Why not?"

I wasn't sure I believed her but there was no use in arguing. We continued for several minutes through the underground of the prison complex until we reached a massive train station built for a much-larger prison population than had ever served their sentence here. Not that I imagined anyone had ever been released.

It was a football stadium-sized central chamber with two train tracks, each with massive machines that looked like they were attached to rockets. There were several prison cars behind them, but they weren't currently attached to the engines. In what was a kind of hilarious bit of black comedy, I noticed the sides of the walls were plastered with advertisements for Butterfly products. Apparently, even employees at a top-secret, illegal black site couldn't escape the Butterfly marketing division.

Much to my surprise, I saw we didn't have to rescue any of my friends. Jane, Christine, Anna, and a few remaining HOPE soldiers were standing over a half-dozen captured Monarch troopers kneeling with their hands tied behind their back. I was both relieved and stunned to realize they'd gotten away on their own.

"Rob!" Jane said, stunned.

"Can we kill them?" Esther asked, hopefully.

"No!" I snapped. "Get them on the train. We need to get out of here. The entire place is about to blow."

"What?" Jane stared.

Esther smiled. "A little present for our Monarch guests. Oh, Colin Reilly is dead, too."

I couldn't see the Monarch troopers' faces behind their helmets, but I assumed their jaws dropped in horror.

"Yes!" Anna said, making a fist of triumph.

"It wasn't me!" I shot out, not sure why I still cared what she thought. "It was Trevor."

"Trevor?" Jane repeated. "Your friend?"

"It's a long story," I replied, which seemed to satisfy her curiosity for the time being.

Jane sighed at my non-answer and looked to one of the HOPE soldiers. "We need to get one of the engines running now."

He nodded and went in to start powering up the machine.

"I don't understand what's going on," Christine muttered, still traumatized by her experience.

That was when I heard Trevor's voice speak in my earpiece. "I know you're listening, Rob."

I was tempted to respond but didn't. I climbed onto the engine instead and directed everyone else to do the same.

"I know you still have some of my men," Phil chimed in through the earpiece. "Please, Rob. Those are decent soldiers with families.

Don't make me call their children and tell them their parents won't be coming home."

"Disarm the Monarch troopers and let them go," I ordered, staring at Esther. "They can find their own way back."

Esther stared back at me. "You must be joking."

I had to wonder if they'd managed to weaponize crazy in the future. Did they have psychopath pills everyone could take or had the Scorpion sought out the most sociopathic soldiers he could find to upgrade into his Elite Scorpion Guard? I honestly didn't know and suspected I'd never find out before one of us ended up killing the other.

"Do it," I demanded. I wasn't going to be responsible for more death if I could avoid it.

I was amazed when Esther shrugged and freed the captives. Anna also shocked me by not shooting the Monarch troopers in the back as they took off. Today really was full of surprises.

"I know this place is about to blow up," Trevor said. "My troops and I have already evacuated, and the ones you just let go are headed to a chopper on the roof. Maybe you're in the midst of escape yourself. Maybe you're unaware of what your terrorists have done. It doesn't matter. You need to surrender yourself to me."

Yeah, fat chance of that. I didn't respond, though. If I did, he'd almost certainly know where I was.

"If you don't, I'll kill Georgia," Trevor said.

Wait, what?

"Rob, help!" Georgia spoke on the other end of the infolink. "Trevor's gone crazy! He took me from my cell and is killing all the prisoners!"

"No," I whispered.

It was impossible to gauge if Trevor was bluffing, especially with Phil right next to him, but I knew the psycho really was capable of anything.

"You have to respond in ten seconds, or I shoot her," Trevor said. "Ten…nine…eight…"

The engine of the train started to power up and prepared to rocket out of the prison complex. This was it. A game-time decision. If I left, there was no way to keep Georgia alive.

"Five..." Trevor said.

I reached to turn on the speech function, only to have it ripped away from my hands by Esther who pointed her assault rifle at me.

"No!" I shouted.

"Stay," Esther said.

The train surged forward, and we departed down a long dark tunnel, leaving the prison complex behind.

A gunshot echoed through the infolink.

CHAPTER NINETEEN

The train tunnel walls zoomed past the windows so rapidly it seemed like we were in a spaceship moving faster than light. I knew if I stared at it long enough, I would've gotten sick and probably vomited all over the place. Not that looking out the window was a problem. My focus was squarely on the communications device—the infolink—in Esther's palm and then the tiny bits of it after she crushed it with a quick squeeze of her hand.

"What the hell are you doing?" I shouted.

"Keeping you alive," she said while dusting the train floor with the remains.

I forced out a single sarcastic chuckle.

"That's hilarious coming from someone who once tried to ki—"

I was interrupted by a loud boom that shook the moving train. More than that, it shook the entire tunnel surrounding us. The explosion reverberated through my teeth. It jostled the train and we all stumbled around, desperately trying not to fall flat on our faces. A swirling flash of orange and red engulfed the windows, but only for a moment. The train kept moving, and the shaking subsided. It seemed we had escaped the fiery blast that chased us. There was a brief silence in the train car as everyone regained their balance, and I could sense Esther gazing at me.

"Trevor didn't want you to surrender," Esther stated. "He just wanted to stall long enough for the reactor to go off and kill us all."

"Jesus," I muttered, staring at the sight disappearing behind us.

"Not my god, Scorpion," Esther said, as if taunting me with the occult elements of my now-erased future.

While the rest of us relatively normal folks still wrestled with the near-death experience of being blown to bits, Cody lumbered over to the side of the train and jammed his ax in the door. He then leveraged his entire body into the blade until the door popped open, exposing the inside of the train to the tunnel whizzing past at a hundred miles per hour, if I had to put a number on it. It seemed to be moving even faster without the window between us.

Still recovering from the blast, the HOPE soldiers scrambled to raise their weapons at Cody, but Esther countered by lifting her own, which was bigger and a lot more intimidating, if I was being honest.

"I would put your guns down unless you think this train interior could use a lot redder adornment," Esther threatened, her voice scarily relaxed. "Then by all means, let's start shooting."

Jane stepped forward, only slightly irritated that her former comrades decided to risk all our lives by opening the door of a moving bullet train. "What are you doing?"

With her guns still raised, Esther backed up slowly to the door. "Remember that thing we came here to do that you decided you wanted no part of?"

Jane didn't say anything. She just scowled.

"Well," Esther went on, cheerily, "Cody and I have to finish it."

Jane subtly glanced in my direction. Her eyes didn't flash concern at me. "Concern" was too passive an emotion for Jane. But there was a certain sharpness to her glare, letting me know that if the assassins made a move, then she was ready to throw down.

"Oh, not him," Esther laughed with a silly giggle. "We learned today that he doesn't become the Scorpion. So, congratulations, Jane. You got your wish. Daddy and his baby girl can go off and play house for all Cody and I care."

It was amazing how quickly Jane's expression went from ready to kill to utter and complete surprise. Anna looked curious. Christine just seemed confused.

"But somebody else will be the Scorpion. I can feel it in the air," Esther revealed, wiping the smile from her face. "That means Cody and I still have a job to do. Now if you'll excuse us."

Cody turned and leapt from the train without warning. He disappeared instantly. At this speed he should've turned into mush the second he hit the ground. I knew he didn't, though, all evidence to the contrary. They were genuine superhumans and the mods to present-day soldiers just couldn't keep up. The fact they'd killed dozens, if not hundreds, of soldiers by themselves was proof enough of that fact.

"Ta-ta for now, bitches." A moment later Esther lowered her gun and gave us a quick salute. She then leapt backwards off the train, also disappearing instantly.

"Stop the train," Jane ordered. "We have to go after them."

Anna's soldiers moved towards the controls but stopped when I casually waved them off. "Let them go."

"Let them go?" Jane repeated as if she didn't even understand the words. "Don't you remember what happened last time they went in search of the Scorpion?"

She asked it rhetorically because there was no way I would forget the cross-country killing spree the original group of assassins went on to find me. Jane chose to let them keep me safe, a decision clearly weighing heavily on her shoulders.

"We can't let that happen again," Jane added. "We're the ones responsible for setting those two psychopaths loose."

"I'm actually going to disagree with Jane on this one," Anna chimed in. "Her assassin friends were very helpful back there. We could use them for—"

"Shut up, Anna." I interrupted. I had never been so annoyed by her voice.

"You can't expect me to—" Jane stepped up to continue her protest.

I interrupted again, louder this time. "Shut up. Shut up. Shut up!"

It was a childish display, unbefitting a guy studying to be an executive or a future terrorist leader. Not that I had any future in either. All the studying, gladhanding, and planning I'd done for the past four years amounted to nothing. It had all gone up in a set of explosions orchestrated by a man who I had thought was my friend.

Worse, I'd become a casual killer. I'd killed someone in self-defense years ago but now I had multiple people's blood on my hands. I'd gone on a fricking military assault, and it had felt good. Assuming they didn't blame me for all the deaths at the Chrysalis—which was a big if—I was still heavily involved in what would probably be considered the worst terrorist assault in US history. Nuclear explosions weren't something even the corporate-controlled media could ignore.

"Rob, are you okay?" Anna asked, as if it was not the silliest question in the world to ask right now.

"I've had two friends for the last few years," I explained while walking to the open train door and pressing the button to close it. "Exactly two. And I just listened to one kill the other while trying to kill me. So please, ladies, if you don't mind, can I have a minute to process that?"

Jane had no response other than to swallow hard, which I assumed was a physical manifestation of burying her pride.

"You rescued me, Robbie," Christine said in the same soft voice that had captivated me as a teenager. "Whatever happened inside that prison...just remember that I wouldn't be here if it weren't for you."

It sounded cheesy, but Christine's optimism made me feel better. She had this rare ability to be forceful yet compassionate at the same time. It was that very tone that inspired so many, me included, to join HOPE.

A hopeful sentiment settled over the room as Anna and the HOPE soldiers also felt touched by Christine's kindness. It was an oddly comforting moment that Jane shattered in an instant. "What I'd like to know is how you got there in the first place."

Anna spoke up before Christine could respond. "That's classified HOPE intelligence that Christine will debrief back at our base."

"Seriously?" Jane just looked at her sideways.

"It's all right, Anna," Christine chimed in, gently. "These two risked their lives to rescue me. They deserve to know why."

Jane appeared satisfied. She allowed Christine a moment to gather herself as she strolled over and relaxed into a seat. Christine then took a deep breath and closed her eyes as if preparing for a long journey. "After our failed heist in their Chicago headquarters," Christine began, "Butterfly found a body in the basement."

Christine was talking about Gunner, the man who'd become the leader of the New Hope assassins after Jane abandoned them to protect me. He also happened to be the first person I ever killed. It was self-defense. Not murder. But still, I made a promise to myself afterward that he would be the last person to die by my hand. It was one that I'd failed to keep. Christine didn't know any of that, though.

"They listed the body as a member of HOPE," Christine went on, "but that was just a cover. The technology they recovered on it was like stuff from a sci-fi movie."

Of course, it was. It came from the future.

"My source…" Christine started before choking over the words with emotion caught in her throat. She hesitated to continue and leaned forward as if a massive weight just dropped on her shoulders.

"Are you okay?" Anna asked, reminding me of their friendship.

"Did you find anyone in the cell beside me?" Christine asked while staring at the ground. "I had a friend there."

"There was nobody," I lied.

I could feel Jane and Anna's eyes both hit me at the same time, each one of them judging me for completely different reasons. Anna wasn't happy that I withheld important details about her mission, but Jane was taken aback by how easily I dismissed her mother as insignificant. Neither of them said anything, probably because it just wasn't the time. Truth be told, I didn't lie about the dead girl we found for either of them. I was merely sparing Christine another moment of tragedy in a world defined by it.

"She was a good kid," Christine reminisced. "Smart. Determined. I thought we were going to do great things together. If only I'd—"

"Christine, focus," I said, trying to get her back on track. Or maybe that was just an excuse I told myself because I didn't want to think about a dead girl who was supposed to become the mother of my child. It made my head hurt. "What happened to the body Butterfly found?"

Christine took another deep breath to reset herself then continued.

"Colin Reilly became obsessed with it. So much so that he pushed his weapons-development program into high gear."

"Aurelia," Anna whispered loud enough for everyone to hear.

It was Butterfly's big secret and apparently the source of all that had gone wrong in our lives. I was so troubled by everything that happened that I couldn't even think about the fact it seemed to have been inspired by technology from the future.

Something wasn't adding up, though. I'd been Colin's assistant for a while, and this didn't seem like him at all.

"That doesn't make sense," I interjected. "I know Colin Reilly. He was crazy enough to try and develop time travel, but what use would he have for it? He wasn't obsessed with the past. He considered himself a futurist. That was the reason why he wanted so much power, so he could rebuild the world in his image. At least that was how he justified it all."

"You're right, Robbie," Christine acknowledged. For some reason, I didn't feel the need to correct her about my name change.

"Time travel wasn't Aurelia's main objective," she added. "It was just a part of it."

Anna was the only one of us shocked by the detail. "How could something as farfetched as time travel be considered secondary?"

"I don't know." Christine shook her head. She didn't have the answers. "We never did find out what the Aurelia weapon was, but it's a long-term project that will take years, maybe even decades to finish. Colin Reilly knew that, but he wanted it now. So, one of his lab techs, a man named Charles Kepler, presented time travel as a possibility and Colin ate it up. He expected development of Aurelia to finish alongside the time travel work. Then, when both were operational, Aurelia would be brought to the past. Well, their past. Our present."

The pieces were falling in place as Trevor's last conversation with Colin started making sense. Trevor was supposed to bring Aurelia back for him, but he didn't. My old friend had other plans. I couldn't believe

I'd so badly misjudged Trevor. Hell, I'd misjudged Georgia, too. Apparently, all three of us had been pretending to be people that we weren't.

"If Colin's dead then I guess his plan didn't work out the way he hoped," Anna said, stating the obvious.

I could tell she was happy Colin was dead, even though he was now going to be replaced with someone worse. A part of me hoped that Butterfly would collapse without him or his board, but the fact was there were hundreds, if not thousands, of employees who would happily replace the ones who had fallen. Colin Reilly had created an entire ideology around corporate rule and loyalty to the company. I didn't know if Trevor would be able to take control of the company himself, but he apparently had moles among those people as well.

"We need to stop Trevor," I muttered.

"There are bigger issues at stake," Anna started to say.

"No, there aren't," I said, dryly. "He's dangerous and can create a far worse future than anything I could do."

"You could?" Christine asked, confused.

"It's a long story," Anna said. "Suddenly, it's a long story that makes a lot more sense than it did a few hours ago."

There was more to discuss. A lot more. But I didn't necessarily trust Anna's instincts. Her fight against Butterfly was always personal, but for me it was simply a matter of doing the right thing. Even when I worked for them, I never viewed my goal to change the company as a crusade. Trevor had changed that.

It wasn't that he hated me. He hated future me. What I did to Butterfly in the years to come created a deep-seated resentment inside Trevor. It caused him to come back in time and befriend me just so he could rub his victory in my face. Talk about a grudge.

First it was my destiny as the Scorpion that eventually led to my father's death. Now it was my fate as a Butterfly executive that led to Georgia's. *How does this keep happening? Why do those close to me keep being punished for the man I would become?* Jane, Christine, and even Anna could see me wrestling with that question. I could feel their faces homing in on me, but none had the opportunity to continue the conversation.

"Rob?" Jane asked.

"What?" I asked, sharper than I'd intended.

"We're here," she said.

The train came to a sudden stop. Wherever we were going, we had arrived.

"Oh," I said, taking a deep breath. "I see."

CHAPTER TWENTY

The train had been automatically slowing for some time during my argument with Jane, but I hadn't noticed. The stress from recent events had me wanting to find a bed to collapse on and sleep for a week. I'd gotten some rest on the drive from Chicago and so had Jane but that seemed a lifetime ago.

Unfortunately, restful sleep wasn't going to happen anytime soon, and I wondered if it was ever going to happen ever again. I was simultaneously exhausted and wired, two states warring within me as I struggled to figure out how I ended up in this position in the first place.

"I see," I said again, looking at what appeared to be some sort of outdoor train station. There was no sign of any people, yet, and I didn't care if there were. The only thing Butterfly's people could do was kill me after all. I wasn't sure I gave that much of a crap about that anymore. Taking a step off the train, I wandered out and tried to get my bearings.

"Rob!" Anna called behind me.

"Just give me a bit," I replied, not looking back. "Please."

Much to my surprise, the train station beyond looked nothing like I expected it to. Instead of being like the brutalist architecture of the military facility we'd just escaped, it looked like someone had gone for a deliberately Victorian look. The place had an almost Hogwarts-esque charm to it with ornate arches, red brick walls, curved metal gates, and an antique ticket center. There was an enormous grandfather clock-styled timepiece by the curved stairs leading out of the station and not a sign of anything electronic beyond the magnetic rails that had led us here in the first place.

There was, however, a sign of what we had done behind the train. The rails stretched out for miles behind us where I could see a mushroom cloud in the distance. It was a fusion explosion. Not radioactive, but the sight of what we'd done left me stunned. This was something Monarch couldn't cover up and had undoubtedly killed anyone that was in the Chrysalis when it went off. We'd managed to rescue Christine but hadn't been able to get anyone else out of that hellish prison. Worse, we'd lost a lot of people getting in and out of there. That was on me.

I could already imagine the headlines that would be on every website, blog, and info feed tomorrow: TERRORISTS NUKE AMERICAN HEARTLAND. It didn't matter that the only place destroyed was an illegal corporate prison; there was no evidence of that anymore. Butterfly would certainly do its best to blame us versus claiming it was one of their reactors going critical. Hell, they weren't even wrong to do so.

"Son of a—" I muttered, staring at the distant sign of devastation. "I did this."

"No, you didn't," Jane said, standing behind me. "This was Esther and Cody's doing. It was always their doing."

"Not in the mood, Jane." I looked down.

"We need to talk," Jane said, her voice soft but firm. It was a different kind of tone than the one she normally used with me.

I looked back at her. "Shouldn't we be finding a way out of this place? I feel like we're in a holo vid and there's a coin puzzle or something we must unlock."

Jane blinked. "You realize I've never played a video game that doesn't involve killing people, right?"

"Oh," I said, frowning. "Sorry, I just…"

"Rob?" Jane asked.

"Sorry, I'm still angry." I frowned. "Not at you, but this entire situation. I feel used and want to lash out. Now is not a good time to talk to me."

"It's not all about you." Jane closed her eyes.

"What?" I asked, confused.

"We've all lost someone today," Jane replied. "I don't know what's going to happen next. Hell, for all I know, I'm going to vanish in a few minutes. Maybe the universe will collapse. I don't know."

I blinked rapidly. "Huh?"

"My mother is dead," Jane said, softly. She started speaking more rapidly and I could tell she was panicked. It was a new emotion for her. "You and she never met, which means I'll never be born. If I'm not born, then that means I can't go back in time. If that doesn't happen, then I can't rewrite the future. If I can't rewrite the future, then my mom should be alive, but she—"

"You're afraid that a time paradox has happened," I suggested.

"Yes!" Jane snapped. "It's like I've gone back in time and killed her myself!"

"Jane, I don't think the universe is collapsing." I looked at her sadly. "This is also not your fault."

"How is it not?" Jane asked me. "I never should've come to this time. I've ruined everything."

I was surprised to see she was as torn up about this as she was. Then again, I should have realized that this went beyond mere temporal physics. I couldn't mourn this girl I didn't know, but it was clearly something that had broken Jane. She'd turned against her father and fellow time-travelers to save me, the person her father had been. How must it have felt for her to find her mother but be unable to form any kind of relationship?

I wasn't in the mood to be reassuring, but I took a deep breath. "Jane, you didn't cause this. Reality isn't collapsing. You're here. I'm here. It was always your plan to change time and you have. Apparently, the future you come from was averted long before this. What did you think was going to happen?"

"I just thought you and Rachel might meet despite all this. You know, once we'd managed to stop them."

Jane looked ready to cry, which stunned me. In that moment, Jane was just a girl rather than the unconquerable badass from the future I'd always thought her to be. "Rachel was her name?"

"Yes," Jane said. "Rachel Chang Anderson. She was a blogger. I never learned how the two of you met but...this could've been the day."

"Trevor." I closed my eyes.

"What?" she asked.

"Trevor could've had her killed," I said, disgusted. "He's from a second future. One where I managed to become head of Butterfly and fix things. He objected."

Jane sighed. It was the only time I'd ever seen her completely confused in our years of knowing each other. Time travel would do that, even to time-travelers. "This is insane."

"Yeah," I replied. "He came back to set wrong what we set right."

"I hate time travel," Jane muttered, feeling her face. "What the hell does this all mean?"

"It means that the future is completely open now. We don't know what's going to happen, or how."

"Are you still having dreams?" Jane asked. "I mean, of the future?"

"More like hallucinations. I don't understand them. I mean, maybe they would make sense if I were a time traveler, but I'm not. I'm just someone who has had his life affected by all this craziness."

"Maybe," Jane replied. "Maybe there are things we just don't know about how time travel works."

"What are your dreams about?" I asked.

"You dying horribly," Jane said, as if she was ripping off a Band-Aid. "The world back under the control of the New Hope Army but worse. It's like a military dictatorship. The Scorpion is a god and kills anyone who thinks otherwise. I always assumed they were just that — dreams. But now it seems they may actually come to pass."

"Great." I sucked in my breath. "I don't suppose you have any idea who will take my place?"

"No," Jane said as she shook her head. "Though I'm pretty sure it has to be someone either in the inner circle of HOPE or someone the other assassins have been in contact with."

As Jane said, time travel made my head hurt.

"I'm sorry, Jane. I'm sure Rachel was a lovely person, but I can't mourn her the way you do."

Jane closed her eyes. "My mother was lovely and sweet but had a core of steel. I never got to know my father as a man, but everyone spoke of how he changed when she died. He closed himself off and sent me to study with the other children to be a soldier."

"How old were you?" I asked.

"Four," Jane replied.

Wow, my future self was a real piece of garbage. At least he wouldn't be hurting anyone else ever again. He wasn't going to exist and that was about the only thing I could take comfort from right now.

"Well, I want you to know…I guess, I'm sorry? I don't know what to say in this sort of situation."

Jane looked down before turning to the train platform where Anna and Christine were catching up. The remaining soldiers looked stoic, except for one who was on the verge of breaking down. I didn't blame him.

"I'm sorry for the way things turned out between you and Anna," Jane lamented.

Her out-of-character apology made me frown. "Our breakup wasn't your fault, Jane. The whole conflict with Butterfly was eventually going to push us apart. She's gone and become a soldier while I tried to reform Butterfly from within."

"You would have succeeded too," Jane replied.

"Would have," I said, realizing all the work I'd done until this point was up in smoke. In an explosion visible from orbit no less. "What do you think happens next?"

"The real war begins." Jane looked grim. "The United States will probably order a full-scale investigation of the incident and use it as an excuse for Butterfly-backed congressmen to declare martial law. Monarch will be hired as a 'peacekeeping' task force and the purges will commence. The country will officially become the Incorporated States of America and all industry put under the purview of the Corporate Alliance."

I took a deep breath. "Even without Colin Reilly?"

The question sounded too hopeful even to me. After all, I had just told myself that Colin had created an entire army of fanatical followers while he was the head of Butterfly. Something more akin to a cult than a corporate culture. People that he'd conditioned to believe that a private enterprise devoted to profit like Butterfly was better for leading the world than democratically elected officials. Indeed, Trevor was probably one of those people, given how he reacted to the idea of my preventing the company's ascension with a mixture of disdain as well as pure hate.

"It's not that simple," Jane frowned. "History isn't just made of great men and women; it's made of events and historical inertia. Colin Reilly may have gotten the ball rolling but there are other people who will pick up the slack."

"You're right. I...I..." I closed my eyes.

"What?" Jane asked.

"I think I need to kill Trevor," I said, simply. It was a conclusion that I reached as I finished the sentence. I was surprised to hear it come out of my mouth. I needed to kill someone? Me? All of this had been about avoiding bloodshed. But it was too late to do that now. I'd helped to kill everyone Cody and Esther had killed just by bringing them along, and I had participated in a military attack that had ended in massive bloodshed. There was no going back now.

"Rob—" Jane started to speak.

"No," I said, taking a deep breath. "I must do this. He's from the future. He's got information that we don't. He...He killed Georgia."

"Was Georgia important to you?" Jane reached over and put her hand on my shoulder.

"No, it wasn't like that," I said as I reluctantly removed her hand. "I never had much time for dating once I dedicated myself to my studies. Also, I couldn't be open about all the terrible things I've experienced. I've been as celibate as a monk."

"Too much information, Dad," Jane said.

"Oh," I said, grimacing. "Right." I stared down at the ground. "I know where Trevor lives, what he does for hobbies, and how he thinks. I can find him."

"Correction: you know what Trevor let you know about his cover identity," Jane said. "You never really knew the real Trevor."

That felt like a gut punch. She was right, though. I didn't know the real Trevor. The grandson of Colin Reilly. The time traveler. The Trevor I knew had been somewhat snooty and arrogant, but he wasn't a killer. He wasn't someone who would have gunned down Georgia. Even now, I couldn't bring myself to believe he did but what would be the point of faking it? I needed answers and that was perhaps my real motivation.

"Yeah," I muttered. "I still have to find him."

"Don't do anything rash," Jane said. "You're not a killer."

"I am," I replied, not knowing how many people I'd killed now.

"Not like me," Jane said. "Not even close. You don't set out to make people die. It just sort of happens."

"I'm not sure that matters to the dead," I replied.

"No," Jane took a deep breath. "Not at all. You're a person who saves lives, not takes them. Right now, you're just angry and need sleep."

"Tell that to the mushroom cloud," I said, turning away.

Jane let me go.

The train station was an insane-looking place with even more weird curiosities than the ones I'd seen on the way in. There were museum-like exhibits of clockwork toys, statues of Colin Reilly dressed like a British soldier in the Boer Wars, and paintings of various executives. It seemed like the place had been set up as the entrance to a theme park rather than a prison. Really, it was just another sign of how strange Butterfly could be and how much they catered to the eccentric whims of its executives.

A part of me was terrified we'd have Monarch soldiers waiting for us when I finally managed to break open one of the gates and found a parking lot full of cars. Apparently, the train served as a way for staff to travel to the prison without tipping people off. Whoever came up with that plan had to have been middle management.

There was no sign of helicopters, tanks, troopers, or Monarch descending on us. They'd probably retreated fully from the explosion. A good thing, too. I'd had enough warfare for one day.

I didn't want to be involved with HOPE anymore. This fighting was the sort of thing that turned me into the Scorpion in Jane's timeline, but I could do something now to keep Trevor from ruining our future. I just had to steal one of these cars and get to him. It didn't matter what happened to me afterward. If I rid the world of Trevor, then it would all be worth it. Somehow my best friend had become my worst enemy and all it had taken was him killing someone very close to us both. I should have realized he'd been trying to get close to me our entire time together at college. Instead, I'd been blinded by my own ambitions and Georgia had paid the price.

"Rob?" A familiar female voice interrupted my thoughts. It was hard to believe I was hearing it again.

"Christine?" I asked, turning around. "Now is probably not a good time."

Christine stood there, wearing her prison jumpsuit, her hair cut very short and looking like she'd been through hell. Still, there was something very beautiful about her and I remembered how much I'd cared for her.

"I just wanted to talk," Christine said.

"You have to be horrified by what's happened." I looked down. "You started HOPE as a passive resistance. Now it's become a terrorist organization."

"Or freedom fighters," Christine said, sighing. "I'm not a violent person but I admit my feelings on how to deal with Butterfly have changed."

I sucked in my breath "Yeah, I suppose they would."

"I've seen that you've changed, too," Christine said, dryly.

"Yeah, not for the better." I grimaced.

"I disagree," Christine said. "You saved me and I'm not going to forget that."

"I'm sorry about your source." I paused and frowned. I wanted to show her sympathy but didn't know how else to say it. I couldn't exactly reveal that I not only knew the girl's name but that in another future she became the mother of my child. It was also why I lied about finding Rachel's body. The fewer questions I had to answer, the less pain I had to cause.

"She and I were...close." Christine mournfully closed her eyes. "The two of us had a relationship that wasn't always friendly but was built on respect. Her loss will be great, but I intend to carry on the work we were both dedicated to. I intend to carry on life for the both of us."

I didn't know what she meant, not really, but nodded. "What are you and Anna planning?"

"To get Aurelia," Christine said. "That weapon may well be the key to all of this."

It seemed like a big assumption that Aurelia was a weapon. Colin Reilly had been willing to bankrupt his company to create it and while I was leaning toward it being time travel—Jane had said as much—I noted that nothing prevented the Alaskan research center from having more projects in the works than just how to crack time. Somehow what was created there had resulted in the defeat of the United States military and keeping it from Butterfly's—well Trevor's now—hands might mean the difference in any upcoming war that might happen. Me becoming the Scorpion was prevented from happening now, but maybe we could stop the Corporate War from happening altogether. But did I want to be a part of that? Especially with all the violence our "liberation" of the Chrysalis had resulted in? I didn't know.

"I want to help but I can't," I said. "I can't go on another mission like this. It was too much. Too many people died. I have blood on my hands and—"

I was going to get more on them. No matter how much I denied it, I had deliberately chosen to become part of the violent resistance against Butterfly. I'd participated in a direct assault against a facility and had gunned down who knew how many people as well as brought Esther and Cody along.

That was on me. Worse, as much as I regretted how it had turned out, I probably would have done the exact same thing again if it meant getting Christine out. It was a nasty realization to have about yourself but if it meant burning down the corporates then it was justified. Perhaps I wasn't so far from Anna as I thought. Perhaps the biggest difference between us was that I didn't trust the government faction she'd allied with to do much better. Maybe no faction was better, and the only solution was anarchy.

Christine shook her head. "That's not what I'm here for." And she drew close to me.

"What do you mean?" I asked, confused, shaken from my thoughts.

Christine put her arms around my neck and kissed me.

"Christine, I—" I said, so stunned that I didn't react physically.

"I want to live life," Christine said. "Please, give me a moment to."

I just stared at her, completely slack-jawed. That was when my infopad beeped, I pulled away and checked the screen. It was modified to be off the Butterfly Network, a precaution I was glad to have made given the circumstances, yet there was a message from Trevor: WE NEED TO MEET.

CHAPTER TWENTY-ONE

Trevor's text sent my head spinning. I had no clue how to react, which was good considering the circumstances. I didn't even know if I should respond or not. The last communication I'd had with the guy ended with him killing Georgia to hurt me. One thing was certain, though, I couldn't figure this out with Christine over my shoulder.

"I have to go," I muttered while slipping out from under her arms.

"Is it something I said? I'm so—" Christine's body deflated.

"No," I said, cutting off her apology before she could make it. "Not at all. I just…"

I searched for the right explanation, but nothing came to mind. Christine deserved to know the truth, even if just a small part of it. In many ways she started this whole conflict by jumpstarting HOPE. But my life right now, which had become consumed by time-traveling assassins and despots, was just too much to dump on her.

In the end, I decided to avoid the issue entirely. "Something's come up. We will talk about this later, though. I promise."

Christine nodded with a faint smile. She didn't like the situation but understood it, which pretty much summed up how I felt about it as well. I slithered away like a snake, not knowing where I was going or why. All I knew was that I had to put both literal and figurative distance between us.

"Good luck," Christine said.

"Thanks," I muttered. "A lot of people have been saying that lately."

"Maybe it's because you need it," Christine said, walking back to the train station.

I fought the urge to turn back and glance at her, eventually succumbing to it. It looked like she was still tougher than I was. She had to be to make it through a place like the Chrysalis.

I was glad she had left, though. If she had still been standing there like a heartbroken mess then I probably would've never been able to focus on texting Trevor back, which I did despite my better judgment.

Trevor said he just wanted to talk. I, of course, was skeptical. But that didn't mean I wasn't interested. There were still tons I didn't know about Trevor's plans. Not to mention how to stop them.

No matter how many times I circled the issue, I kept coming back to the same conclusion: I needed to kill Trevor. I didn't *want* to kill him. I didn't want to kill *anybody*. I'd spent so much mental willpower fighting back my destiny as a genocidal dictator that even the thought of ending one life left a knot in my stomach. The visions I'd been having, the bombings, the raid on the Chrysalis—all of it was starting to take its toll. But I just didn't know any way to stop Trevor other than taking his life.

Maybe if he really were "just looking to talk" I'd have the chance to attack him. He'd probably be guarded, which meant if I had any chance of doing this it would be best to keep Anna's hot head far away. Unfortunately, that would also limit my chance to escape, but maybe I was prepared to take that risk.

I might not want to kill Trevor, but did I *need* to kill Trevor? I wasn't sure despite the fact everything about our relationship had been a lie. Despite the fact he'd—probably—killed Georgia. Hell, despite the fact I was now someone who'd killed multiple people and been involved in a jail break. I never wanted killing people to be easy, but if Trevor was responsible for the executive bombings, then he was a monster and had probably set himself up to take over Butterfly in the chaos. I didn't know how he planned to do that, but I clearly didn't know him nearly as well as I thought. Maybe if he died, at my hands or otherwise, Butterfly would be left decapitated. Leaderless. Broken. It would be so easy, and that kind of thinking frightened me.

"What the hell have I gotten myself into?" I muttered to no one in particular.

I ended up stealing one of the cars from the train station's parking lot. They had a row of company vehicles with keys at the front desk. Luckily, none of them had voice recognition or other identity verification systems required. They were also butt-ugly, in an orange-and-black color scheme. I didn't tell Jane or Anna what I was doing because, well, they wouldn't let me go off on my own.

The location Trevor provided was an abandoned farmhouse halfway between the train station and the crater that was formerly the Chrysalis. He promised to come alone if I did. I didn't believe him, though. I couldn't help but think of all the times I'd spent with him and Georgia—it made me more committed than ever to putting Trevor in the ground.

The morning light was peering over the distance by the time I reached the farm. It was surrounded by cornstalks and looked undisturbed by the huge explosion that rocked the Earth not that far away. Butterfly fusion generators didn't leave fallout, but it was still surreal to be so close to a national disaster. Soon the ruins of the Chrysalis would be surrounded by reporters, the military, and Butterfly personnel…if it wasn't already.

The farmhouse was an ugly-looking thing. A three-story wooden structure that looked to be well over a hundred years old and built by hand. I was never a big Superman fan, but I imagined Clark Kent—the quintessential do-gooder farm boy—would've grown up in a house just like this. There were no cars or tanks surrounding the place, showing that if Trevor had brought his goons with him, he had them well hidden.

I parked my car out front and searched for any signs of life. I didn't find a single one. In fact, it looked as if nobody had been at this place in decades. Yet, when I walked through the front door, I found Trevor calmly waiting for me at the homely kitchen table. The place was decorated like it was ready to receive guests, and I realized the property was yet another Butterfly cover. There was probably an underground listening post or an armory or something here—it existed just to sell the illusion the Chrysalis was a small facility instead of a massive underground complex.

"I'm surprised you actually came," Trevor greeted with a pleasant smile.

He'd changed into an expensive-looking suit and had no sign of any armaments. I guessed if he wanted to be a Butterfly executive then he had to dress the part. I was tempted to pull out my gun then and there to put him down. I really wanted to kill him. To kill him for Georgia and his years of lies, but I couldn't. Unfortunately, my anger failed me. In that moment, all I could think about was all the laughs we had shared as friends, and I wondered how it had all gone so very wrong.

"Me too," I grumbled while strolling over to the table and taking a seat across from him. "I don't often accept invitations from people trying to murder me."

Trevor chuckled. He was really playing up the casual conversation vibe. "Don't be so dramatic. Controlling Butterfly is my goal. You were just standing in the way of that."

"Was Georgia?" I asked through clenched teeth. I was starting to doubt if I could really bring myself to kill Trevor. Thinking of Georgia helped me get angrier, though, and that rage made me think I was just brave enough to pull this off.

The relaxed smile faded from Trevor's face as he took a deep, sobering breath. "HOPE and Butterfly are on the verge of war, Rob, and people die in war. That's just how it is."

"It might've been war. But you made it personal." I looked him straight in his eyes to make sure he understood every word I was saying.

I was trying to be intimidating, the kind of scary badass that could have become the Scorpion in another world. It didn't work.

"Can't it be both?" Trevor asked, rhetorically. "After all, this is my family's legacy we're talking about."

"Didn't seem to me like you cared too much about family legacy when you killed your grandfather," I said, sighing.

I let the anger fade away and just tried to focus on Trevor. Every time I contemplated reaching for the gun my hand clenched up. I just couldn't do it and hated myself for it. Dammit.

Trevor hesitated for a moment, and his eyes sharpened ever so slightly, a reflex he tried to hide from me. It seemed that I had hit a sensitive subject.

"I did that to save it. Colin Reilly's leadership was bringing Butterfly to ruin. He should've squashed HOPE like a bug the minute it formed. Now look where we are."

I wasn't sure I agreed with Trevor's assessment. Colin Reilly had worked to stamp out HOPE, but always in a half-hearted inconsistent way. He'd always been cautious about making martyrs out of them. Colin wanted to take a slow and steady path to eroding the liberties of Americans as well as building up his public support. That included letting HOPE be the ones to attack Butterfly rather than the reverse, or at least having it appear that way. Every time HOPE launched a terrorist attack or became more militant, it benefited him in the public eye.

"You should've thanked him," I remarked, deciding to play some mind games. I'd gotten a lot better at them over the course of all my college classes. Of course, Conner University called them "business techniques."

If I wasn't going to kill Trevor, then I could at least get information from him. This was a whole new ballgame and I had to understand the specifics. Time travel had changed the rules yet again and I needed to know how this weird piece of technology fit into them.

"Thanked him?" Trevor's face lit up with surprise, and not in a good way.

"Without him there would be no Aurelia," I explained, trying to work my way through the paradox of time-travel logic, "which means you wouldn't be here."

I might've tipped my hand letting Trevor know I was aware of his secret weapon, but I didn't have time to play his games. I needed answers, and pushing his buttons was the only way to get them. Trevor didn't look shocked, though. If anything, he looked impressed and mildly intrigued by my resourcefulness.

"Your HOPE friends told you about it, didn't they?" Trevor asked.

Trevor eyed me down, waiting for an answer. That was information he didn't need to have, though. Not that Trevor appeared particularly keen on getting it. He looked curious more than anything and quickly moved on when it became obvious that I wasn't going to reply.

"It's true that Aurelia helped bring me to this time," Trevor said, leaning back in his chair, "but my grandfather doomed himself by creating it."

"How do you figure?" I asked, genuinely wondering where he was going with this.

Trevor unbuttoned his jacket and casually leaned back in his creaky old wooden chair.

"The idea that Butterfly's CEO would divert resources into developing something as crazy as time travel weakened his influence with the other executives. Colin knew it but continued to hold out hope that someone would bring Aurelia to him from the future. When no one showed he deemed the project a failure and sought to scrap it. But what if the reason no one showed was because he stopped development of the time-travel tech before it was finished? So, the poor fool had no choice but to keep it going. The whole thing became an endless loop that made it easy to position myself for a takeover."

"Someone did come back, though," I stated, putting the pieces together from something utterly insane. Somehow, we'd gone from a four-dimensional chess match to a multiverse free-for-all. "You brought Aurelia here. Only you plan on using it yourself."

It wasn't a question.

Trevor looked rather pleased by it too, like a proud teacher finally breaking through to his student.

"See? Now you're catching on. I was able to use future tech and business information from the future to leverage my position from the moment I arrived. I couldn't rely on market data because that would change the more that I altered things, but I was able to give myself a heads up. Plenty of people who would be the big names in Butterfly later were able to be approached. I control perhaps twenty percent of Butterfly already. By tomorrow, I'll have a majority stake in either my control or my puppets. Aurelia will allow Butterfly to become the predominate power on Earth."

But knowing his plan and understanding it were two entirely different things.

"You really think a weapon from the future will tip the scales in your favor?" I asked.

"A weapon?" Trevor scoffed, amused by the question. "Is that what you think Aurelia is?"

"Isn't it?" I looked at him sideways.

"I have plenty of super weapons, Rob," Trevor went on. "Aurelia is far more than that."

"What is it then?" Now I was just lost.

In the past twelve hours I'd learned a lot about my former best friend, but the old Trevor I knew wasn't an idiot and I doubted this one was either. He knew I was fishing for an answer.

"Why do you want to know?" Trevor teased with a smirk. "So, you can run and tell your girlfriend? The beautiful Christine? Or are you planning to get back with Anna?"

The comment shot my blood pressure up from calm to boil. "She's not my—!"

I caught myself before I let him get completely under my skin. Not that it mattered. The smug look on Trevor's face told me he was already quite enjoying himself. But he didn't arrange this meeting just to mock me. He had an agenda and I needed to know why. "What do you want, Trevor?"

"I meant what I said," Trevor insisted, putting on the fakest smile imaginable. "I don't want to kill you. I just want you out of the way, so you don't stop me."

"You don't have to worry about that," I lied before shifting to the truth. "I was only with HOPE to get my friend back. I'm done playing freedom fighter."

Both of us were lying. Still, I had no idea what I was going to do. I partnered with Anna to get Christine back. Now that she was safe, I saw no reason to continue fighting for the future with violence. I'd chosen to work for Butterfly to avoid massacres like the one at the Chrysalis. I thought—no, I believed—that there was a better way. And just like Trevor viewed me as being in the way of his plans, I viewed him being in the way of mine.

Trevor didn't appear satisfied by my response, though. He smiled, but it wasn't a content smile. It looked hungry and sinister. The more I looked at it, the scarier it became.

"Good to hear," he said. "But what if you did the opposite? What if you joined me, instead?"

A hard chuckle forced its way from my chest. Seriously. I had zero control over it. "You must be joking."

"You were right," Trevor confessed, humbly. "I had let my plans for you get personal. But it wasn't you I hated. It was the future you. The you that would eventually twist my family's company into a weak, emaciated version of its former self. But you're not him yet, and there's no reason to believe you will be."

It felt like I'd had this conversation before, except the other way around. Jane once warned me about the villain I was destined to become. Now Trevor was trying to prevent me from being a hero instead. His proposition was laughable for the obvious reasons.

"Why would I join you when I still want to be that person?" I asked.

Trevor didn't flinch. He was undeterred by my resistance. "Because you're also pragmatic. We're both trying to stop this conflict before it gets out of hand. You through peace and me through an iron fist. The only difference is mine will be immediate and yours will take a decade."

"It'll be worth it," I declared, full of conviction.

It was all bluster and bravado, though. Trevor had ruined any plans that I made for peace. In ten years, I might have been an executive at Butterfly with real power but now I was probably going to be labeled as a terrorist for killing Colin Reilly, even if it had been Trevor's finger on the trigger.

Trevor favored me with a condescending leer. "Will it? Think about all the damage that will be done in that time. All the lives that will be lost. I'm looking to bring about an end to all the fighting here and now. To stop the bloodshed before it starts."

The visions returned. Not completely, but in flashes. Quick shots of bodies piled in fields and bloody streams trickling through the streets. Bullets were everywhere, zooming from every direction. There were no sides to this war anymore. Just chaos.

"Butterfly's corporate cult is tired of the old guard," Trevor continued, snapping me back to the farmhouse. "Colin Reilly wound up an entire generation of people waiting to take over the world and then told them to wait. It's ready for new, young leaders to step in and fill the void. We can lead Butterfly together and mold the world into what it should be."

"You mean control it," I corrected, now finally feeling like I could shoot Trevor. How could he ever believe that I'd forgive him for killing Georgia?

Trevor didn't deny my word choice. If anything, his eyes gleamed with pride. "Is there a difference?"

"Sorry, Trevor." I shook my head. It wasn't even a choice. "But I think I'll pass on the fascism."

He frowned. Not a surprised frown. Just a disappointed one. "Well, I guess I'll have to show my big gun then."

"Huh?" I asked.

Trevor pointed to a doorway behind me. "Come on in."

I turned around, ready for an ambush.

That was when Georgia walked into the room.

Dammit.

CHAPTER TWENTY-TWO

"Georgia?" I said, staring at her as she took a seat at the side of the table. I felt like such a fool.

Georgia had changed out of her prison fatigues and was wearing a pleasant white blouse and blue skirt now. She had on a wide-brimmed hat to cover up where her head had been shaved in the Chrysalis. Certainly, she'd looked better, but she wasn't dead and had at least had the time to take a shower.

"Why?" Trevor asked, gloating. "Because you heard me shoot? That didn't mean I had the gun to her head."

I stared at him then her. "I don't understand."

Trevor snorted. He was in full cocky, corporate executive mode now. "Work it out, it's not that difficult."

I remembered when Jane had busted one of my eardrums firing a gun nearby my head to convince the Scorpion Elite I was dead. Hopefully, Trevor had managed to fire it a little further away.

"Georgia is working with you?" I took a deep breath and stared.

Georgia looked down. "I'm sorry, Rob, but I had no other choice."

"I thought you were with HOPE?" I asked, not sure how to deal with this latest twist in the insanity of my life.

"I was, but Trevor...He..." Georgia choked up as she tried to explain. "He said he'd kill my mom if I didn't join him."

I narrowed my eyes. "Bullshit."

Trevor smirked.

Georgia frowned then her attitude immediately changed. "Alright, you caught me. I'm on Trevor's side. I think he knows the right way to go forward."

"You think you can trust him?" I stared at her suspiciously.

"I don't know," Georgia frowned. "I don't know anything more. I always looked up to my parents and the job they had at Monarch, but when I started working at Butterfly, I realized how wrong everything was. I tried working with HOPE, but look where that got me. Trevor's offering me a third option."

I shook my head. "Trevor is worse than both! He put a bomb in the Butterfly boardroom and—"

That was when the truth dawned on me, and I turned to Trevor slowly.

"It was you, wasn't it? You didn't just blow up the boardroom. You set off the bomb at Connor U's Security Center, too."

The thought made me sick to my stomach. It had been in the back of my mind, but I hadn't wanted to acknowledge it. Yet, it was also the only thing that made sense. Trevor had been in control from the start. The explosion at the school had made Colin Reilly vulnerable, vilified HOPE, and made everyone scramble in the aftermath. It meant that Trevor had an opportunity to assassinate the people standing in his way to taking over the company, assuming he really did have a bunch of Monarch agents already under his control.

"Yes," Trevor said, unapologetic.

"Why?" I had to ask, despite knowing the answer.

"There were a couple birds I hoped to kill with that stone, one of which was your girlfriend Anna," Trevor gloated. "She's the evil heart of HOPE and has plans far worse than setting off a couple of bombs. By eliminating her before it happens, things will be better."

"I hate to admit it," Georgia went on, "but Trevor's the only one of us who has seen the future. Surely, he knows the best path."

I blinked. "You know about time travel? And Anna isn't like that!"

It bothered me that my defense of my ex-girlfriend came after my questioning of whether she knew about time travel.

"She knows everything," Trevor said, chuckling. "What she's saying about your ex is true as well. In my future, when you quote-unquote reform Butterfly, Anna remains a terrorist. She kills millions of people in my time before she's finally stopped. Proudly owns her nickname, too."

"Don't." I stared at him.

"That's why they called her the Scorpion. The—" Trevor started to say.

I stood up from my chair and shouted at him. "Shut up!"

This was all too much to handle, and I felt like hyperventilating. I didn't want to acknowledge it all. I'd failed utterly to reform Butterfly from the inside, even if Trevor said I might have had a chance to succeed without his interference. My best friends were both monsters, people who'd killed scores of innocents to make a play for ultimate power, and now they were claiming that all my efforts to avoid a Scorpion rising were for naught. If it wasn't me then it would be Anna and the only difference between us would be a matter of scale.

Trevor frowned in disappointment. "Come on, Rob, you can't make an omelet without breaking a few eggs. My way is better. It's the way the future should have played out."

"You're wrong." I rubbed my temples, trying to wrap my brain around what he was implying. It wasn't true, it couldn't be.

"I'm not," Trevor said, chiding me. "I lived through it. I know what I'm talking about."

A laugh escaped my chest. "You have no idea and that's what makes this whole thing so sickening."

"What do you mean?" Trevor asked, confused.

"I didn't want to do this, Rob," Georgia said, not realizing she'd already destroyed any trust or good will she'd built up with me over the years. "However, it's what had to be done. You're someone who can help us build the future. Trevor has told me about the great things you accomplish in his timeline. You are someone that makes a difference and that is a rare ability in any era."

I snorted at them. "You've already destroyed my reputation."

"I'm in charge of Monarch now," Trevor said, as if it was that easy. "The three Deputy Chiefs are all my men. I can wipe away your record with a hand swipe."

Georgia looked at me with an almost pleading look. "Please, Rob. This isn't just my family we're talking about. It's everyone's family. The entire world."

I didn't blame Georgia for joining Trevor. Raised by Monarch board members. Arrested in front of your classmates. Tortured in a state-of-the-art prison. I would jump at the chance for a savior too. Assuming she wasn't a psychopath like Trevor at heart, which I was increasingly unsure of. All this made me realize just how disconnected I was from the people I'd considered my best friends.

I'd been so focused on my studies and getting ahead at Butterfly that I'd missed the obvious staring me in the face. Then again, it was crazy that I'd succeeded in the future, so time travelers had to come back and warp my destiny. Twice! It made me wonder if Abraham Lincoln or Ramses II ever had to deal with something like this. Was time just going to be a free-for-all from now on? If "from now on" had any relevance anymore?

I sat back down, still unable to comprehend everything. "How did you get so much power? I mean, everyone still believes you're a college student."

I was manipulating Trevor now. Playing the defeated fool. I was good at playing weak. I'd been weak for most of my life.

Trevor felt like he was in control again. He stood and started walking around the table. "Colin Reilly was a painfully short-sighted man thinking he could control a time traveler. With that kind of power there was no reason for me not to make sure things turned out the way I wanted them to. The only way for me to lose was to do nothing, and that wasn't going to happen."

I thought about my visions. I wasn't sure if they were being erased or just painted over. Maybe that was the reason I kept having them. I was the point of divergence for both the futures and now they were crashing together. "You think you have everything figured out."

"Almost everything," Trevor said as he sat back down. "There's still you."

"What are you talking about?" I asked.

"My offer to join me still stands," he said with a smile.

"And my answer will stay the same." I made a point to keep my face devoid of emotion.

"In the future you were my mentor, Rob," Trevor's smile remained as he spoke. "And in the present, you became my friend. We were all friends. Don't you remember what that was like? The fun we had. The dreams we shared. The three of us were good together. We could be good again."

I looked over to Georgia. She had her gaze fixed on the table. She couldn't even look me in the eyes.

"Think about it," Trevor went on. "The three of us in charge of Butterfly together. The assistants running the show. Like it always should have been."

"You still don't see the big picture," I said, shaking my head. "Which means all your complicated plans and ideas are based on a flawed premise."

"What do you mean?" Trevor's smile disappeared and he looked confused.

"I mean that you're not the first-time traveler," I said, dryly. It was worth it to reveal this critical bit of information just to see the stunned look on his face.

Trevor furrowed his brow then looked at me before shaking his head. "No, not you. You had a family, birth certificates, and more. I would have known if you were a time traveler. I looked it all up."

"Not me," I said, simply. "Others who were unhappy with the future they came from and tried to stop it. Just like you."

"You're lying." If Trevor had been expecting me to say anything, it wasn't that.

I stared up at him. Now I was the one in charge of this conversation, and I had to admit that it felt good. "No, I'm not."

"Who were they?" Trevor demanded. "What did they want?"

"It doesn't matter," I said, looking up at him. I was furious now at his stupidity. "What matters is that even if you succeed in this stupid plan, there will be more time travelers coming to stop you. Changing the future is a dead end, Trevor. Just an endless cycle of people trying to swim against the tide."

It was a revelation, really, what the evil heart of this matter was. Time travel didn't fix anything. It just makes things worse. Aurelia was something that inspired Colin Reilly to devote billions of dollars to a thing people had previously dismissed as impossible. As long as it existed, it meant that we'd never be able to know peace. Any progress we made would be stymied by people going back in time to change things. That made me realize I'd been going about this all wrong. I needed to kill the source of the problem. Stopping Trevor here might delay things, but Aurelia and the Butterfly time-travel experiments were a clear and perpetual danger to all of human history.

"I need to go," I said while pushing my chair away from the table.

"No," Trevor said, staring. "We have a lot more to discuss."

"Let him go, Trevor," Georgia said, her voice warm and affectionate. "He'll come around eventually."

"I don't recall asking for your opinion," Trevor said, taking out a gun hidden under the table and shooting Georgia in the head.

It was like a bolt of lightning shot down my spine, paralyzing me in place. I couldn't move. I couldn't breathe. I couldn't blink as my eyes refused to look away from the giant hole in Georgia's skull that oozed a pool of blood all over the table.

"If you thought hearing her death over the infopad was bad, then I can't imagine what seeing it in person is like," Trevor said, reveling in my pain.

I stared down at her corpse.

"She served her purpose," Trevor said to my unspoken question. "She was getting annoying as well."

"You bastard," I said, wanting to break his neck with my bare hands.

"Yeah, I am." Trevor tilted his head back to yell deeper into the house. "We're ready."

A squadron of Monarch troopers entered the room, all six of them in full armor and heavily armed with rifles. He didn't need them. Trevor was just trying to make a point.

"What's wrong with you?" I shouted, as if the words were ejected from my lungs.

Trevor casually put his gun away. He gestured to Georgia's still-bleeding corpse. "If you're not going to join me, Rob, then there was no reason keeping her or any of your other friends around. Because nothing's stopping me. Not you. Not your girlfriend's army. Certainly not the sands of time. This is what destiny looks like. It's time you understood that."

I wanted to pull out my gun and put him down but that wasn't going to help matters. Besides, I didn't want to kill him in anger. If I were to do it, then the act needed to be controlled and calculated. A rational decision to save the world. Maybe I was just fooling myself. It was one thing to kill a stranger in self-defense, but it's another to kill someone you knew, however much of a monster they'd turned out to be.

"There's no such thing as destiny," I whispered. "Only mistakes by assholes like you and your grandfather."

And me.

"As we speak," Trevor continued, "Monarch is off prepping for the martial law the United States is about to declare. They're going to arrest all the anti-Butterfly politicians and cite their ties to HOPE as an excuse. Some of it is even true. I'll be a figurehead for Butterfly among the shareholders. They don't know I already control a majority of stock through proxies that I've blackmailed. I've brought from the future the deepest, dirtiest, and filthiest secrets of the richest men in the world. By the time they realize I'm in control, they'll be powerless to stop me."

"This is how the war gets started Trevor," I said, staring at him. "The corporations don't win. Nobody does."

"You'll have plenty of time to share the details with us," Trevor said, motioning for one of his troopers to detain me. "The Chrysalis may be gone but it's not like we don't have smaller facilities."

I lifted my hand and a red dot suddenly appeared in the center of Trevor's immaculately pressed shirt. The trooper beside me stopped moving and looked to his boss.

It took him a moment, but once Trevor realized the dot was there, it moved up to his forehead. Half of the troopers pivoted their rifles off me and aimed them at the cornstalks out the window. It didn't matter. They could have X-ray goggles and still wouldn't be able to spot Jane out there. How did I know it was Jane? Who else? I hadn't told her but clearly she'd followed me out and with good reason it seemed.

Best daughter ever.

"What the hell," Trevor said, looking down.

"I learned a few things working for Butterfly," I replied, wishing I could kill him but not mentally there yet. "The funny thing was I fully expected to kill you. I just decided not to. Were you planning on capturing me the whole time?"

"Honestly, I just wanted us all to be friends again," Trevor said, casually adjusting his jacket as if a gun wasn't aimed at his head. "It seems we've grown quite untrustworthy of one another."

"Seems so," I said, standing. "With good reason it turns out."

Trevor's hands clawed the table as he balled them into fists. His face hardened, leering at me with a scowl.

"If you leave, Rob, I can't be held responsible for what happens to you next. We shouldn't let someone like Georgia stand between us. There will be other girls."

"Statements like that make me wonder how we were ever friends." I backed towards the door. "Goodbye, Trevor."

The look in his eyes was unmistakable. I didn't know if Trevor's offer for me to join him was legit. Maybe he had an ulterior motive. After all, it didn't take much for him to execute Georgia on the spot. He should've known I was going to turn him down. I just hadn't expected him to respond by…I couldn't even think the words. Trevor was truly insane enough to believe we could rule together. He was a psychopath and probably always had been. And he thought I was one, too.

I reached backwards and felt around for the doorknob. It was now locked. Trevor smirked and the troopers quickly closed in around him, protecting their boss from the sniper outside. I moved swiftly by throwing a chair out the window. I jumped through it within a second of it shattering and hit the ground with a roll. Gunfire followed me as I ran along the side, disappearing into the cornfield. I knew exactly where Jane was waiting on a revved-up Monarch A-7 motorbike. The sniper rifle was on a tripod, showing she'd been bluffing toward the end. Smart move. I didn't want any more bloodshed today. Too bad a lot more was coming whether I wanted it to or not.

"Get on!" Jane shouted.

I did and we were gone.

CHAPTER TWENTY-THREE

"You idiot!" Anna shouted, her voice trembling with rage and concern. "What the hell were you thinking?"

Anna, Christine, Jane, and I were all sitting in the middle of a living room with brand new, untouched furniture. The place had a weird all-white decor with plastic coverings on a pair of couches and a big leather easy chair. There was a fireplace with a flat-screen TV inside it, showing a burning fire in what was easily the biggest waste of utility I'd ever seen in a home. We were in the middle of an Iowa housing project that had constructed a dozen homes for future megacorp middle-management. A FOR SALE - CONTACT ORANGE REALTY sign was firmly planted in the yard. Anna thought this would be the perfect place to crash while we waited out the aftermath of the Chrysalis attack and to contact the rest of HOPE.

Honestly, I was hoping there would be more soldiers present because this felt too much like I was alone with my friends. I wished there was a sign of the others to distance myself from those I cared about. I couldn't look at Anna the same way anymore, knowing there was a chance she could potentially become the new Scorpion. At least based on what Trevor had been about to tell me. There was also the fact that Christine and I had kissed. I couldn't lie to myself and say I didn't have feelings for her. I'd always been attracted to her. Or maybe it was just because I hadn't seen her in so long.

Now I was in a room with all these people when I just wanted to crawl into a hole and hide. There was the fact I had mixed feelings about not killing Trevor. I never wanted to kill anyone in my life—not even Colin Reilly—but what Trevor had done was unthinkable. He played me, making me believe he killed Georgia, just to later use her as a pawn, and then kill her for real right in front of me. My anger towards him made me presume I could assassinate someone for the greater good. It was a nasty feeling, believing that I could end up doing exactly the sort of thing that Esther and Cody had been sent back to do. I never wanted to think I had anything in common with them, but here I was ready to step into the role of murderer. The very thing I swore never to become.

"I'm sorry," I said, not really having a defense. "I thought it was more important to go after Trevor. He's a time traveler just like Jane."

"That's no excuse." Anna felt her face like she had an enormous headache coming on.

"Isn't it?" Jane asked. "It seems a very valid excuse to me."

"I still can't believe time travel is real," Christine muttered, shaking her head.

"You filled her in?" I asked, looking at Anna.

"Of course," Anna said, staring at me with laser eyes. "HOPE members don't keep secrets from one another."

It was an obvious dig, one which went completely over Christine's head.

"It just feels so surreal," Christine said. "Especially the fact that I'm a part of it all."

"You were a very important figure in my timeline," Jane muttered, giving me a dirty look for some reason.

"All I've done in this time is get captured, tortured, and imprisoned." Christine looked embarrassed.

"No!" Anna said, surprising me with the force of her words. "You did so much more!"

I was surprised by the passion in Anna's tone. "You helped organize us and build a national movement to resist the evil of the megacorporations!" Anna said, her voice raising in pitch. "Don't ever think that wasn't important. If not for you, HOPE wouldn't exist and there would be no one resisting the corporations."

Christine looked almost amused by Anna's statement. "Yeah, for all the good that has done."

"We struck a blow against tyranny," Anna said, clenching a fist and shaking it in the air. "The Chrysalis was a major Monarch base that was integral to its evil plans. The complex's destruction. Colin Reilly's death. These aren't small things."

"They're going to blame HOPE for the explosion," Christine replied. "I mean, the sheer amount of environmental damage from—"

"It doesn't matter," Anna interrupted. "The important thing is that people understand that the time for negotiations, meetings, truces, and protesting is done. It's a war now. We need to strike while the enemy is confused and decapitate them."

I almost argued that we'd already done that, and it just made it easier for Trevor to take over. That would have been the height of hypocrisy, though. "How bad is it?"

Christine reached over and pulled out a remote control before aiming it at the fireplace. The image of burning flames was replaced with a report from BBN that showed senators and congressmen being arrested right from the Capitol. It seemed history was playing out the way it was originally intended.

The big difference was when they showed an image of Colin Reilly behind a podium with Trevor giving a speech. Trevor looked older, in a suit and makeup to give him the appearance of a man in his thirties rather than his early twenties. A ticker of news scrolled beneath him. It read: INTERIM CEO OF BUTTERFLY APPOINTED AFTER TRAGIC DEATH OF BELOVED BUSINESSMAN.

"So…bad," I said, taking a deep breath.

"Very bad," Christine replied. "The army is already refusing to stand for the arrests and the Speaker of the House has gone into hiding. Like Anna said, it's Civil War 2.0."

"The first one worked out," Anna remarked rather dryly. "We just need to be more thorough with the slavers. Lincoln should have hung all of them."

I wasn't sure I disagreed, but this wasn't the Antebellum South. I'd spent the past few years getting to know Butterfly's employees and most of them were just people. Even the soldiers of Monarch were decent folks just trying to live. The problem was that my plans to reform things from the inside were completely shot. I hadn't realized it, but they'd been shot from the moment Trevor entered my life.

"You shouldn't give into those urges," I said, trying to figure some way of talking Anna down.

It was hard to believe she would one day become the Scorpion, but it also made a disturbing amount of sense. Anna had always been angrier, harder, and more devoted to the cause than me. She also had managed to claw her way up to leading veteran soldiers twice her age. I could see her eventually becoming someone that people would follow across the world. That couldn't be allowed to happen, though. I just had no idea how to stop it. I still cared for Anna on some level. Or at least, that was what I told myself. Three years was a long time.

"We're past the point of urges," Anna said, staring at me like I'd lost my mind. "You're past that point. You were there fighting with us. You brought the psycho killer Terminators with you, too. They were your idea."

Anna had me there. "You're right. We're past the point of recriminations."

Jane gave me a sideways look. "Perhaps."

"Trevor was the one who set the bomb at Connor U," I said, thinking that might have an impact on Anna. "He tried to kill you."

She looked shocked for a second, then sighed. "I had a tip the place held disciplinary files from some unruly students. Men and women who questioned Butterfly on campus. I thought it was a good opportunity to find some recruits. I never thought snooping around in there could cost me my life."

That explained what she was doing in the building and shed some light on another mystery.

"Was the tip from Georgia?" I asked.

Anna nodded. "The girl wasn't a true believer, but she knew enough to tell right from wrong. She supported our cause and tried to help. It was a dangerous game, and one that ultimately got her killed."

Anna still believed Georgia died before the Chrysalis exploded. I chose not to tell her what happened at the farmhouse. I just didn't see the point in it.

"I'm sorry, Rob." Anna looked at me, then lowered her head.

I hadn't expected that. "Excuse me?"

"I knew Georgia was friends with you and I took her information anyway," Anna said. "Sometimes I forget that real power is letting others pay the price for what we're doing here. I'm willing to give my life to serve the cause, but I shouldn't assume everyone else is as enthusiastic to—"

"Take others' lives?" Jane asked, interrupting.

Anna glared at her.

"This is bigger than just Trevor," I said, trying to divert the conversation. "Even if we manage to stop what's coming, there's just going to be another set of time travelers ready to come back and muck with reality. Someone who may be willing to erase us by going back even further."

"How would we even know?" Christine asked.

"We wouldn't, I guess." I frowned. "I think the future is in flux, though. I keep getting visions of what's going to happen, and they've been changing."

Everyone looked at me like I'd grown a second head.

"Oh, *now* it's unbelievable?" I asked, sarcastically.

"It was unbelievable before," Anna said. "But what do you think?"

"I think time travel is an existential threat to everything," I said with a grimace. "We've already seen how it can ruin lives and destroy all we've been working for."

The three women all glanced at one another, trying to read the others' reactions before forming their own.

"People will constantly go back in time to undo the mistakes of their ancestors and remake the world how they see fit," I continued. "Eventually, the timeline is just going to fall in on itself. History will crumble. Either time travel will end up never being invented or mankind will just wipe itself from existence."

"Mankind didn't need time travel to destroy itself in my time," Jane replied. "We were on the verge of extinction thanks to entirely mundane means. Time travel gave us a chance to set things right."

"Except, that wasn't the Scorpion's goal," I replied. "It was just an elaborate suicide attempt after he wiped out all his enemies. A coward's way to avoid having to face the consequences of his actions."

That had been the biggest twist. The Scorpion Elite hadn't been people who'd revolted against the Scorpion. They'd been following his final orders. My future self had seen the ruined disaster he'd left the world and decided to wipe himself from the timeline. I couldn't even imagine the level of hubris I'd have to develop to think that was the right way out. But, then again, I'd thought I'd be able to reform Butterfly from the inside too.

"Maybe," Anna said with an intrigued smirk. "You can't deny he had a pretty cool name, though."

I glared at her but refused to acknowledge what Trevor had told me about her future. She wasn't the Scorpion yet, any more than I was when Jane first arrived. That meant we could prevent her from becoming a monster, which was a discussion for another time.

"What we need to do is stop time travel from ever happening," I said, keeping us on topic. "The best way to do that is by shutting down Aurelia. It's the only way of making sure we won't have any more visits from Trevor-like people in the future."

Or Esther and Cody. I hadn't forgotten about them in all this madness. A part of me wanted to tell them that Trevor was the new Scorpion, but that seemed a tad too cowardly. If I wasn't willing to kill Trevor face-to-face, then I didn't want to do it by manipulating a pair of lunatics into doing it for me.

"And what about your BFF?" Anna asked. "Ending Aurelia might protect the future, but it won't stop what's happening here and now."

"Trevor is still consolidating his control over Butterfly," I said, simply. "He's missing something, otherwise he would've used Aurelia as a weapon already. Assuming it *is* a weapon. We can strike the facility and destroy it along with all their time-travel research. Then he'll have a choice to either start from scratch, which he won't be able to do, or abandon the project entirely."

Trevor stated that Colin Reilly lost a lot of respect from his fellow board members due to the amount of money he poured into Project: Aurelia. It was possible that if he tried to restart the project, he'd lose whatever control he'd managed to build up. Then again, it was possible I just wanted to find some way to turn all of this into a story with a happy ending. The more I thought about it, though, the more I realized there was no way to do that.

"You realize if you do this, Rob, there's no turning back," Anna said, looking at me. "We let you tag along on the last mission, and you didn't embarrass yourself, but this is the big leagues. An attack of this magnitude will require HOPE calling in our government backers to join the battle. If we win, we might be able to crack Butterfly open like an egg. But if we lose, then we'll probably be fighting them forever."

I honestly thought that was already a given. "I may not be very good at cold-blooded murder but I'm willing to fight."

"I believe in you, Rob," Christine said as she reached over and gave my hand a squeeze. "I'm not much of a fighter, either, but I'm with you."

"Just help us expose Butterfly's crimes to the world," Anna said, talking to Christine. "Social media still works. We'll set you up a secure line and you can start sharing the truth about what happened to you. You can be the voice of the Resistance."

I wasn't sure if Anna really believed that this would do any good but now was perhaps the best time to try to reveal Butterfly's crimes to the world. With the executives dead and Trevor's hold tenuous, it might be the one moment in history where the propaganda machine couldn't control the narrative. The United States government could push back and maybe regain some control of the country. A more cynical side of me believed Anna might also just be pushing Christine forward to help justify more violence against Butterfly. Then again, it would be the height of hypocrisy to turn against her for what she *might* do.

Christine looked uncertain before nodding. "If you say so."

It seemed weird seeing her succumb to Anna's command, and I squeezed Christine's hand to reassure her, just like she had done to mine. She smiled at me. I smiled back at her. And for an instant, everything felt okay.

It was a pleasant moment and ended when Christine's soft eyes sharpened into a hard gaze that focused on everyone in the room. "Rachel died getting us information on Aurelia's defenses. All I ask is that you make her sacrifice worth it."

Anna and I both took her wish to heart and nodded firmly. Jane, on the other hand, was already on her way out the door. She didn't need to say it, but I knew. Out of everyone here, she was the one most truly ready to end this.

Except for me.

It was time for me to take charge of my destiny.

CHAPTER TWENTY-FOUR

Aurelia was being developed in a facility outside Nome, Alaska, which was officially one of Butterfly's energy research plants. It was a converted US military base and had been covered with massive geodesic domes, reinforced concrete bunkers, and its own fusion power plant. It also was the center for the largest Monarch base in the world, having literally thousands of troopers stationed there with state-of-the-art military equipment.

I'd hoped to convince HOPE leadership to let me carry out the attack, but ironically, reality had caught up with me. The United States Army generals who had been covertly supporting HOPE laughed in my face. They weren't going to let a college kid with approximately one battle under his belt and no military training lead an assault. They did let me come along, though.

I stood on a ridge—a "safe" distance from the conflict—next to a Jeep with Jane and Anna inside. A tall, harsh-looking man named Major Jones oversaw us. He had barely said two words but was taking the job of keeping us safe seriously. Even so, I could tell that Jane resented anyone being her babysitter. I couldn't blame her since she'd been fighting in these kinds of conflicts since childhood.

"How did you convince them to attack this place?" I asked, watching the battle through a handheld infopad that fed live military information from the drones hovering over the conflict.

The US military had orders to take Aurelia intact and I wasn't sure how I felt about that, especially since I didn't even know what it was.

Time travel was bad enough, but the thought of a futuristic super weapon in the Army's hands didn't exactly give me a warm feeling inside. They were my closest ally right now, though, and advancing on the base with tanks. They'd given the Monarch troopers the option to surrender and threatened overwhelming force if they resisted. The base commander had refused to comply and now they were sitting ducks for a force that far outnumbered them. It seemed too easy.

"I left the time-travel details out of my briefing," Anna said, the door to the Jeep open. "They do know the place is a weapons-research facility instead of being devoted to studying fusion like people claim. Trevor's already utilized Butterfly's propaganda machine to push competing stories about what's really going on. The government, at least what's left of it on our side, is losing control over the narrative. But, if those aligned with us can decapitate Butterfly while the company is still disorganized then they can stop Trevor's takeover before it's complete."

"Yeah," I said, not entirely sure of their plan. The biggest advantage the military had was force, but not everyone's loyalty was secure. If it was a choice between serving their country and Butterfly, most would choose their country. But nothing was that easy anymore. Megacorporations had spent so long commingling the two that it was difficult to tell who the legitimate authorities in the nation were. Trevor took full advantage of this and was able to play the victim in the aftermath of the Chrysalis explosion. Social media was already infested with bots and hackers making it seem like a conspiracy of senators gone rogue. It seemed the "official" narrative was that some military officials aligned with HOPE were trying to overthrow the legitimate government to install a fascist state. Trevor was projecting his own plans on his enemies, and it was difficult to argue with him since the truth at this point was simply a matter of perspective.

"You don't sound sure," Anna said, unhappy.

"I just wish we had more control of the situation," I said, reluctantly.

Anna snorted. "The military does things their way, and we would have been hopelessly outnumbered without them."

"Yeah," I said again, this time with more conviction.

That had been part of the point. As bad as it would have been, excluding the Army from this mission would have allowed me to move freely through the base. I wanted to destroy whatever they were researching here. Anna had outmaneuvered me, though, and turned the plan I'd been hatching into her own. I wasn't sure the US military ending up with time travel was any better than Butterfly.

Either way, I'd informed them about Trevor's involvement, but I wasn't sure how much they'd believed me. The destruction of the Chrysalis had the potential to turn the entire country against HOPE and remove any political support for those backing it, even in secret. On the other hand, if they could link Trevor to all the terrorism then maybe his takeover of Butterfly could be thwarted. It would take more than my word, though, to do it.

"Do not overestimate our chances," Jane said.

"What do you mean?" Anna asked.

Jane sighed. "Trevor came to this world with full knowledge of the way history played out. This may not be his timeline anymore—far from it—but he still knows who the power players are."

"I wonder what you think of all this." I looked at Major Jones.

"Quit playing games," Major Jones said, not bothering to look at us. "This is serious."

He had no idea how right he was when my pad shorted out seconds later. The skies above us started to swirl and crackle with blue lightning, and I was suddenly reminded of the brutal vision I had back at Anna's base. I barely recalled the bright, blue image when a glowing spear of light descended from the heavens and struck the Earth. I turned away at the last second, but still was almost blinded by the flash that radiated outward.

"What the hell?" I asked, falling to the ground and picking up snow to throw in my face. The pain was searing.

After a few seconds, my eyesight cleared, and I turned to look at the battlefield beyond. It was a horrifying vision of an almost completely paralyzed field of tanks, fallen helicopters, and overturned Jeeps. The blast from the sky had totally shut down all the military's machinery and left it completely vulnerable. Monarch's forces proceeded to pour out of their base and begin a slaughter of them all.

I turned to Major Jones to see what his reaction was but caught my breath when I realized he was lying face down on the ground. Rushing over to his side, I turned him over and found a face frozen in terror. His eyes were completely burned out, turned into nothing but empty sockets. The major was obviously dead, a casualty of the strange new weapon employed against the soldiers below.

"Anna! Jane!" I called while standing up. "Are you alright?"

"Unfortunately," Jane said, walking up to me. "I pushed Anna down behind the car seats when I saw the Blue Cascade."

Anna stumbled out of the back of the Jeep, throwing up on the ground. She looked like she'd just been put in a centrifuge and could barely balance herself.

"The what?" I asked, confused. "What the hell was that thing?"

Jane closed her eyes and took a deep breath.

"It's a weapon created by Butterfly. It scrambles machinery and leaves the people inside them blinded or worse. We're lucky we were at the edge of it."

"Lucky?" I asked, stunned. "Major Jones wasn't lucky!"

Jane looked over to the dead body and nodded.

"It seems even a few feet proved the difference between life and death."

"Why didn't you warn us?" Anna shouted, standing up. She balled her fists together and advanced on Jane despite how suicidal that was. "All those soldiers below are going to die!"

"I didn't know!" Jane said, raising her voice to defend herself. She looked shell-shocked by the sudden turn of events. "The Blue Cascade isn't supposed to be ready yet! When the New Hope Army stormed this facility in my time, it was stolen along with Aurelia. We eventually finished it, and the Scorpion used it to…"

Her voice trailed off, but she didn't need to finish the sentence. We both knew what she was about to say.

Anna didn't care, though, and pointed a firm finger up at the sky. "But it's finished now! And they're using it against us."

"Yes," Jane said, shaking her head. "Somehow history has been changed."

"Trevor," I whispered. "He was always going to the labs with his ideas. One time he disappeared for about three months and wouldn't say what he was up to. I didn't think much of it at the time."

"Why would you?" Anna said. "Trevor isn't a scientist. I saw that in his school files."

"He wouldn't have to be a scientist if he came from the future with a flash drive or laptop full of plans," I replied. "That might be another way he wrestled away control of the company. He gave scientists inventions they hadn't created yet and patented devices that would make the company a fortune."

Jane cursed under her breath. "Then forget Aurelia. If he has the Blue Cascade, then there's already no stopping him."

I had to take a moment to think about the situation. That was when the calculating tactician part of me—a side that had been more focused on boardrooms than battlefields these past few years—took over. "Now's our chance to get inside."

"What?" Anna asked. "Are you insane?"

"All of the Monarch forces are occupied!" I shouted, gesturing towards the wasteland of a battlefield below. "This is our only chance to get inside the facility! We can destroy the Blue Cascade, Aurelia, and every crazy tool and weapon Butterfly is developing for its arsenal."

"You're insane." Anna stared.

"Are you coming or not?" I asked.

"This is suicide," Anna said.

"Probably," I said.

Jane went to the back of the car and pulled out a trio of tote bags. "Here are Monarch uniforms."

"Where the hell did you get these?" I asked.

"I prepared them in case we wanted to try something other than a direct assault," Jane replied, her voice dry and cold.

"You knew this attack would fail." Anna looked ready to launch herself at Jane.

"I suspected the attack would fail," Jane said as she started changing. "I didn't know what form it would take."

Anna lunged at Jane, only for me to grab her by the arm.

"Now is not the time!" I snapped. "If there's to be any hope for the future at all, we must stop them. Imagine that blue wave of death coming down on Chicago or New York."

"This Aurelia thing is what you're really after." Anna glared at me.

"Trevor seems hell-bent on activating it," I replied. "It's probably the last piece of the puzzle. The one thing that will cement Butterfly's control over the world."

"If you want revenge for your dead comrades," Jane added, "then stopping it is the only way."

Anna shot Jane a nasty glare before taking a deep breath. "Yes, I do. We'll do it your way."

"Rob's way," Jane corrected.

Anna didn't look happy, but she nodded and started to change.

I looked away with a bit more reluctance than I wanted. As much as Anna and I had parted on bad terms, she was still a very beautiful woman and my first love. It was hard shaking those feelings, even knowing how much she'd changed over the years. The fact I'd kissed Christine recently also confused me. There was no time for love, though, when the entire fate of the world depended on our next actions.

We ended up changing as fast as we could as explosions emerged from the battlefield below. They almost deafened us the same way the Blue Cascade had almost blinded us.

"What the hell is that?" I asked, staring downward.

"The US military bombed their own position," Jane replied. "They saw what the Cascade had done and didn't want to surrender the field."

"Why the hell would they do that?"

"General Page," Anna muttered. "He's the leader of the forces down there. He's a lunatic."

I stared at Anna, wondering what it would take to make her think that.

"Yes," Jane replied. "Another figure that was instrumental in the New Hope Army's founding. He will be assassinated in two years, the army largely turning against him. The troops underneath him pledge their allegiance to the Scorpion instead."

"That past is dead," I replied.

Anna just seemed to absorb it, nodding. "I'll bear that in mind. At least this means that Monarch won't be retrieving its soldiers."

Wow, that was cold blooded.

"It also means this place is going to be overrun with the US Army in a bit, if they have any reinforcements to deploy," I said. I was already imagining this battlefield becoming even more of a massacre than it was. I couldn't understand why Anna was loyal to the people who would do all this.

Then I realized it didn't matter to her who was backing her as long as they supported her. The ends justified the means. It made me realize I couldn't trust anyone but also, perhaps, Anna wasn't wrong. Whatever brought down Butterfly in the long run. Sometimes you had to make compromises with those you didn't like or trust. Either that or I was fooling myself to make myself feel better about studying business for years.

"Unlikely," Jane said. "The Blue Cascade required an hour to recharge between shots, but we don't know how much it's been modified since Trevor brought the plans back. It's highly likely he will deploy it against the general's location next."

That was Anchorage, Alaska. The forces of the military had been assembled there, but it was a city with three hundred thousand souls. I had no doubt that Trevor would use the weapon and kill everyone there to wipe out the least bit of resistance. That caused me to change faster since we were now under a ticking clock.

I was aware it was still a ridiculous idea. We were going inside a heavily armed military base—devastating counterattack aside—as three of the most-wanted people in the world. We were going to stop a superweapon and a time-traveling psychopath. It was insane, ridiculous, and liberating all at once if we managed to achieve our goal, whether we lived through the process or not.

The three of us headed down the hills and moved across the vast snowy expanse toward the edge of the base. Much to my surprise, we met almost no resistance. Even as Monarch soldiers were brought in on stretchers by the few survivors, we slipped into the location with no one questioning our presence. It was almost disappointing as the chaos and confusion provided a cover that made it frighteningly easy to get inside.

The interior of the base was a confusing mass of nearly identical buildings, people running around in a panic, and strange machinery I didn't recognize. It was like we'd wandered into Area 51 and I half expected gray aliens to pop up at any point.

"Okay, where the hell do we go now?" Anna asked, looking at the flames and smoke visible just outside the fence. I could see the hatred in her eyes and didn't blame her. She was the one who'd told the military about this place after all.

"I don't know," I said, looking around. "It's not like we can ask people. I'm making this up as I go along."

Jane looked at the open doorway to one of the buildings, walked in, and walked back out with a plastic map in hand. It was the kind that buildings put up for people in case of fire or other emergencies.

"Thank God for corporate culture," she remarked.

"This is too easy," I said.

"Don't jinx it," Jane said, handing over the map. "By the way, Christine is on the television."

"Wait, what?" I asked.

"She hijacked the BBN signal," Jane replied. "She's telling the whole world that Trevor is responsible for the deaths of Colin Reilly and the Butterfly board. Also, that he was the one who caused the blast at the Chrysalis."

"Huh. Did that happen in the original past?" I stared at her.

"Nope!" Jane said. "Should be interesting."

Anna took the plastic map and stared at it.

"There's a big building marked 'central lab' that way."

Anna pointed to the largest of the geodesic buildings.

"Well, I guess we have our target then," I muttered.

CHAPTER TWENTY-FIVE

I couldn't speak for Jane or Anna, but I knew I was expecting the lab to be a mad scientist's wet dream of death rays and buzzsaws. This was Butterfly's top R&D weapons department, where they designed and tested a million and one ways for Monarch goons to flay, torture, and maim anyone stupid enough to oppose them. Stupid like us.

What I didn't expect was an oversized warehouse filled wall to wall with computer servers. They were perfectly organized in rows that towered all the way to the ceiling. The place was absolutely freezing, too. Completely insulated. Which made sense. What better place than Alaska to hide a massive server farm that needed to be kept cool?

I'd heard of Butterfly's server farms before, even seen pictures of them, but nothing even remotely like this. This was a building full of bleeding-edge quantum supercomputers that were all seemingly interlinked. You could run not just the entirety of Butterfly from here but perhaps the United States. Several of these machines were supposed to be only theoretical, another sign of just what Trevor had managed to alter about our world's technology.

As I was taking it all in, Anna summed up my feelings perfectly. "What the hell?"

"I was not expecting this many computer servers," Jane stated in her patented, deadpan tone.

We wandered the aisles while spinning round and round, looking for something—anything—that stuck out amongst the endless landscape of computer equipment.

"Where are all the weapons?" I said to no one in particular.

"I don't know," Anna replied while pointing straight ahead. "But there's Trevor!"

I looked and realized Anna was getting ahead of herself. In the distance, in what I could only assume was the center of the room, the server towers stopped, revealing a raised platform with seven people on it. I couldn't make out if any were Trevor, but one of them had his back to us, typing away at some sort of large console. The others were all armored Monarch troopers who started approaching us as soon as we came into their view.

"I'll keep them busy," Jane stated and started casually jogging towards them.

"How?" Anna asked, confused by Jane's confident declaration. "There's six of..."

Her voice trailed off as Jane dove headfirst into the line of troopers, tackling half of them to the ground. She then instantly popped to her feet and engaged the other three, alternating punches and kicks that didn't let up for a second. Her feet and fists moved back and forth between the troopers while she danced around every one of their attacks, even as the three she knocked down got back up and joined the fray.

Anna's jaw dropped as she watched Jane in action. "My God."

I'd seen the white-haired girl fight enough to know she had things handled.

"She'll be fine," I said. "Come on."

I led Anna to the next row of servers, where we had a clear path to the raised platform. Our feet clanged against the metal steps as we climbed to the top, where we found Trevor, still with his back to us and intensely typing away at the console.

Anna drew her pistol and aimed it at him. "Hands off the keyboard."

"Then you're going to have to shoot me." Trevor kept his eyes on the large screen filled with computer code attached to the console.

Anna cocked the hammer back on her gun. "I won't say it a second—"

Trevor swiftly flung a knife in Anna's direction. The blade struck her in the shoulder, and she screamed while collapsing to the floor.

"Anna!" I shouted.

I expected him to have one for me next, but he went right back to typing frantically. Whatever Trevor was trying to do was more important than dealing with me. His fingers moved like crazy, entering code into the monitor faster than my eyes could keep up. I wanted to check on Anna, but the fact that Trevor ignored me to continue his work was enough for me to realize I didn't have a second to waste. I had to stop him.

I took off running and Trevor kept on typing right up until the moment I tackled him to the floor. We rolled several times before slamming into the platform's railing. The two of us were tangled in a mess. I had no idea where his head was. I just began punching whatever body part I knew wasn't my own.

Trevor had a more graceful response. He spun off me, grappled my head in some sort of hold, and then flipped me over like a pinwheel. It was an expert maneuver, proving he'd obviously been trained way better than I had. I was disoriented but could focus just enough to see Trevor raise another knife into the air.

"No!" I screamed while feebly lifting my arms to defend myself.

Jane suddenly appeared beside him and grabbed his wrist before the blade came down. Before Trevor realized what had happened, Jane quickly disarmed him and drove the knife into his thigh. He screamed and dropped to a knee, but Jane had already turned her attention to helping me up.

"Thanks," I said.

Jane nodded and moved to help Anna off the floor. "You okay?"

Anna cringed while removing the knife from her shoulder. "Yeah. I'll be all right."

I briefly looked over my shoulder just to confirm what I already knew. Sure enough, the six Monarch troopers were lying in the aisle. I couldn't tell if they were unconscious or dead. I wished Jane had spared their lives, but right now I had bigger things to worry about.

I turned my focus over to Trevor and grabbed him by the shirt, fully prepared to beat the answers I needed out of him.

"Where's Aurelia!?" I shouted with a fist cocked and ready to strike.

"I'm right here, Mr. Stone," a woman said from behind me.

It was a voice I didn't recognize, and I turned to find only Anna and Jane behind me. They weren't looking at me, though. They were looking at the screen above the console. The extensive code was still there, but it was no longer in black and white. The entire code shimmered in gold while swaying up and down. Almost as if it were…alive.

"It's an AI," I muttered while trying to wrap my head around the revelation.

"Technically," the code said, pulsating as it spoke, "I'm an operations interface for an AI, but yes."

While it was cool to be talking with a machine, I still struggled to comprehend how an artificial intelligence fit into all this. "I thought Colin Reilly was developing a weapon?"

"Anything is a weapon if wielded properly," Aurelia replied.

Or improperly, depending on how you looked at it. She was just a computer program, though, and could only reply in the context of which the question was asked. I tried to think of ways to utilize that when Trevor's laughter interrupted me.

"What's so funny?" I asked, annoyed by the sound.

Trevor continued giggling while removing the knife embedded in his thigh. "Your ignorance."

"What do you mean?" I asked.

Trevor went on when he looked up and saw the confusion on my face. "What's the most powerful ammunition on Earth?"

Again, I had no idea what he was talking about, and my brow wrinkled even further.

"Information," he said, answering his own question. "And Aurelia is a weapon to control it."

"I don't understand," I replied.

Trevor paused as he smiled and then quickly shifted his focus to the console. "Aurelia, shut down all systems!"

"No!" I shouted, turning to the screen.

Nothing happened. The flowing golden code remained the same. She appeared to have listened to me. I was so overwhelmed by everything going on that I didn't even question it. I should have. Trevor had brought Aurelia from his future, where I had been a high-ranking Butterfly executive.

"Please," I said to her. "Tell me what he's talking about."

"My function is to collect and assess all data transmitted across digital networks," Aurelia replied.

Jane stepped up. It seemed as if she was finally interested in this development. "What networks?"

"All of them," Aurelia answered.

"H…how…" Anna stammered in disbelief. "How is that possible?"

"Butterfly subsidiaries have stock in every global telecommunications grid across the globe," Aurelia responded, her oddly human voice sounding clear and without emotion, "which allows me to make a record of all data those grids service. Pictures. Emails. Infopad calls."

"Even if it's behind a firewall?" Jane said.

It concerned me that she was just as clueless as Anna and me.

"No encryption is beyond my computing power," Aurelia replied. "I see everything, everywhere, all the time."

"And Trevor just activated you?" I asked while looking at him cradling his injured leg on the floor.

He scowled at me. I was clearly learning things he didn't want me to know.

"Yes and no," Aurelia replied. "Collecting the information is easy. These servers here have been doing it for years, but it's processed as code. Unreadable without an interface like myself. That interface is what Mr. Reilly just uploaded."

The entire room went silent as the three of us tried to comprehend what we were hearing. Half a minute later, Anna was the first to speak. "How do we use you against Butterfly?"

213

"I'm sorry, Anna Cross," Aurelia replied. "I cannot provide tactical recommendations based off your question."

"And why not?" Anna sneered.

"Because you are not an authorized user for my system."

"And he is?" Anna shot an angered look in my direction.

"Of course," Aurelia answered. "As CEO of Butterfly, Robert Stone has full access to all my capabilities."

Although I knew my fate, it was still a surprise to hear it out loud like that. It seemed future me had been doing quite well for himself. Rising to the top of an international conglomerate. Brokering peace with the Scorpion. Controlling a dominant AI with the ability to monitor the entire world. No wonder Trevor couldn't stand me. But now I was drawing Anna's ire, as well. She looked at me as her face contorted between shock and anger.

"You—You actually do it. You take over Butterfly."

Anna was shell-shocked. I couldn't imagine what she was feeling, having learned that her ex-boyfriend would rise to become the head of the very organization she despised. Mind you, there was no way it was happening now, but that didn't seem to occur to her. All that mattered was my becoming the leader of her enemy.

I ignored her, though, to ask a more pressing question on my mind. "And Trevor's access?"

Aurelia answered without delay. "As Vice President of Public Relations, Trevor Reilly has restrictions to his commands. I believe he was in the process of hacking my code to unlock them when you interrupted him."

I turned to Trevor, still on the floor and still trying to kill me with his stare. "Can I revoke his access completely?"

"Affirmative," Aurelia replied.

"Then do it," I said, wondering if it could really be that easy. Turning to him, I said, "Trevor, you're fired."

Trevor laughed at the *Robocop* reference. I hadn't even been trying to make it, but it seemed appropriate right now.

"One moment," Aurelia said as her flowing code became more active. "Command completed."

Trevor lifted his hands off his bleeding leg to begin a slow, dramatic clap. "Bravo, Rob. But what now? This is the power my grandfather dreamed of. You have a god of the web at your disposal. What are you going to do with her?"

The thought never even dawned on me. After all my run-ins with time travel and witnessing the Blue Cascade's devastation, my only objective had been to destroy the dreaded things inside this place. But now that I had the most powerful one of all in the palm of my hand, my conviction had begun to waver.

"Destroy her, Rob," Jane said without a second thought.

"What?" Anna objected with her brow furrowed. "No!"

Jane didn't look to her. She stared at me instead and shook her head. "Nobody should have this kind of power."

"She's wrong," Anna argued. "The right people should have it."

"Think of the man who envisioned this thing," Jane said, her voice as soft as I'd ever heard it. "He was a controlling narcissist with a God complex. That alone should tell you something."

"Exactly!" Anna exclaimed while clutching her injured shoulder. "So, it should be his enemies who wield it."

Anna stepped closer to intimately continue her argument. "Think about it, Rob. Butterfly can't hide anymore. We can expose them to the world. Their secrets. Their lies. With this kind of intelligence at our fingertips, HOPE can win this war in a month."

She made a good point, and it was also the warmest she'd been to me since we were in high school. The caring in her voice reminded me of a simpler time when it was just us against the world. I was ashamed to say her speech made me long for those days.

Then Jane took a step forward to match her. "I've seen what happens when HOPE uses weapons Butterfly developed. They become the very thing they hate. Don't let it happen, Rob. Please. This is too much for anyone to control."

"So, what then?" Anna snapped in Jane's direction. "We just let Butterfly win?"

"Never," Jane replied in a more calm, reserved tone than her opponent. "I've fought them before, and I'll fight them again."

Even though Anna was the one visibly heated, I could tell Jane was just as passionate about her position. She had this blank stare that by all accounts seemed emotionless, yet it bore through you with pure, unwavering conviction. That look, combined with experience, told me that when Jane told you she was ready for a fight, you damned well believed her. Her resolve was not enough to convince me she was right, though.

The situation in front of me presented a once-in-a-lifetime opportunity to affect the future, and flashes of that future began coming back to me. Visions of Monarch and HOPE soldiers engaged in battle rolled over my eyes in waves. Scorched cities rose in the background as a blue wave of destruction leveled everything in its path.

This premonition had always seemed inevitable. In fact, I felt myself on the precipice of it in this very moment, but I also felt something different. I sensed the ability to take a step a back and set a new course. One that would eliminate that destiny for good.

"Things are different now," I pointed out. It was hard to make sense of all this, but I was doing my best. "You said it yourself, Jane. The Blue Cascade was not activated this early in your timeline, but Butterfly has already used it in this one. With or without Trevor, they will utilize it to destroy everyone and everything in their way."

I looked up to the screen and watched the golden code, glowing as if waiting patiently for my command.

"But Aurelia can change things," I said. "Forever."

Anna nodded with a smile, pleased with what she was hearing.

"Good. Now tell her to give me—"

"Aurelia, open up access," I said.

"To whom?" Aurelia asked.

"Everyone," I replied.

"Understood," Aurelia said without hesitation.

Anna's confused gaze shot back and forth between the screen and me. "What are you doing?"

I ignored her question and continued giving Aurelia my orders.

"Now distribute those user IDs to every e-mail in your system."

The golden code pulsed faster as Aurelia began calculating. "That is a total of—"

"I don't need to know the number," I said. "Just do it."

"Executing." The golden code swirled rapidly on the screen.

"Wait. Don't—" Anna futilely held out her hand to stop the order.

"Command completed," Aurelia stated.

Anna's face grew wide in horror. "No!"

"Yes," I said, smug. Whether it was the right decision or not, I'd given the public access to the truth.

All the truth.

Anna turned to me with a scowl that might as well had been shooting fumes from her ears. "What did you just do?!"

I put my head down, contemplating the decision.

"For years I've felt torn between two futures, each one pulling me in a different direction. So, I said screw it and wrote my own."

Anna bared her teeth at me. I swear I had never seen her so mad. "You stupid little—"

"Hold that thought," Jane interrupted. "Trevor's gone."

I looked back at where he'd been lying, but now there was only a small puddle of blood that dripped through the platform's metal slats.

Dammit.

CHAPTER TWENTY-SIX

Upon seeing Trevor was gone, my first reaction was to pick up the gun Anna had dropped when she was stabbed. I was sure she wanted it, but I wasn't exactly getting the best feeling from her piercing stares. The last thing I wanted was her holding a firearm, and luckily her injured shoulder meant she was in no position to beat me to it. I then followed Trevor's blood trail off the platform before she had a chance to object.

It led me through more rows of servers and out a door on the opposite side of the building. Once back under the sharp Alaskan sun, it wasn't hard to spot Trevor limping away from us. He was moving pretty fast considering the amount of blood he left in his wake, but it wasn't the pace of his escape that had me worried. It was the battalion of armored Monarch troopers he was headed for.

We were at the back of the base, so they didn't appear to be soldiers headed for the battle. They were outfitted more like guards, supervising a crowd of parka-bundled scientists as they shuffled their way into transport vehicles. It was an evacuation.

Jane, Anna, and I ran to catch up to Trevor, who yelled as he approached the scene.

"Shoot them!" he shouted.

The troopers all turned their helmeted heads and instantly raised their rifles. I braced for them to fire, but they never did. They were waiting for their leader, the trooper out front, who lowered his weapon slowly.

"Rob?" he said, curiously.

It was hard to recognize his muffled voice, but I was relieved when the trooper removed his helmet and revealed Phil Boulder's face underneath.

Anna's and Jane's stances were still tense and ready to scatter. I didn't blame them. But I was also tired of fighting. Trevor was on his last leg, almost literally. And I had to take a stand.

"I'm not here to fight, Phil." I raised my hands with the pistol dangling from the trigger guard around my finger.

"Then what are you doing here?" he asked, dropping the helmet to the ground.

"Don't ask questions!" Trevor exclaimed, his gaze darting back and forth between us. "Just shoot!"

The Monarch troopers' rifles, which had been relaxing, snapped back to attention.

"Hold your fire," Phil ordered, loudly.

Trevor seethed in his direction. "What are you doing?"

"Thinking for myself," Phil replied, calmly.

Trevor was furious. His body language practically screamed it. Menacing scowl. Fists clenched at his sides while the blood still seeped from his leg. Yet despite all that, his voice was exact and measured. "You're not paid to think. You're paid to do what you're told."

Phil had no reaction. He just blankly stared at his boss as if his mind hadn't decided what to do.

"That goes for all of you," Trevor continued, now addressing the troopers as a whole. "You're paid employees. If you don't follow orders, your families don't eat. Now pull the damned trigger!"

They didn't. In fact, I could see their heads all tilt in Phil's direction, waiting for his command. I had to wonder what they thought about being attacked by the United States military and witnessing the Blue Cascade kill thousands of them. Many of them were veterans. On the other hand, I also knew that Phil had barely survived an attack I'd been part of. As far as he knew, I was a HOPE terrorist. It could go either way.

"I'm going to ask you again, Rob," he said, ignoring Trevor and talking to me directly. "What are you doing here?"

My body stayed still, but my mind raced trying to think of a response. I needed to say something, but I had to be careful. My life literally depended on it.

But I never got the chance to speak.

One by one, chimes started echoing around the crowd. Everyone knew what they were. The sound was unmistakable. It was the ding an infopad gave when a notification came through, but the scientists and troopers all looked around confused. They had no idea why they were all getting it at once.

"Check it and find out," I said, answering Phil's question.

Everyone dug into their pockets and pulled out their infopads, still confused by the message on their screens.

"What is this?" Phil asked.

"Open it," I said.

Phil clicked his infopad's screen, and it made another chime.

"Aurelia?" I called.

"Yes, Mr. Stone?" she replied, her voice emanating out from Phil's infopad.

Here went nothing. "Show them all what Trevor has been up to the last seventy-two hours."

The air grew tensely silent. I couldn't see what Aurelia was playing for them. Whatever it was, though, was enough to completely captivate their attention. Every scientist and trooper stared at their infopads, completely speechless by what they were witnessing.

When Phil had seen enough, his horrified, gawking expression shifted in Trevor's direction. "It was you this whole time?"

For a moment I expected Trevor to deny it or try to spin the revelation into some kind of conspiracy. He laughed instead, completely owning the moment.

"Oh, don't act so surprised. This is what corporate culture is. Cutthroat. Ruthless. Kill or be killed. I know that better than anyone. And so should all of you."

Phil's shocked face morphed into a sneer of rage. "Take him."

Several troopers stepped towards Trevor, but he stepped back while also removing a small square device from his pocket.

"Not so fast," he threatened. "Unless you want the Blue Cascade directly above our heads to vaporize this whole base in an instant."

Could it really be that simple? Could a tiny box in his hand control the most brutal weapon I had ever seen? Trevor was certainly no stranger to lying, but I believed him, mainly because he was just that sore of a loser. He would kill us all rather than be taken in by the very people he wanted to control.

"You're insane, Trevor," I said, speaking as his friend. "Certifiably crazy."

He held the Blue Cascade trigger in my direction like a gun, his thumb delicately hanging above the button. "I'm insane? Really? That's funny coming from someone who just ended the world as we know it."

"What are you talking about?" I asked, utterly confused by his mad rambling.

"Aurelia!" he exclaimed, as if he was insulted that he had to explain. "You've ended everything by releasing her to the world. She was going to solidify my hold over the other megacorporations. Recluse. Infocorp. Scarab. All eleven of them. They would've been mine. Now all the secrets, the backstabbing, the entire way of corporate life will be out in the open, and our tenuous coalition will crumble. It'll be worse than war. It'll be anarchy. The complete and total collapse of everything. All because you have some self-righteous need to—"

A loud bang cut him off, followed by a hole suddenly appearing in his head and blood spraying out over the troopers behind him. Trevor's body seemed to hover for a moment before collapsing. Everyone then instantly turned in my direction, and I couldn't understand why until I looked down and saw the smoke drifting out the barrel of the gun in my hand.

I killed him. It was me. And I hadn't even realized that I did it.

With the veil of the Scorpion hanging over me, I'd been avoiding this moment for so long. It was preposterous to be afraid that murder was a slippery slope to genocide. But that was the insanity of my life. To try and avoid death at all costs. The first person I killed was Gunner, the assassin from the future. I felt awful afterwards and that was in self-defense. Now, after struggling so long with the idea of ending Trevor's life, when I finally pulled the trigger, I felt nothing.

The eyes upon me didn't last long, though. They soon shifted to the Blue Cascade control box, which had fallen from Trevor's hand as he collapsed, bounced several times on the dirt, and came to rest only inches from Anna's feet.

The tense silence returned as Anna's gaze sharpened on the object, like a lion about to devour a meal. Her eyes zoomed from the box, to me, to the Monarch troopers, and then back to the box, and I could practically read her thoughts with every move.

Then she darted down to pick it up.

"Anna, wait!" I shouted, not that it mattered.

The troopers all raised their weapons at once, but they weren't fast enough. By the time their sights were trained on her, Anna had already snatched the device from the ground and dashed to grab one of the scientists, using him as a human shield between her and the rifles.

The scientist was young and dorky looking. Even younger than me, if I had to guess. His glasses were thick, and his hair was scraggly. And he looked terrified as Anna dug a knife into his neck, the same knife Trevor had flung into her shoulder only minutes ago.

"What are you doing, Anna?" I said with my hands up, one of which aimed the pistol to the sky.

"I'm not leaving here empty-handed," Anna said, coldly.

I tried to focus on Anna as she slowly shuffled away from us, but I couldn't help noticing Jane staring at me. She had this weird, wide-eyed look on her face. She wasn't necessarily shocked or even afraid. She was nervous, though, as if she had something urgent that she needed to share.

"That's Charles Kepler," she mouthed, silently.

Oh, no. Anna's hostage was the future father of time travel. I'd read about him in the old history book she'd brought me. Though I couldn't imagine him being the father of much right now. He looked barely old enough to shave. Yet in a matter of decades this man would be responsible, either directly or indirectly, for turning my life upside down.

I doubted Anna knew who she was holding. It made sense, though. He had to be here to work on the time-travel side of Aurelia, and if she were to grab someone at random, then of course it would be him. That was just how my luck was going lately. Or maybe I was destined to have fate constantly working against me.

I debated whether I should tell Anna who he was. After all, our original mission was to end the time-travel program completely. That didn't mean killing its creator, but Anna might not see it that way. Or maybe she would see more value in him alive, the same way she saw value in giving Aurelia to HOPE. Either way, she was becoming too extreme and unpredictable. I couldn't risk telling her the truth.

"He's just a scientist," I pleaded. "Let him go."

"Not a chance." Anna shook her head. "He's my way of understanding this thing. To use one of Butterfly's tools of death as a force for good."

"I'm just a lab tech," Kepler shook his trembling face, "and the Blue Cascade isn't even my project. I have no idea how to—"

"Shut up!" Anna shouted, digging the knife in just enough to draw a drop of blood. "You science nerds are all the same. I'm sure you'll figure it out."

"I can take the shot, Rob," Phil said from behind me.

It was strange for the Monarch troop leader to quickly defer to me as an authority, yet it felt oddly natural when I held out my hand, signaling him to hold off on firing.

"He doesn't deserve to be your prisoner, Anna," I urged while taking a step towards her. "Butterfly scientist or not. Take me instead."

Her sneer sharpened. "There's no way I'm taking a traitor like you with me. Not after what you did."

I grimaced and shook my head. "I had no choice."

"There's always a choice!" Anna snapped. "Before, we just had one enemy to fight. But now the megacorporations will split and we'll have to take them all on at once. Trevor was right. It'll be anarchy."

"Now I have the key to make sure HOPE comes out on top." Anna slipped the control box into her pocket and began backing away faster.

As Anna turned to run away, I felt the gun in my hand moving on its own. In fact, I aimed it straight ahead. I couldn't tell if it was pointed at Anna or Kepler, not that it particularly mattered. I could've shot either for an effective result. Kepler dead meant time travel would never exist. Anna dead meant HOPE may never get its Scorpion. All I had to do was squeeze the trigger and the job was done.

It was that thought alone which compelled me to force the gun down at my side and watch as Anna took off through the base with the scientist as her prisoner.

The light grumble of chatter began to rise behind me, but I didn't care to turn around. I just kept staring deeper into the base, even as I felt Jane walk up and stand beside me.

"Did I make a mistake?" I asked.

"No," she said while placing a hand on my shoulder. "You stopped yourself from becoming the Scorpion."

At first, I thought that was a ridiculous thing to say. I'd already avoided that fate by joining Butterfly. My ties with HOPE were over. Then I understood what she meant. The Scorpion wasn't a fixed person I would become. It was an idea I would embody. A mindset that the ends would always justify the means, regardless of what stood in my way and the price I had to pay to achieve them. In that regard, the Scorpion would always be something I'd be fighting. He would be a specter lingering over me for the rest of my life.

EPILOGUE

"Well, congratulations. You did it," Jane muttered. "I don't know how you did it, but you have successfully destroyed the future."

The two of us were standing on the rooftop of the Butterfly Building in Chicago. The building was frantic as employees inside scrambled to secure their future amidst a sinking corporate ship. I no longer worked here, but Phil helped get us past the Monarch guards who barely seemed to register any of their previous fanaticism. Indeed, the entirety of Butterfly's once grandiose corporate culture and fanatical loyalty had been sucked dry thanks to my actions.

Sadly, my friendship with Phil was destroyed as he reacted to both me and Jane with abject fear in his eyes. He was a General now, as most of Monarch's leadership was now on trial for war crimes including Georgia's mother. However, as far as he was concerned, I was a terrorist and a murderer myself. It's just I had the backing of the law behind me.

Maybe he was right.

It had been over a year since Aurelia was unleashed, and the city's streets—every city's streets—were a mess. There were a couple of fires burning and the constant blaring of sirens permeated the air. It seemed the dissolution of the megacorporate alliance and the complete extinction of secrets across the world led to chaos. Who knew? Good had come of it too with the dissolution of the Blue and Red Zones with their reincorporation back into the United States.

Unfortunately, the constant influx of new scandals and revelations by Aurelia meant any stability was a thing of the past. It seemed there was no politician or corporate leader not involved in something unforgivably evil or corrupt. The truth had set us free, but it had also scorched the Earth.

There had been attempts to tear down the internet and rebuild it but as soon as any new servers went up, Aurelia infected them as well. People had started deleting as much as they could and storing their confidential records on hard copy, but it had already been the biggest shock to human record-keeping in history. Aurelia could sort through propaganda, lies, and junk facts every bit as well as she could decrypt anything.

I'd mostly stayed out of the limelight during all of this, working for Christine's pardon and later successful Senate run. There had been some death threats and even a few assassination attempts but Jane had taken care of those. Now it was the first order of business as Christine's aide to supervise Butterfly's nationalization. It was "too big to fail" but needed a new leadership composed of US loyalists.

Jane and I took the elevator up to the rooftop to watch it all unfold. It was scary and, I was ashamed to admit, thrilling at the same time.

"Honestly, I'm not sure what I've done," I said, looking down. They'd repaired the damage to the building, but I could still see scorch marks from the bombing if I looked closely.

Butterfly's stock had plummeted once Aurelia was out in the open. The puppet government they'd established turned against them, and with the other megacorporations now gunning for their spot at the top, I'd be surprised if the company lasted a month. Its assets were being frozen, and all the executives left with any real power were being arrested for treason. Anna would've been happy...if she weren't so insane.

"You found the Achilles Heel of Butterfly," Jane replied, watching the tiny dots below. "Truth."

"The truth shall set us free," I said, thinking about Aurelia and what she'd managed to accomplish where weapons like the Blue Cascade had failed. "I just never thought it would be so literal."

Aurelia had her tendrils in everything from infopads to supercomputers and had given everyone access to it all. The technology was decades ahead of its time and benefited from the fact it had been designed to work with the standardized hardware that Butterfly had built its fortune on. Governments and other megacorporations were already attempting to purge her from the world's servers, but unless they shut down the entirety of the infonet, it was simply impossible to remove her.

The immediate effect was that everyone had been able to confirm what Christine said on TV about Trevor and what his grandfather had built. They learned about the coup, murders, terrorism, secret camps, and more. Aurelia prevented Butterfly's propaganda and information warfare specialists from combatting the endless stream of exposed crimes that were coming to light. Some people hadn't cared. They were die-hard corporatists that only wanted to win, but they'd ended up being a minority in the grand scheme of things.

"I think it was Trevor who actually did most of the work," I replied. "Butterfly could stand the loss of its board and the promotion of Colin Reilly to dictator, but his death followed by the destruction of the—"

"Yes, yes," Jane replied. "People don't deal well with change. Trevor assumed that everyone would recognize him as CEO and chairman, but they didn't know him. He may have been Colin's grandkid in the future, but he was just another student in the present. He might have been able to bribe and blackmail a bunch of people into cooperation, but they were never as loyal as he thought they were. Phil proved that."

"I'm surprised he sided with us," I said. "I mean, we helped kill a lot of Monarch soldiers."

"A lot of them were ex-US soldiers to begin with," Jane reminded me of a fact she'd brought up earlier. "They were only with Butterfly because they thought they were protecting America from collapse. The fact that collapse was due to the megacorporations dissolving America's social safety net to enrich themselves couldn't be seen until it was right up in their faces."

"Maybe," I replied. "Still, I'm surprised."

"The slaughter outside the lab was the kind of thing that makes you realize you're on the wrong side of history," Jane replied. "I suspect Phil was also feeling a lot of guilt for what he saw in the Chrysalis. It was run only by the most fanatical of the corporate cult."

"Yeah, but it's not the same between us," I said.

"No," Jane said. "Even if he sided with his country, we killed a lot of his friends. Just be glad that the country has turned against Butterfly."

"Trevor pushed things too far," I said, understanding now how things had gone down. "He acted like a supervillain. Executing hundreds of people, using a satellite weapon, killing his grandfather, and spinning a fission explosion to smear his enemies. He's going to go down as one of history's worst terrorists."

"Instead of you," Jane replied.

I grimaced. "Let me guess, the Scorpion did worse."

Jane nodded. "You were much better at doing what Trevor did. Mind you, he didn't exist in my reality. We're completely off the rails now. Nothing that has happened remotely resembles what my future was created from."

"Except there will be a Scorpion," I said, feeling sick to my stomach. "Anna."

Even though Anna was pissed that I didn't give her exclusive access to Aurelia, which didn't stop her from having a field day with the tech, presumably with Kepler's help on how to best utilize the AI. What little of Monarch's spy network remained intact reported that Anna had emerged as a kind of folk hero amongst HOPE leadership by uniting virtually every extremist group she could find. Not many had been willing to ally with a young black woman, but there was an entirely new radicalized number of youth that had seen what the megacorporations had been willing to do. They'd leveraged the information about corporations, politicians, bankers, and even movie stars to claim that a global revolution was necessary against them all.

I wasn't sure she was entirely wrong. HOPE had the benefit of the truth on its side, after all. Unfortunately, she also didn't care about collateral damage in their wake, and her followers only cared about her interpretations. Global capitalism as a whole was her enemy, and they were ready to party like it was 1917. That was the year the Russian Revolution began, by the way.

"Yes," Jane replied. "We created her."

"Did we?" I asked.

"I hoped when you came clean about your future as the Scorpion it might make her finally understand what you've been going through," Jane said. "I think, in retrospect, it only inspired her instead."

I stared at her. "No. Anna's becoming extreme, but she's not evil."

"Not yet," Jane replied. "But neither were you when we first met. And now with Kepler as her prisoner, who knows what she's capable of doing to take the other megacorporations down next."

That was the most depressing part of it all, in my opinion. Butterfly was on its way out the door, but its assets wouldn't vanish overnight. The other eleven megacorporations would become like vultures picking at a carcass. They may have covertly supported Colin Reilly's takeover of the government, but they'd kept their hands reasonably clean of outright treason. Already, politicians were starting to hedge their bets about reining in future corporate meddling and were pointing to Butterfly as a sick aberration rather than a symptom of a much larger problem.

"Just a few bad apples," I muttered.

"A few bad apples spoil the barrel," Jane said, dryly. "That's the entire saying. Like my country, right or wrong. If my country is right, let it be kept right. If my country is wrong, let it be set right. Blood is thicker than water was originally blood of the Lamb is thicker than the water of the womb. The popular interpretations of the saying are the exact opposite of their true meaning."

"Yeah," I said, looking down.

"You don't really think any of the megacorporations would support Anna, do you?" Jane asked, surprised. "She's a rogue."

"A rogue that's gaining a lot of global support," I replied. "The other megacorporations are eager to pick up Butterfly's research with its fired scientists. It's possible time travel might still become a reality."

"Let's hope not," Jane said. "I could imagine you being next to travel back in time, and one Robbie is enough."

"Rob," I corrected her.

"Well, I'm not calling you Dad," Jane said, smirking. "You're more like a distant relative now."

I snorted then frowned. "I'm sorry about your mother, Jane. I'm sure she was a wonderful person."

Jane looked away. The wound was still raw. "She wasn't my mother any more than you're my father."

I nodded. "Maybe destroying Butterfly was enough and you don't have to be my bodyguard now either."

"We can't let Anna run free," Jane said as she shook her head. "Not after all we've been through."

"Seriously?" I said, taking a deep breath. "We don't have to do anything anymore. You can have a normal life. *We* can."

Jane frowned. "I'm never going to be normal, Rob. Neither are you."

She had a point there. It wasn't like there was an outlet for her skills either. The military wasn't likely to accept her any more than it would me. There had been a lot of people who felt I should be tried for what I'd done. Not just the attack on the Chrysalis but also the release of the Aurelia. Countless government and corporate secrets had been released, many of which I was connected to as an executive assistant to Butterfly's CEO. I wasn't entirely sure I wasn't a fugitive from the law.

Privacy for a lot of people had been massively violated and the repercussions hadn't always been positive. Marriages, friendships, and relations between nations had been irreparably strained—if not outright destroyed—by Aurelia's release. Hate groups and radicals were starting to turn analog to bypass her propaganda. They were using old-fashioned leaflets as well as rallies to talk about the oppression of the new AI editing the world's communication. Overall, I was glad I'd made the choice I had, but there were still consequences that I would have to deal with over the course of the next few years. Hell, the rest of my life.

"Not to mention Cody and Esther," Jane said, dryly. "Would you really leave them to go on whatever rampage they have planned?"

I didn't have a good answer for that either. We knew members of HOPE and the military faction that Anna had been a part of were going to be their targets. They'd declared war on Anna and weren't afraid to get their hands dirty to stop her from becoming the new Scorpion. It wasn't a matter of if they were going to strike. Just when.

"Those two need to be behind bars," I admitted.

"Or dead," Jane said. "After everything that happened, you might be the only one who could talk them down."

"I never gave them any orders!" I said, flabbergasted.

"You did," Jane replied. "You recruited them as weapons and gave them their purpose back. It's the only reason you're still alive."

"We'll figure something out." I sighed.

I honestly never wanted to see Cody, Esther, or Anna again as long as I lived. As much as I'd cared for Anna, she'd forfeited whatever friendship we'd had. It'd been the same with Trevor, except her betrayal stung much worse. By the time I'd gotten my will together enough to kill him, he was dead to me. Anna? She was a mixture of a hundred different conflicting emotions that still burned every time I thought of her.

"So, what are you going to do now?" Jane asked, almost sensing that I needed a change of topic.

I took a deep breath, looked down once more at the end of an era, and smiled.

"Now? Now we go get some pizza. Chicago style. I may only be an assistant to a US Congresswoman, but I can afford that much."

"Technically, you're an assistant—" Jane started to say.

"Don't," I replied. "That joke wasn't funny a year ago."

As if on cue, the infopad in my pocket began to ring. Jane and I looked to each other as I cautiously pulled it out and answered it. "Hello?"

"I wasn't sure you'd pick up," said a cheerful voice on the other end. It was accompanied by a hologram of Christine displayed on the screen. She was wearing a powder blue suit and I could see the back of her office in Washington DC behind her.

"Rob?" Christine asked when I didn't respond. "You there?"

"Yeah," I said, the word practically ejecting from my mouth. "Jane and I were just reminiscing on top of Butterfly Headquarters. We haven't even begun to meet with people yet."

Christine let out a short, nervous laugh.

"I don't blame you. Returning there must be insane."

"Yeah," I muttered. "None of us have had any time to ourselves."

Ever since we kissed, not a day went by that I didn't think about that moment. I wasn't sure if there was more to our relationship, and I wasn't quite sure how to ask her about the future. You'd think a year would have been long enough to figure out whether we wanted to date or not, but her new status as America's most radical Congresswoman prevented that. Now was not the time for either of us to be dating.

I took a deep breath, preparing myself for what I knew was going to be an odd conversation.

"What's been happening with you, Christine?"

"I've been meeting with some old friends," Christine said. "Ones you might recognize."

"You mean with Anna?" I asked, worried that she'd tried to make contact. Christine had a very different idea of my ex than me.

"No," Christine replied quickly, as if to separate herself from what Anna had been doing. "Political friends. Ex-classmates, Conner University students, and Butterfly executives. People not involved in Colin Reilly's schemes but who want to try to rebuild without the fascist dreams of their former leader."

I was surprised to hear that. For as long as I'd known her, I had pictured Christine as a protestor in the street. But the thought of her negotiating with all her old enemies felt natural.

"No more civilian activism?" I asked. "Working with the big boys now?"

Christine shook her head.

"I haven't spoken to Anna or anybody in HOPE since I was with you. No. That part of my life is over. It's time to stop running in the shadows and work in the light. To enact change the way it's supposed to be done."

I caught sight of Jane leering at me and turned away from her to smile.

"That's great, Christine. I'm happy for you, but something tells me you didn't call to catch up."

"No. I didn't." Her voice turned solemn. Not glum, but from friendly to serious. "I have someone here who wants to speak with you."

She handed the infopad over to someone who spoke for nearly a minute without me uttering a thing. It was a voice I was familiar with but didn't know personally. A voice I never expected to hear talking directly to me.

When he was done speaking, I hung up in a daze and just stared at the infopad, too dumbfounded to say anything.

"What was that about?" Jane asked, curiously.

I continued to stare at the screen as I answered her.

"She put me on the infopad with the President of the United States. He said Butterfly is just too big and too tied into our government infrastructure to collapse. Letting it fail might mean it brings the entire country down with it."

I could sense Jane waving her hands, motioning for me to go on.

"And…?"

I looked up with the baffled expression glued to my face.

"And he wants me to save it."

Jane's brow wrinkled, confused by the proposition.

"How?"

"The government is stepping in to restructure the company and wants me to have a seat on the board. They think it'll be a good public-relations move to honor me as a hero rather than condemn me as a terrorist. Oh, I'm getting the Presidential Medal of Freedom, too."

The words felt both powerful and dirty as they left my mouth. It didn't make any sense, but I was glad. Wasn't I? This was a chance to work from the inside against the megacorporations and use their tools for good. Except, well, hadn't I failed doing that before? Was the US government any better? I honestly didn't know.

"Congratulations?" Jane more asked than stated.

Suddenly, I wasn't hungry for pizza anymore.

TO BE CONCLUDED IN

DESTINY'S END

BOOK THREE OF THE DARK DESTINY SERIES

AUTHOR'S NOTE

I'd like to thank you for reading this book. The publishing industry is changing dramatically since the advent of eBooks. It is now very difficult to get any book noticed, regardless of quality. If you enjoyed this book, you could do some very simple things to help me attract attention.

Word of mouth is the number one source of success for novels, so simply telling family and friends about the book is a great start.

Here are a few other ways of helping, if you are so inclined:

* Post a rating or review on Amazon.com
* Post a rating or review on Goodreads
* Talk about the book or write a review on Facebook
* Tell folks about the book in a blog post.

If you like any of my other books, please feel free to check them out. A lot of my series are interlinked, and you never know when you'll find someone familiar showing up.

ABOUT THE AUTHORS

Frank Martin is an author and comic writer that is not as crazy as his work makes him out to be. A fan of storytelling in all its forms, Frank always enjoys exploring new genres and mediums. He currently lives in New York with his wife and three kids. You can check out updates for all of Frank's writing at frankthewriter.com, on his Facebook page at facebook.com/frankmartinwriter, or follow him on Twitter and Instagram @frankthewriter.

Bibliography

A Weapon's Journey
Modern Testament (comics)
Mountain Sickness
Skin Deep/Ordinary Monsters

Dark Destiny (Dark Destiny, Vol. 1)
Destiny's Paradox (Dark Destiny, Vol. 2)

C. T. Phipps is a lifelong student of horror, science fiction, and fantasy. An avid tabletop gamer, he discovered this passion led him to write and turned him into a lifelong geek. He is a regular blogger and also a reviewer for The Bookie Monster.

Bibliography

Novels
The Rules of Supervillainy (Supervillainy Saga #1)
The Games of Supervillainy (Supervillainy Saga #2)
The Secrets of Supervillainy (Supervillainy Saga #3)
The Kingdom of Supervillainy (Supervillainy Saga #4)
The Tournament of Supervillainy (Supervillainy Saga #5)
The Future of Supervillainy (Supervillainy Saga #6)
The Horror of Supervillainy (Supervillainy Saga #7)
Tales of Supervillainy: Cindy's Seven (Supervillainy Saga #8)

I Was a Teenage Weredeer (The Bright Falls Mysteries, Book 1)
An American Weredeer in Michigan (The Bright Falls Mysteries, Book 2)
A Nightmare on Elk Street (The Bright Falls Mysteries, Book 3)

Esoterrorism (Red Room, Vol. 1)

Eldritch Ops (Red Room, Vol. 2)
The Fall of the House (Red Room, Vol. 3)

Agent G: Infiltrator (Agent G, Vol. 1)
Agent G: Saboteur (Agent G, Vol. 2)
Agent G: Assassin (Agent G, Vol. 3)

Cthulhu Armageddon (Cthulhu Armageddon, Vol. 1)
The Tower of Zhaal (Cthulhu Armageddon, Vol. 2)

Lucifer's Star (Lucifer's Star, Vol. 1)
Lucifer's Nebula (Lucifer's Star, Vol. 2)

Straight Outta Fangton (Straight Outta Fangton, Vol. 1)
100 Miles and Vampin' (Straight Outta Fangton, Vol. 2)
Vampiraz4Life (Straight Outta Fangton, Vol. 3)

Wraith Knight (Wraith Knight, Vol. 1)
Wraith Lord (Wraith Knight, Vol. 2)
Wraith King (Wraith Knight, Vol. 3)

Dark Destiny (Dark Destiny, Vol. 1)
Destiny's Paradox (Dark Destiny, Vol. 2)

Brightblade (The Morgan Detective Agency, Book 1)

Space Academy Dropouts (The Space Academy Series, Book 1)
Space Academy Rejects (The Space Academy Series, Book 2)
Space Academy Washouts (The Space Academy Series, Book 3)

Psycho Killers in Love

Anthologies (as editor)
Blackest Knights

Curious about other Crossroad Press books? Stop by our website:
http://crossroadpress.com
We offer quality writing
in digital, audio, and print formats.

Subscribe to our newsletter on the website homepage and receive a
free eBook.